OTHER BOOKS BY JESS MOWRY

Rats In The Trees
Children Of The Night
Way Past Cool
Six Out Seven
Ghost Train
Babylon Boyz
Bones Become Flowers
Skeleton Key
Tyger Tales
Phat Acceptance
When All Goes Bright
Knights Crossing
The Bridge
Reaps
Drawing From Life
Midnight Sons
Magic Rats
Double Acting
The Coyote Valley Railroad
In The Dead Of Night
Ghost Ship
Spencer's Spirit
The Insiders
The Light

TO MARIE LAVEAU

VOODOO DAWGZ

JESS MOWRY

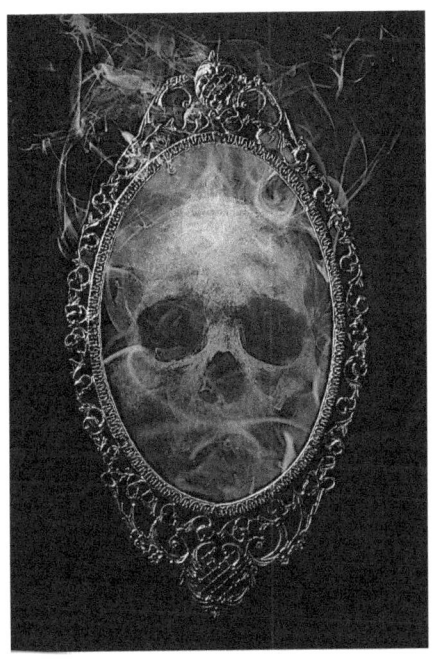

VOODOO DAWGZ

The little kid sneezed when he pulled the trigger.

That was his only big mistake because everything else was a perfect setup for putting Kody underground.

But, Kody had noticed four other boys hanging out across the street, their backs to a wall in the blazing sun. That wasn't normal in New Orleans, and Kody's brain had buzzed a warning that something was wrong with that picture. The oldest boy looked about fourteen, while the youngest was maybe twelve. There hadn't been much to catch Kody's eye; they looked like most of the many street kids who cruised the French Quarter day and night selling vampire teeth and Voodoo dolls, magic charms -- or sometimes their own -- or tap-dancing for tourists. All wore only jeans and sneaks, their shirtless bodies gleaming with sweat like polished African idols. But, Ursulines Avenue wasn't a place where things like that were usually sold, and kids with nothing else to do mostly hung out in front of bars or little corner markets. These dudes weren't toting dancing shoes, but all wore black bandannas. Kody's mind was lazy from a monster Cajun lunch, but had come alert as he'd entered the alley, stepping from sunlight into shadow, though his eyes still hadn't adjusted and he hadn't spotted the kid.

But then the little boy sneezed.

Kody dodged instinctively. The gun's muzzle-blast could have wakened the dead in the narrow confines of the passage, spitting yellow-orange flame in the dimness. Kody slammed into his cousin Raney, who walked a pace behind him, but the bullet ripped through Kody's arm instead of drilling his heart.

The other boys dashed away up the street, awkward in their ass-baring saggers and leaving the little hit-man alone, though Kody still couldn't see him clearly, except he was also shirtless in jeans. The courtyard gate was locked behind him -- iron bars with spikes on top -- and the alley was only four feet wide, so Kody and Raney were blocking escape. The big gun's kick had surprised the kid, especially since he'd held the piece in that showtime sideways gangstuh grip that almost guaranteed a miss at anything more than ten feet away. Kody focused on his face, which looked more confused than anything else since Kody hadn't bitten the dust. Then the kid stared at Raney, who definitely wasn't the kind of dude you got to target twice.

Raney didn't know much about gang-banger games, but he must have known he couldn't run or the kid would get a free shot at his back. To Kody that was obvious: he charged the wide-eyed little boy before he could pull the trigger again, and Raney followed close behind roaring like an alligator.

This overloaded the little boy's brain... people usually ran *away* from small black kids with big black guns. He dropped the steel with a cobblestone clatter and tried to make a bust for the gate. That wouldn't have done him any good -- even if he'd cleared the spikes he would have been trapped in the courtyard -- and though he grabbed the gate's top bar he couldn't seem to pull himself up despite his frantic struggles. His baggy jeans tumbled around his ankles, comically baring his cocoa-brown butt since he'd gone on this mission commando. Kody grabbed him and yanked him down.

The kid was maybe eight-years-old, with a chubby chest and baby-fat arms but packing an awesomely blubbery belly that hung almost halfway to his knees... which explained why he hadn't been able to climb. He had to lean backward to balance its bulk, which jiggled like Jell-O contained by skin, and though he tried to punch Kody's face, his belly swung like a pendulum, pulling him sideways and making him miss. He was slick as snot with smelly sweat, and Kody lost his grip, but Raney grabbed him around the neck and slammed him against the rough brick wall.

Like Kody, Raney was only thirteen but made of solid muscle. His chest jutted out like a pair of bricks, his biceps bulged like paving stones, and his belly was armored by ripples of bronze. He wasn't any taller than Kody, but fighting him would have been a mistake for anything less than a bulldozer.

Even the little kid wasn't that stupid and went as limp as laundry. He suddenly burst into buckets of tears as Kody snatched the smoking gun, an ancient army .45, and jammed it to his forehead in a grip that *wouldn't* miss.

"The hell is this shit?" Kody yelled.

"Yeah!" bawled Raney, clutching the kid by his throat. The boy's face was shadowed by a wild bush of hair partly tamed by a black bandanna -- the same as the other boys had worn -- which probably explained the shit.

3

Raney glanced at Kody. "You all right, cousin?"

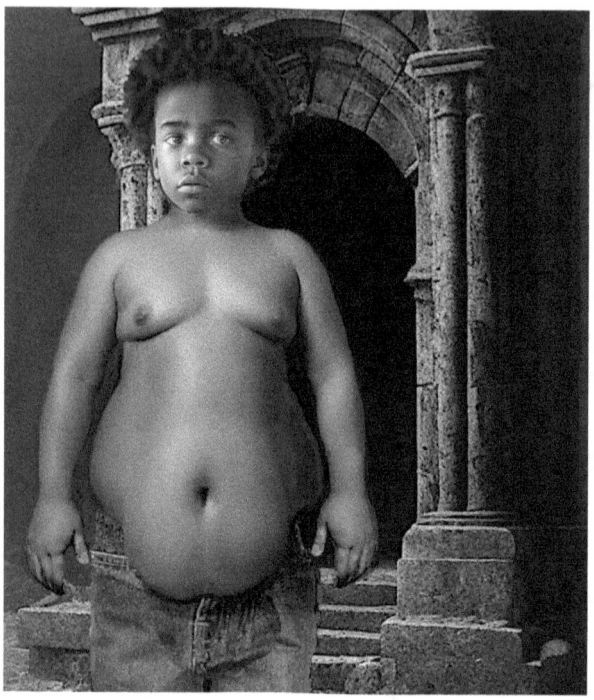

Kody was a chubby boy of the rolly-poly persuasion, sooty black with bobby breasts, and a belly far overlapping his jeans, its navel a funnel-shaped cave into night… though it couldn't compare to the little kid's, which looked more like an accessory melded onto his middle. Kody's face was pear-shaped with chipmunk cheeks and a wide snubby nose, full pouty lips and obsidian eyes beneath a bushy cap of curls, and scowling now as he checked his arm, which was leaking blood but didn't hurt much and seemed to be working okay. The bullet had missed his biceps muscle, cutting clean through its padding of fat. "Pretty much," he puffed, shaking sweat from his hair.

The little kid could barely breathe. His black-coffee eyes rolled back in his head as Raney's fingers throttled his throat. He managed to make a death-rattle sound.

"Easy, cousin," said Kody. "We don't wanna send him to coffin city." He shifted the gun between the kid's eyes. "*Yet*, anyway."

"Please!" rasped the kid, wheezing for air. "Don't hurt me, man!"

"Hurt *you!*" roared Raney. "You just try an' kill my cousin, you dirty little weasel!"

"I had to!" gurgled the kid.

"The hell you sayin'?" Kody demanded, jamming the gun muzzle tighter.

"Hold up, cousin," said Raney, turning his head to scan around. On this sultry day in early June this part of the Quarter was silent as death. "We can't stay here an' figure this out. Somebody might of heard the shot an' maybe called the cops."

Kody nodded, trying to think while his arm was beginning to pulse with pain, and blood was still leaking out.

Raney, like Kody, wore jeans and sneaks, and nothing else but skin. His face, like his body, seemed forged of bronze, with a solid square jaw and determined chin, yet he seldom wore an aggressive expression and his eyes were usually childlike in lack of calculation. He scanned the shadowy alley again, which led to the little courtyard. The liquid music of trickling water echoed between the ancient brick walls. Then he faced the sunlit street. "Y'all think his friends be comin' back?"

"Probably not," said Kody. "If they'd been packin', we'd both be ghosts."

Raney snorted. "I hate this city-ass shit, man! Guns an' gangs an' thugger crap!" He considered the gasping kid, then turned to Kody again. "So, what we gonna do with him? Feed him to my 'gator?"

"No!" cried the kid.

"Shut up!" bawled Kody, surprised by a sudden flame of rage despite the fact this kid had shot him. He was starting to feel sort of dizzy and weak. He glanced down at the cobblestones but there wasn't a lot of blood. Maybe it was the smothering heat, especially here in the alley, which felt like an oven tomb. He wiped more sweat from his eyes.

"Aunt Simone won't be back till dark. Guess we better take him inside." He met the kid's eyes along the gun barrel. "You mess with me an' it's dirt-nap time! You hearin' me, you... damn little nigger?"

"Yeah," gasped the kid, trying to nod, which wasn't the easiest thing to do with Raney wringing his neck.

Kody gave the gun to Raney, then dug a big brass key from a pocket to unlock the rusty wrought-iron gate, pushing it open on hinges that creaked like horror movie sound effects. His jeans rode dangerously low on his hips beneath his lolling belly, baring the plump midnight moons of his bottom, and he yanked them up an inch or two while stepping aside for Raney.

Raney gave the kid a shove, and Kody added a kick to his butt. "Get movin', shithead!"

The kid, his jeans still around his ankles, and leaning way back to balance himself, seemed to be following his belly, which wobbled and wallowed against his bare thighs as he duck-footed over the paving stones in a waddling, bent-kneed, sway-backed gait.

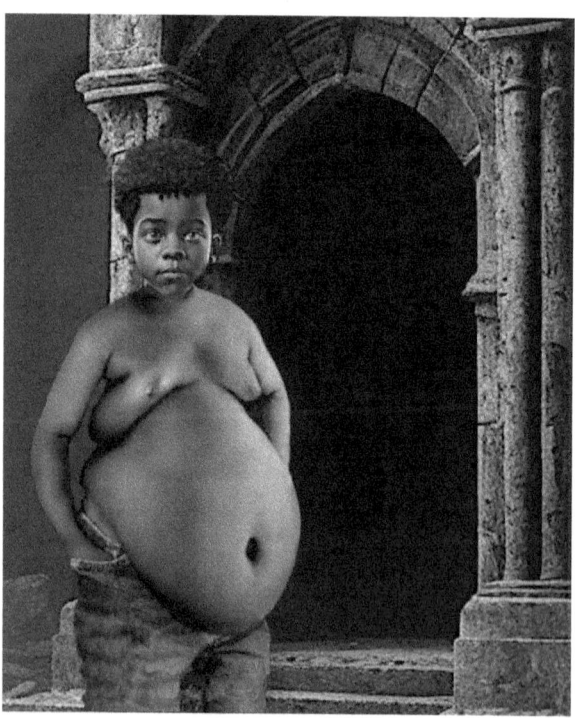

6

Like many French Quarter houses, the one belonging to Kody's aunt was a gauntly narrow two stories tall. It showed its shuttered backside to the street, while its real front faced the courtyard, a forest of ferns and steamy foliage. A mossy fountain was brimming with lilies of the funeral variety, and a fat bronze cherub with a vase on his shoulder eternally filled it with water. There was a wooden table and chairs, and a fire pit circled by blackened bricks where Voodoo rites were held.

The gate clanked shut behind Raney's back with a death-row kind of final sound. Kody yanked open a rusty screen door and shoved the kid into a dark little foyer below a narrow staircase. The ancient house smelled musty and damp, of rotten old wood and crumbling brick. The little kid was sobbing again, and the black bandanna slipped over one eye. He started to pull up his jeans, but Kody grabbed his hair. "Leave 'em down so you can't try an' kick us."

"How I get up dem stairs?" the kid sniffled.

Kody gave him another shove. "Crawl, shithead! Like a coffin worm! You just might need the practice!"

TWO

Kody's room was a spook-house. Its walls were paneled in worm-eaten oak as black as death after two-hundred years, and wooden lathing showed like bones where plaster had dropped from the ceiling. Two tall windows faced the street and opened onto a gallery that overhung the sidewalk. Heavy curtains of deep-purple velvet made the gloomy room look cool, but that was just an illusion. There was a rusty air-conditioner, but using it was a luxury reserved for Kody didn't know what. His aunt often said the house owned *her* instead of the other way around. Naturally, it was haunted, but most houses were in the Quarter.

The space was almost filled by a bed, a massive old mahogany thing. Its headboard was carved with an eerie scene of ghoulish grave-robbers at work in the night beneath a sickle of moon. You couldn't quite see their faces, and were somehow glad you couldn't. The bed's tall posts were topped with skulls that grinned a toothy welcome… Marie Laveau, the Voodoo Queen, had supposedly had it built. An ancient clothes-press stood in a corner, looming like a monster's coffin, and there was an ebony chest of drawers with a murky mirror above. Faces and things would appear in the glass… Kody preferred the faces to things, even if they were only bone. Cobwebs clung in shadowy corners and draped the blades of a ceiling fan with spectral threads of spider silk. The fan was turning slowly now, stirring the heat like a witch's brew, and all three boys were dripping sweat.

Kody shoved the kid into the room. He hadn't made him crawl up the stairs, but climbing wasn't easy for him packing that blubbery bulk of belly, so Kody and Raney had taken his arms and not gently frogmarched him up. Then, using the strap from his travel tote, Kody tied the boy's hands behind his back and then to a skeletal bedpost, where he stood with his belly dangling down, its tunnel-like navel leaking sweat that puddled on the black floor boards. Raney raided his aunt's sewing box to make a bandage for Kody's arm after dousing the wound with antiseptic from the bathroom cabinet. The bleeding had just about stopped; and Raney went out to the kitchen fridge to snag a forty-ounce of malt.

"Here, cousin," he said, returning. "Good ol' snake-bite remedy."

"Thanks," said Kody and took a long swig.

Raney plopped down in a plush velvet chair and mopped his face with the back of a hand. "Had enough action for one day, cousin, so what we do for a love scene?"

Kody went to one of the windows, staying warily off to one side, and parted the drapes to scan the street. A few people passed on the opposite sidewalk, mostly tourists armed with cameras and searching for the "real" New Orleans of vampires, Voodoo and grisly ghosts, but there was no sight of the thugger kids. A middle-aged white couple stood in their place, probably reading the sign at the alley, which advertised the Voodoo rites, touted tours of the haunted house, and boasted of Kody's creepy old bed.

"Ain't sure," said Kody, closing the curtains. "Nobody tried to kill me before. ...'Least nobody alive." He fingered the gun, which felt hot in his hand but also somehow comforting, then checked the clip, finding five bullets left. "Well?" he demanded, facing the kid. "Why you try an' cap me... *boy?*"

For a moment the little dude tried to come bad, which wasn't an easy part to play: for one thing he was way too cute with a button-nosed cherubic face, while the black bandanna still over one eye made him look like a kid playing pirate. He'd been watching the other boys swigging malt and had wistfully licked his lips several times while trickles of sweat ran down his cheeks. "Ain't tellin' you fuckin' nothin'!" he spat.

"If I gotta get outta this chair..." Raney warned.

Kody took a direct approach, jamming the gun to the little kid's chest about where he figured a heart would be, an inch from the

Hershey's Kiss of a nipple. "Don't dance with me, boy! My name ain't Barney!"

"Okay!" cried the kid, almost sobbing again. "It was nothin' personal."

"*What!*" yelled Kody. He jabbed the gun muzzle tighter. "The hell you tellin' me, nigger?"

Raney raised an eyebrow.

The kid began to cry again. "I wanted ta join da Skeleyton Crew, an' dey tole me I gotta cap somebody ta show 'em I was worthy."

For a moment Kody almost felt sick, like a bony claw had clutched his guts. Maybe it was only the smothering heat. Or maybe the pulsing pain in his arm. But no, he thought, it was something else... it was knowing he'd just been a random mark for this baby-banger's initiation!

Kody almost pulled the trigger! Something seemed to laugh in his mind... thirteen years of hopes and dreams, of staying in school, getting good grades, and trying like hell to be a good person; and this snotnose *nigger* had tried to kill him just because he'd turned a corner!

"It coulda been him," the kid went on, jerking his baby-chub jaw at Raney. "Dey tole me ta cap da first mark I seen, 'less dey was ol' or white."

"What the hell difference that make?" rumbled Raney.

"Ol' people don't count, an' cappin' a whiteboy is trouble."

Raney shook his head. "I hate this thugger bullshit!"

"You said that already," said Kody.

"Can I have a drink?" asked the kid. He looked down at the gun to his heart. "I sorry, okay?" he added, then sneezed.

"Bless... Shit!" muttered Kody. "'You're sorry!'" He lowered the gun, not trusting himself, and took his finger off the trigger. "I feel like throwin' up."

"You an' me both," said Raney. "But I don't wanna lose a good lunch 'cause of him."

Kody snagged the bottle and tilted it to the little kid's lips. The boy gulped fast and sloppily, dripping amber foam on his chest.

"Tanks," he finally panted, with a fourth of the bottle inside his belly and more than a little all over it. But then a new look flashed on his face, of sudden and total terror. "Oh, shit!" he cried, and more tears fell. "Now dey gonna kill *me!*"

"What you sayin'?" growled Raney.

The kid began to cry again. "I ain't worthy!" He stared around in wide-eyed horror, as if a ghost had materialized and rattled its mouldering bones. "An' I lost his gun!"

Kody glanced down at the .45. "Your 'mentor's' piece?" he asked. "That big bad boy who bailed his butt when you didn't drop me?"

Raney made a disgusted sound. "Kids really that stupid 'round here?"

"They do it in Cleveland, too," said Kody. "Why dad send me down here in summer." He almost laughed. "He thinks I'm safer in 'Nawlins."

"I can't go home!" cried the kid. "Dem niggers be waitin' for me!"

"The hell!" roared Raney. "Y'all think we just gonna let you go like you just flipped us off or somethin'?"

"But I *can't* go home!" howled the kid.

Kody studied the boy: his tears looked on the real, but little... niggers... lied so much they half believed they were telling the truth. He felt the gun's heat in his hand again, which seemed strange after only one shot. He tossed the piece to Raney, then untied the kid from the bedpost.

"What you doin'?" sniffled the boy.

"Gettin' you outta my sight, shithead. Just lookin' at you make me 'shamed to be black. My grandfather was a Panther. You probably never heard of them. *He* was fightin' for somethin' good. But now what we got? Rag-ass gang-bangin' babies like you who kill your own brothers for turnin' a corner!"

"Hold on," said Raney. "You can't turn him loose."

"Looks like I'm doin' it, don't it?"

"No!" cried the kid. "You can't!"

Kody scowled. "Pull up your Pampers an' get the hell out!"

"No, man! I can't! Dem niggers be waitin'!"

Kody suddenly grabbed the kid and shoved him to one of the windows. Then he parted the drapes.

"No!" the kid pleaded, trying to get away from the glass.

"Go out on the gallery!" Kody ordered. "Put on a thug-o-rama show to prove how bad you think you are!"

The kid fell to his knees at Kody's feet. "Please!" he sobbed. "Don't make me go out dere!"

Kody raised the luggage strap like a whip above the kid's bare back. "Go on, nigger!"

Raney cocked his head. "We could do without that nigger stuff, cousin. My daddy'd go upside my head if I called somebody that."

"That's what he is!" bawled Kody. "A dammed, stupid, worthless, nigger!"

"No, please!" cried the kid.

Kody snorted. "I thought you lost 'his' gun? So, what you worried about?"

"He gots another one!"

"So, why didn't he finish what you tried to start?"

"He don't got no bullets for it."

"Mmm," said Raney thoughtfully. "I think he be on the real 'bout them other weasels wantin' to kill him." He flipped the pistol in his palm. "What if we give this back to you?"

The kid kept on crying. "Den I gotta cap somebody else."

"So what's the problem... boy?" said Kody. "Don't wanna play big bad baby no more? ...Or, you startin' to figure out what bein' a 'gangstuh' really means? ...You already got enough enemies, fool, just for bein' black, you don't gotta go out an' make 'em!" He snatched the gun from Raney and jammed it to the kid's forehead. "This ain't no video game... *boy!* I pull this trigger, it's death on the real! The lights go out, an' it's dark forever, an' there's nothin' but worms in your future!" That suddenly seemed like a cool idea!

The kid shied away from the gun like a puppy away from a mess he'd made, but then his eyes widened in sudden new fear as he stared over Kody's shoulder. "What's dat?" he cried.

"What?" asked Kody, alert for a trick.

The kid aimed a trembling finger. "In da mirror! I seen a *face!*"

Raney smiled. "Y'all owe us five dollars, darlin'."

"...Huh?"

"*He* won't hurt you," said Kody, glancing at the murky mirror. "Not like your little gang-baby boys."

"...You gots a ghost in dis house?" asked the kid.

"This is 'Nawlins, darlin'," said Raney. "You don't got a ghost, your neighbors would talk."

The boy struggled to get his feet against the wobbly weight of his belly spilling over his thighs. Kody grabbed him under the arms and pulled him to a version of vertical. When Kody did nothing else, the kid shambled back to the bed and sat down, but kept his eyes away from the mirror. "What I do now?" he whimpered.

Kody put the gun on the dresser, where it reflected in the glass. "What about your folks?" He poked the kid's belly with a finger, which almost sank out of sight. "You sure ain't been homeless."

The kid wiped his eyes with the back of a hand. "Only got mom, an' she... on crack. Da Skeleyton Crew let me hang with 'em, an' I been eatin' good. Dat what da game all about."

"You play, you pay," said Kody. He poked the kid's belly again. "That was the play, but now is the pay, an' it cost a lot more than you thought, huh?"

The kid sneezed again and looked ready to cry.

"Bless... Shit!" Kody yanked off the kid's bandanna. "Wipe your snotty-ass nose. ...Are you on somethin'?"

"Nah. Gots me a summer cold, is all. Mom always say dey da worst."

Kody glanced at Raney and shrugged. "Any ideas, cousin?"

"Y'all could give him back the gun."

"Funny, man, but no cigar."

"I wouldn't kill you if you did," said the boy. "Swear ta god, man! You was right, dis ain't cool shit."

"I don't wanna find out if you lyin'," said Kody.

"Only one way to find out," said Raney.

"Why I don't wanna." Kody studied the kid again. "Figure those punks would hurt your mom if they can't get you?"

"I dunno," the kid sniffled.

"Didn't think about that either, did you?"

The boy hung his head, "Nah, I didn't."

"Well," said Raney. "Your 'friends' don't know what happen to you. Your baby bow-wows bailed they butts an' left you on your lonesome, darlin'. ...Y'all really that stupid?"

The kid puffed his baby-breasted chest. "Had a B average in school."

"I mean to believe in that gang-bangin' bull."

"Just said I don't believe it no more."

"Trouble is, darlin', I don't believe you."

Kody said, "Maybe they think we called the cops an' you're in jail now."

"Dey find out about dat," said the kid. "Dey said dey could get me anywheres if I wasn't worthy. Even outside a grave."

"Beyond the grave," Kody corrected. "But they're still only kids. An' I hate to say it, but you're probably smarter than them. ...Which ain't sayin' much." He paused to think again. "For all they know we capped your ass an' dumped your corpse in the river. ...Where you live?"

"In da Projects. By Cemetery Number One. Same as dem."

"Like fish in a little ol' pond," sighed Raney. "Y'all can only feed on each other. Ain't bad enough you poor as dirt an' dumb as Mississippi mud, you gotta go killin' each other, too."

The gate buzzer sounded.

"Oh shit!" cried the kid. "Dey come for me, man!"

Kody grabbed the gun off the dresser.

"Damn!" muttered Raney, now on his feet. "Wish I had my 'gator gun!"

"Chill out," said Kody, though scared himself. He pointed to the coffin-like press. "Get in there... what's your name?"

"Newton," said the kid.

"Get in there an' keep your ass quiet!"

"What should I do?" asked Raney.

"Lock it when he gets inside. I'ma go see who it is."

"My belly ain't gonna fit!" cried Newton after backing into the press.

"Suck it in," said Raney.

"I am!"

"Then you gonna get squeezed a little."

"How I gonna breathe, man?"

"Y'all don't shut up an' get in there, you might not have to anymore!" Raney locked the clothes-press door after fairly gently compressing the kid. He slipped the key in his pocket and looked ready to wrestle something. "I got your back, cousin."

"With what?" said Kody. "Those muscles of yours ain't bulletproof."

"Just be careful, cousin. I don't wanna see your face in that mirror."

"I don't wanna see yours out of it." Kody left the room and descended the stairs, the gun gripped in both hands. He wondered if the ghost was watching and what it might think if it was... like, why black kids were killing each other instead of picking cotton? He eased the screen door quietly open and crept along the house to the gate, pushing through foliage tangled with ivy while rats scuttled squeaking out of his way. He stopped at the corner to plan his next move... should he risk a peep? That could get him a face full of lead. He sucked a deep breath and called, "Who's there?"

"Hello?" said a man's voice, sounding white. "Are you giving haunted house tours today?"

Kody blew out a sigh of relief. He was sweating as much as Newton, and his jeans were as soddenly soaked as if he'd been drenched in a thunderstorm. He tugged them up to a more decent level, slipped the gun in a back pocket, then cautiously eased around the corner. There was the middle-aged couple he'd seen out on the street a few minutes ago. He definitely didn't feel up for a tour, but life went on and his aunt needed money like everyone else on the physical plane. He made himself smile, a Voodoo boy, a magic descendant of African chiefs. He usually wore a loincloth and a necklace of bones while giving these tours, but it was too late to put them on. Fortunately the bleeding had stopped so the bandage looked like a decoration bound around his arm.

"Sho'," he said, unlocking the gate. "Right dis way, folks. Ah hopes y'all ain't scared of ghosts."

THREE

"**A**ren't you frightened?" asked the woman. "All alone in a haunted house?"

Kody paused at the door to his room. Although two-stories, the house was small, and the tours only took about half an hour unless there were lots of questions. The furniture was tattered and old, giving the place a ghostly look, enhanced by the shadows and cobwebby corners -- his aunt encouraged "spider art" -- and also the musty graveyard smell. His aunt had a TV and some modern things, like a microwave and a Mac computer, but they were usually kept out of sight so the house was like a living museum... or living in one, anyhow.

In the parlor stood an idol of Ethu, a little black eight-year-old boy with horns. He was carved life-size from ebony wood and looked almost real in the shadows. Like Newton, he packed an awesome belly that hung almost halfway to his knees, and posed leaning backward to balance himself. A candle eternally burned at his feet amongst a pile of offerings -- toys and things a young boy would like -- but also cigars and a bottle of rum. A believer had left him an I-pod, and he wore the headphones over his ears atop his bush of genuine hair... a lot of which was Kody's. His eyes were glass -- Kody assumed -- as black as night and filled with joy, which often made visitors smile. Kody had formerly played Ethu's role in the nighttime Voodoo ceremonies, until he'd gotten too old for the part, attaching goat horns to his head with glue... which hurt like hell to remove. His aunt had been using a neighbor's son, but he'd gone to live with his father this summer, so Ethu wasn't appearing live until she found a replacement.

There was also an altar to Baron Samedi -- or Semetery, as some people called him -- the Keeper of Graveyards and Guardian of the Dead. He was sometimes portrayed as a rough wooden cross draped in a long black funeral coat with a top-hat crowning the vertical beam, but Aunt Simone had her own eerie version, a skeleton clad in similar garments who ruled the room from a twilight corner.

Offerings were encouraged, and the woman added fifty cents to the pile of coins at the skeleton's feet, plus another quarter for Ethu. Kody always suggested dollars, but his mind was somewhere else right now... between the spill of his belly in front and the weight of the gun in his pocket behind, his jeans kept slipping off his butt, and he didn't know how to get rid of the steel without maybe freaking his guests.

On a wall hung relics from slavery days; a leather bullwhip -- which might or might not have been authentic -- a branding iron for runaways, and various cumbersome shackles and chains, which were chillingly on the real. With one hand holding onto his jeans like a cherub retaining his modesty, Kody explained the purpose of each; there were leg-irons, manacles, ponderous collars, all so huge and medieval-looking they might have been made of *papier-mâché* if they hadn't been so obviously heavy. There was also a six-foot "trader's chain," like a cartoon leash for a showtime pit-bull, with an iron collar and huge padlock. Kody clamped it around his neck and invited the man to hold the chain. The man declined with nervous politeness... white people usually did.

Kody's room and Marie Laveau's bed were the last things to see on the tour, and Kody hoped Newton wouldn't sneeze. "Ghosts are people, too," he said, which got the usual tourist chuckle.

"Have you seen it?" asked the man, who had introduced himself and his wife as Mr. and Mrs. Trout.

"Ah feels it, suh, in mah bones," said Kody.

"Do you know who it was?" asked Mrs. Trout. "Is it a he or a she?"

"He a he, ma'am," said Kody. "But we's never been rightly introduced. Mah aunt could tell y'all more if you like, if y'all come back fo' the ceremony. Ah can gives you a half-off rate since you's already taken the tour."

"Does your aunt cast Voodoo spells?"

"Yessum, ma'am, But only good ones."

17

Mr. Trout laughed. "Is she out casting any right now?"

Kody smiled. "She help at the *Vieux Carre* Children's Center. Dey's real busy now with school bein' out an' so many kids with nowhere to go."

"What if I wanted to get rid of somebody?" asked Mr. Trout. "That's hypothetical, of course."

"She could spell him a job in another town, suh. You don't gotta hurt folks to better yourself."

Kody cautiously opened the door. He still wore the collar around his neck and deliberately rattled the chain, which should have sounded a warning to Raney. He wasn't sure where his cousin had gone -- for a dude as solid as Raney, he was pretty good at vanishing -- but he'd also disposed of the forty-ounce bottle and straightened the velvet bedspread where Newton had sat on his sweaty bare bottom. The key was out of the clothes-press door, which meant Newton was still inside. It had to be hotter than hell in there, though Kody wondered why he cared.

"Look at that bed!" cried Mrs. Trout, and hurried over to study the carvings.

"It would sure take me out of the 'mood,'" laughed the man, giving Kody a wink.

Mrs. Trout snapped several pictures, her camera flash bright in the room's brooding shadows. "Does anyone sleep in it now?" she asked.

"Ah does, ma'am," said Kody. "But, ah's descended from African chiefs, so's ah's safe from evil spells." He told the usual tale of the bed and spoke for a time of Marie Laveau, who might have been the most powerful woman in the history of New Orleans. "She surely be de most famous," he finished.

"We heard she's buried in Saint Louis Cemetery Number One," said Mr. Trout.

"Her grave be there, suh," said Kody. "But nobody know where her bones went to! Dey took 'em away a long time ago 'cause somebody woulda stole 'em!"

Mrs. Trout shuddered. "Why would anyone steal her bones?"

"'Cause dey be powerful *gris-gris*, ma'am... dat's magic stuff, like accessories. Y'all could cast some mighty big spells with magical bones like hers! ...Dey's a tour every day from da Voodoo Museum over on Rue Dumaine. Say you was here an' dey gives you a discount. ...Now, Miz Laveau, she get lots of letters. An' special-delivery packages, too. Delivered right to her tomb."

"But, you said she isn't in it."

"Her bones be gone, ma'am, but her spirit come back every night."

"To read her mail?" asked Mr. Trout, smiling.

"Sho'," said Kody. "She gotta keep current."

"Could we go there alone?" asked Mrs. Trout. "And save the price of a tour?"

"Ah wouldn't advise it, ma'am." Kody glanced at the clothes-press. "Dere be Projects across da street."

The man and woman exchanged knowing glances. They might have been white from a small Kansas town, but they knew what "Projects" were all about.

Kody added, "An' dey lock da graveyard gates at three. Ah's heard lots of stories 'bout careless folks gettin' locked in dat spooky ol' place overnight. One guy was only twenty years ol', but his hair had turned *white* by mornin'!"

The woman actually shivered, but seemed to be enjoying the tale. "Can you do magic and Voodoo? You seem to know so much about it."

Kody shrugged. "Ah can do me a few simple spells. But mah aunt always sayin' ah don't pays attention, an' don't practice much as ah should."

"Not doing your Voodoo homework?" asked Mr. Trout with a smile. "And no doubt playing video games," he added, pointing to a controller that sat on the ebony dresser.

"Ah 'spose y'all could say dat, suh. But, Voodoo a lot more den magic. It be a good an' ancient religion with roots goin' way back to Africa. Some say it was da first religion, an' da word itself mean spirit. But, most people don't know nothin' about it, 'cept what dey seen in horror movies."

"It does seem like black magic," said Mrs. Trout.

Kody patted his night-colored chest. "It *our* magic, ma'am, if you knows what ah means. But, black ain't da color of evil, ma'am... evil come in all colors. An' Voodoo ain't evil, just misunderstood. No offense, ma'am, but it funny how white folks likes elves an' wizards, leprechauns an' Harry Potter, Lord Of Da Rings an' dat kinda magic, but y'all think Voodoo is evil 'cause dat what you been taught. But, Voodoo gots laws like everythin' else. 'Cept dey be laws you best not break. An' one of 'em's usin' magic fo' evil." Kody glanced at the clothes press. "Y'all might say, if you play, you pay. But da price be your soul lost fo' ever!"

"Could you hurt someone by sticking pins in a doll?"

"Maybe, ma'am. But dat be a bad thing to do. Besides bein' mostly Hollywood shi... stuff. If ah really hads me a enemy, ah try an' make 'em mah friend."

"Throw a love-spell on them?" chuckled the man.

"You can't *make* nobody love you, suh. You can only show 'em *why* dey should love... kinda like settin' a 'zample... an' let 'em decide fo' demselves."

Mr. Trout took his wife's hand. "I think I'd agree with that."

"Could you call up your ghost?" asked Mrs. Trout. "I've always wanted to see one."

"She loves vampires, too," said Mr. Trout. "She's read every one of Ann Rice's books."

"Maybe, ma'am," said Kody. "But ah wouldn't know what to do with him, an' ghosts get awful mad when dat happen… gettin' called up for no good reason. Why, dere was a guy last summer... da cops found him dead in a house up da block! He was layin' in one of dem pentacle drawin's he'd made with chalk on da floor. ...Dey like a protective circle fo' you."

"But, what happened to him?" asked Mrs. Trout. "If he was safe in his circle?"

"He died of starvation, ma'am! He'd called up somethin' *nasty*, but he didn't know how to put it down! An' he couldn't leave his ring of protection or den it woulda *got* him! Dat's one of da rules of magic, ma'am... never call up what you can't put down." Kody flexed his chubby fingers. "But ah gives it a try if you like? No extra charge."

The woman shivered again. "No, thank you! I'd much prefer a friendly ghost."

Mr. Trout laughed. "She collects Casper memorabilia, too." He regarded the grisly old bed. "I don't care for the theme of those carvings... skeletons, coffins, and grave-robbing ghouls... but it's an impressive piece of work. ...We sell antiques on-line."

"Mah aunt was offered fifty-grand."

Mr. Trout whistled. "Can its history be verified?"

"Dey's lots of stories 'bout Miz Laveau, but ain't too much in da way of facts."

The man laughed again. "We hear that all the time in our business... 'George Washington slept in this bed,' and other such tales of fake provenance."

"Well, suh, I kinda think, if she did have it built, she only use it fo' unwelcome guests, to give 'em bad dreams so dey didn't stay long."

Mr. Trout stepped to the coffin-like press. "This is also a fine old..." Then he started. "What's that? I heard a sound in there."

"Prob'ly jus' a rat, suh. Dey's rats all over da Quarter."

Mrs. Trout smiled nervously. "Not your ghost?"

"Well," said Kody, improvising. "He usually don't come out in da day. ...'Course, we been talkin' 'bout spirits an' such, so maybe dat got him interested."

The man slipped an arm around his wife: for a moment they looked like teens on a date. "We'll be back for the ceremony."

"Starts right after sunset, suh. Y'all come early an' get da best seats."

The man gave Kody twenty dollars as his wife arranged her hair at the mirror. "Keep the change, son. And thank you for the tour. We'll tell our friends back home."

"May I take your picture?" asked Mrs. Trout.

"Sho', ma'am," said Kody. "But, you might wanna wait till tonight. Ah dresses up in bones an' such. Fo' da atmosphere."

"That would be fine," said Mrs. Trout.

Kody escorted his guests to the gate, made sure it was locked behind them, then ran puffing back up to his room with the heavy chain clanking over his shoulders.

Raney was stepping in through a window, shiny with sweat from the heat outside as if he'd taken a shower. "We oughta get us another

21

forty," he said while closing the drapes.

"Made us a ten dollar tip," said Kody. "You could go to the market."

A small fist pounded the clothes-press door. "Get me da fuck outta here!" Newton howled.

Raney tossed the key to Kody. "What we gonna do 'bout him?"

"I don't know," said Kody. "I really think he's scared to leave, an' those other punks *would* try to kill him. It's some kinda stupid gang 'respect.'"

Raney snorted. "Ain't nothin' 'bout gang shit I respect!" Then he considered. "But, don't forget, if he kills one of us, he be 'worthy' with them. Guess he don't gotta use a gun, an' they's lots of knives in the kitchen."

"Lemme out!" wailed Newton again. "Dere somethin' *nasty* in here!"

Kody unlocked the clothes-press door and Newton leaped into his arms. "I'm scared!" he cried, clutching Kody.

Kody peered into the shadows, seeing nothing except the clothes he'd brought... T-shirts, jeans, and a Cleveland Browns hoodie. "Ain't nothin' in there," he said, setting Newton onto his feet. "Check it out."

"Is so, dammit! Somethin' *tickled* me in da dark!"

"Probably just my hoodie sleeve."

"No! It was *cold!* A-an' it *whispered!*"

Raney laughed. "Y'all owe us another five dollars, darlin'."

Kody checked the press again, moving his shirts around on a shelf.

"Hey!" Newton yelped. "Dere's a skeleyton!"

"It's only a skull," said Kody. He patted its smooth ivory dome. "It's part of my Voodoo homework."

"It *whispered* ta me!" cried Newton, hastily backing away from the press.

"It's never said nothin' to me," said Kody. "An' I been tryin' to get it to talk ever since I was your age."

Raney smiled. "Too bad it don't talk when tourists here, that be worth five more dollars."

Newton warily eyed the skull after reaching the other side of the bed. "Maybe it heard what you said ta dem people? 'Bout callin' up ghosts, what I sayin'."

Kody closed the door. "No tellin' what it hear or see. Or what it thinks if it does. I used to worry a little... like, when I was takin' a shower. But then I decided the hell with it. After all, it's dead, so why should I care if it saw me naked."

Newton yanked up his jeans. "No damn dead thing gonna see *me* naked!"

Raney laughed. "How long it been since you seen *yourself* naked?"

"...Huh? ...Oh." Newton regarded his belly. "I always been chubby. Mom used ta cook in a Cajun joint, 'fore... like I said."

"She musta been good," said Kody.

"Got dat right," said Newton, leaning backward even more and proudly patting the pendulous proof.

"So, why she get on crack?" asked Raney.

"...Maybe 'cause of me. ...Like, 'sponsibilities."

"I'm sure it wasn't you," said Kody. "You seem like a pretty good kid... when you're not actin' a thugger fool."

"...Guess I was, most da time. ...I'm thirsty. Gots any more brew?"

Raney turned to Kody. "So, what we gonna do with him? I still don't trust him, cousin."

"I said I was sorry," said Newton.

Kody touched his bandaged arm. "That don't make me feel any better."

"How is it?" asked Raney.

"Hurts a little, but you cleaned it good, an' I never got infection before. I could tell Aunt Simone I cut it on somethin'... like, choppin' wood for the ceremony."

"She know you was lyin'. She always does."

"Well, maybe she won't even axe. Another forty would help." Kody gave Raney the twenty dollars.

"I get us a couple," said Raney.

"I'm hungry," said Newton.

"Thought your gang was feedin' you, darlin'?"

"Wasn't no time for lunch today."

"Guess killin' somebody was more important."

"There's crawfish pie in the fridge," said Kody.

Raney frowned. "Y'all watch your back with him, cousin. They's

23

lots of sharp things in this house."

"I got it covered." Kody took off the massive chain and clamped the huge collar around Newton's neck. Then he locked the end to a skeletal bedpost.

"Don't leave me in here *alone!*" cried Newton. He tugged at the big rusty chain like a puppy, while staring wide-eyed at the press.

"Chill out, little man," said Kody. "I'ma put the pie in the microwave."

"Take me with you! Please, man! Don't leave me in here with dat nasty ol' ghost!"

"Where he tickle you, darlin'?" asked Raney.

"He wasn't dat nasty."

"I'll be back in a minute," said Kody.

"No! Please, man! It *scared* me!"

Raney laughed. "Wouldn't be much of a ghost if it didn't."

FOUR

Night was beginning to settle in; that quiet time between daylight and dark when cooking aromas haunted the air like friendly beckoning spirits. In New Orleans there were many food scents and all of them were tantalizing... Cajun, Creole, and French cuisine, barbecued ribs and broiled steaks, crispy fried chicken and succulent shrimp, catfish, gumbo, beans and rice. No wonder the place was called Fat City, and Kody got chubbier every year. He'd only been here a few days, but his belly was hanging at least an inch lower and his jeans would hardly stay on. For that he could blame his cousin Raney, who ate all the time when he was in town as if he'd been saving his appetite for Kody's yearly summer stay. Their days began with massive breakfasts -- sausage and eggs, hash-brown potatoes, biscuits, gravy, and hot buttered grits -- followed by a monster lunch at one of the many restaurants. They topped it off with gigantic suppers, snacked while playing Kody's games, and raided the fridge after midnight. But, Raney could eat like an alligator and never gain an ounce -- or if he did, it went to his muscles -- while Kody only got fatter.

They hadn't gone out for dinner tonight because of Newton chained to the bed and terrified of being alone, but Raney had shown off his cooking skills after making a run to the Red & White Market, producing a boatload of 'gator burgers. He'd also bought a pecan pie and a can of whipped cream to crown it.

Kody had opened the windows, though leaving the drapes securely shut, and the shadows had settled so deep in the room that Raney was almost invisible taking a nap in the ancient chair, while Kody stood out on the gallery, barefoot in only his jeans. There weren't many signs of life at this hour, though Bourbon Street was beginning to boom a couple of blocks away. Its rhythm was like the heartbeat of jazz, and would quicken and throb as the night grew older. Later there might be mysterious drums from over in Congo Square.

Newton was also asleep. He'd gobbled up everything given to him and washed it down with a whole forty-ounce... his capacity for stuffing himself seemed almost supernatural. He lay sprawled on the bed in the heavy slave collar, his arms flung out like a crucified kid, his belly bulging like a balloon that looked about ready to pop.

Kody leaned on the wrought-iron rail and balanced the skull from the press in one hand, while holding the gun in the other. "Talk to me," he said to the skull, while peering into its empty orbits, its noseless nose an inch from his own as if regarding Yorick. "Who were you? Tell me your story." Kody opened his mind and waited.

The air was still hot, and he glistened with sweat as if someone had polished a midnight. More sweat dripped from his cave of a navel to spatter the cobblestones below. It usually took him a week to adapt, and the titanic meals made him sleepy and slow like the pace of life in New Orleans.

The skull only smiled as skulls always do, and Kody set it down on a plastic patio chair. He parted the curtains to check on Newton, then returned to the rail and sighed. There were girls out there in that hot steamy night, some of them no doubt looking for boys, and he was stuck here with a... *damned little nigger!*

At least his arm had mostly stopped hurting. Getting shot sounded dramatic, but the wound wasn't more than a two-inch gash in the chubbines padding his bicep. It probably should have had stitches, though a bullet scar would be cool to take home like a souvenir of his summer adventures. But, one was more than enough.

He tensed for a moment as two younger boys came walking around the Chartres Street corner, but they were toting tap-dancing shoes and sharing a bottle of beer. Another movement caught his eye, but it was only a scuttling rat. A white kid appeared, maybe seventeen and dressed like a showtime vampire, strolling along in a black satin cloak as twilight deepened to gunmetal dusk.

It was tempting to try to forget the gang; the Skeleton Crew were only young kids… but they were also deadly. Raney would soon return to the bayou, but Kody was here for almost three months, and the Quarter wasn't a very big place. Sooner or later he'd meet them again. And, worse, they knew where he lived.

He scanned the darkening sidewalks: he almost *wanted* to see them below, creeping along like rats in a gutter and hoping to catch him off guard. There were four them, but he had five bullets; plenty to even the odds. He stroked the gun barrel thoughtfully, almost enjoying its promise of power, the feeling of reassurance it gave, the comforting knowledge that it could protect him. As he'd noticed before it seemed strangely warm, but that was somehow comforting, too. He glanced at the skull on the chair.

"What choice I got?" he asked. "If I turn Newton loose with this gun, he might try cappin' somebody else. Maybe just to save his own life, but that's no justification. An' without the gun the others might kill him."

Again, he opened his mind and waited, but the skull only smiled in sepulchral silence.

"Lotta help you are," said Kody. "Raney was right, y'know? It's all so stupid an' childish. They're ignorant kids playin' gangster games they seen in movies an' rap videos. It ain't bad enough they're poor as dirt, but they gotta put each other in it."

He fingered the gun once more. "Maybe the world would be better without 'em?" Then he shrugged. "Aw, why am I talkin' to you about this? You might have owned my great-great-grandfather."

From Royal Street came a clopping of hooves as a carriage of tourists went rattling past, crossing Ursulines Avenue. Kody opened his mind again, but couldn't "see" or feel the gang.

"So, why use magic?" he asked the skull, while waving the gun in its toothy face. "Magic takes practice an' lots of hard work; a gun only needs its trigger pulled… an' even a little nigger can do it."

He picked up the skull and returned to his room. He put the death's-head back in the clothes-press and lay the gun on the chest of drawers. The mirror was like an obsidian window instead of only a looking-glass. Sometimes he thought he could see a faint flicker, like something hovering deep inside, but nothing definite swam into view to gaze at him with empty sockets. He switched on the room's feeble lights, candle-shaped bulbs in ornate wall brackets that mostly annoyed the gathering gloom. The ancient gas lamps were functional but his aunt only used them for tours. Newton woke up and looked around. "I gotta go ta da batroom."

Raney also stirred and yawned. "Aunt Simone back yet?"

"Nah," said Kody. "But, I should start buildin' the fire."

"How was Voodoo practice?" asked Raney.

"Dead things ain't talkin' to me tonight." Kody tossed Raney the slave collar key. "Newt's gotta go."

Raney got up and stretched. "What we gonna tell Aunt Simone?" He glanced at Newton. "'Bout him?"

"Ain't thought about it."

Raney raised an eyebrow. "So, what you been thinkin' about? He's our problem now."

Kody shrugged. "I dunno. Guns an' shit. ...Stupid niggers. They go together."

Raney frowned. "Stop sayin' that word, it make *you* sound stupid. An' them ain't our worries right now." He glanced at Newton again. "Simplest thing be to throw him out. It him they wanna kill, not us."

"No, please!" cried Newton.

"Don't get him started again," said Kody. "...Guess we could keep him on the under. 'Least for tonight."

"Don't put me back in dat coffin!" wailed Newton.

"It's not a coffin, dammit," said Kody.

"Then where we gonna hide him?" asked Raney. "They gonna be tourists all over the house."

"We'll think of somethin'," said Kody. "Just take him to the bathroom, aight? I'ma get dressed for the ceremony."

Raney unlocked the chain from the bed and led Newton out of the room. Kody took off his sweaty jeans, put on a red velvet loincloth and a necklace of bright polished bones, then checked himself in the mirror. A skull appeared where his face should have been, but he was used to things like that and decided it wasn't a sign. ...At least he hoped it wasn't.

28

"If you come from the light, welcome," he murmured, a simple spell of banishment his aunt had taught him long ago. "If you don't, go back to the dark."

Not waiting to see if his magic had worked -- besides, it was only a skull -- he padded into the shadowy parlor to place new candles around the Baron, then did the same for the idol of Ethu. He paused to study the huge-bellied boy with his short little horns and impish grin as Raney returned from the bathroom with Newton duck-footing behind on the chain. "Smile, Newt," said Kody.

"Huh?" said Newton, as if being asked to do something weird.

"I know it ain't cool for a thug, but try."

"Da fuck I got ta smile about?"

Raney growled, "Not bein' worm food if nothin' else."

Newton produced a lopsided grimace and looked like a baby with gas.

"Practice a while," said Kody. "But use the bathroom mirror."

FIVE

Aunt Simone was as black as space and as beautiful as the stars therein. She was also a super-size lady, and Kody thought she looked freezerburn cool in the courtyard's flickering firelight. Tonight she was clad in a satin dress of shimmering electric blue perfectly cut to her full-figured form. Her wrists were encircled with African bracelets woven from colorful telephone wire, and she wore a necklace of ruby glass beads. A headband of feathers adorned her long hair, while gold rings sparked on her fingers. She'd been born and raised in the mountains of Haiti, and her Voodoo was totally on the real... though there were also some French Quarter fronts who were only after tourist dollars and couldn't have cast an actual spell if their souls had depended upon it.

The house had been empty when she had moved in -- around the time Kody was born -- because its ghost had scared everyone out who'd ever tried to live there. But, Aunt Simone had given it hell; the neighborhood still remembered that night when wails and shrieks had ripped through the air until Aunt Simone had commanded, "BE STILL," and now it mostly skulked around, playing tricks like tickling Newton or putting skulls in Kody's mirror. It seldom tried to scare a tourist unless they were smugly skeptical, and then it might tingle the back of their necks or whisper scary things in their ears.

But, there was a lot of showtime in magic; people expected mysterious tricks, and Aunt Simone held a smiling skull, which began to glow eerily blue.

"Voodoo is an ancient religion," she said, surveying her group of guests. "Its roots lie deep in Africa, and its power and wisdom were brought here by slaves."

She gestured beyond the circle of light, and Kody appeared in a brilliant blue flash, a deep muffled boom and a billow of smoke. There was a pretty good crowd this evening, at least thirty people filling the chairs around the ceremonial fire. They had already taken a tour of the house in the greenish glow of the flickering gas, which always set a ghostly mood, though the ghost, as usual, hadn't helped. The courtyard resembled a Haitian jungle overgrown with ferns and vines, and the fountain added a shivery sound as the fat little cherub recycled its water. The table was draped with a crimson cloth, and upon it were skulls and other *gris-gris* -- feathers, beads and bony old things -- but there weren't any pins, or dolls to impale. People also expected those, like Mickey Mouse in Disneyland, but Aunt Simone didn't play with toys.

Kody peered over the dancing flames while standing half concealed in shadow and glistening with baby oil. He wore the heavy old trader's chain in addition to his loincloth, his belly hanging over the latter and almost a loincloth all by itself. Raney had bandaged his arm again, this time using a red satin rag so it looked like part of his costume.

Mr. and Mrs. Trout were there, and Kody smiled in conspiracy, which made them willing participants. Then he glanced to the alley

31

gate, where Raney was standing guard. Raney was also in loincloth, a boy-god gleaming with baby oil, while holding a spear and watching the passage. Usually this was only for show -- "keeping evil spirits away" -- but tonight he was packing Newton's gun.

For a moment there was silence, except for the crackle of burning wood and the trickling splash of the fountain, while the smoke drifted slowly away from Kody. The people, all white, were gazing at him, and he realized he'd missed his cue. Still, nobody was smirking... after all, he'd come back from the dead and was probably sleepy or maybe surprised.

His aunt covered coolly by asking his name, to which he responded, "Nathan, a slave." His aunt remarked it *wasn't* his name: his true name had been stolen from him. But before she sent him "deep in the past," she invited audience questions. The people asked most about plantation life and how he'd been treated by his master. "Nathan" had been a blacksmith's apprentice... many slaves had been skilled in trades and weren't just used for picking cotton. He patiently explained to a guest that blacksmiths didn't often shoe horses; that was a farrier's trade. Of course, few people believed he was dead; most were aware this was only a show, but they learned some truths that wouldn't be told on air-conditioned plantation tours.

Then Aunt Simone "took him back to Africa," and the massive old chain fell off by magic to clatter around his feet. He answered questions about his life before he'd been captured by slavers. The guests were pretty cool tonight -- occasionally there were obnoxious drunks -- but these people wanted to hear the truth and Kody was glad to oblige. His "real name" was Tau, he said; and he spoke of his life on the Ivory Coast, hunting, fishing and growing to manhood. His people had been prosperous before the Europeans came, with castles as mighty as those of England.

But then the slave-traders attacked, and spears had been no match for guns. He told of his voyage on a crowded ship, chained to the planking in dark stinking holds, a torture itself for any people who'd lived all their lives in the sun and fresh air; of how so many had died on the way -- men, women, children, babies -- their bodies thrown into the sea like trash to feed the sharks that followed the ship. He told of the auction in New Orleans -- the slave market was a restaurant now, which probably puzzled the ghosts -- and of seeing his mother and father sold while he was bid on by somebody else and never saw them again.

"Why?" he asked with tears in his eyes... tears that were always on the real. "What gave them the right?"

The people were silent and meditative when "Tau" had finished his story. Aunt Simone asked, "Will you stay and play the drums for us?"

Kody went to an African drum and began to beat a slow rhythm. He glanced at Raney again, who'd been alertly watching the alley, but everything seemed to be cool. Then, Kody scanned the windows above in the other three buildings surrounding the court. Two were houses, closed for the summer, their occupants fled to cooler climes, while the third was a store that faced Royal Street and had no courtyard access. Its lower floor was a tourist trap, selling souvenir shirts and vampire junk, along with "genuine Voodoo dolls complete with authentic hexing pins and made by a real Voodoo priest" (not), but its upper floor was unoccupied and dusty windows stared down at the court like black empty eyes in a skull.

The show hadn't changed from previous summers, and Kody knew it all by heart, his aunt describing Haitian rites and the various Voodoo spirits:

"The Voodoo of Haiti has several gods; the greatest of whom is Baron Samedi, represented tonight by this skull."

There were gasps of wonder among the crowd as the glowing skull floated from Aunt Simone's hand to hover by itself in the air.

"There is also Maman Brigitte," Aunt Simone continued, "the Baron's beautiful wife." Then she smiled. "And little Ethu, their child. You have seen his idol tonight in the house, but perhaps he will join us in spirit..."

Kody beat a dramatic roll. There was another flash and boom, and Newton appeared in a billow of smoke!

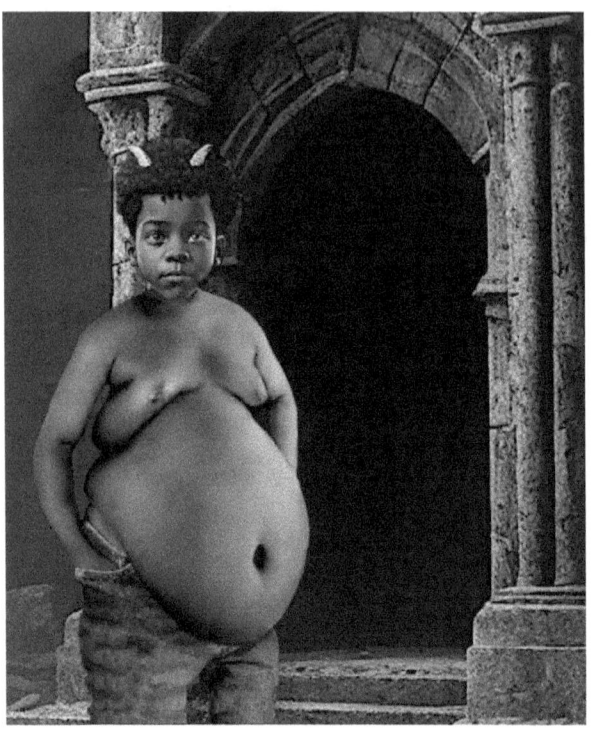

He might have been a little bit drunk, but at least he didn't get stage-fright. He was wearing nothing but baby oil and a few bright feathers beneath his belly secured at his hips with a slim leather strip -- though he didn't need them to conceal anything -- along with a pair of short little horns that poked through his woolly jungle of hair. There hadn't been time to teach him much -- except to smile and stop fronting bad -- but Aunt Simone had been delighted with Kody's "new little friend." Kody had said he was spending the night, adding there were "problems at home"... which wasn't really a lie.

"Ethu" held a cigar in his fingers, and suddenly it was alight. He grinned in a very impish way and took a casual puff.

Aunt Simone continued, "There is nothing evil in Voodoo. And, despite what you may have seen in films, we seldom stick pins into dolls. ...Although, and as with any religion, there are always false priests and charlatans who seek to misuse its power for personal gain or material greed." She turned to Newton. "Ethu is the god of children, and children are always pure in heart. Yet, being innocent, they are often prey to evil influence, so Ethu is their guardian."

"Um," said Newton, taking his cue. "If dere is evil among us ta-night, let's bring it ta light an' banish it!" He gestured to the floating skull, which started to cruise the audience and peer into people's faces. There were many reactions of nervous surprise.

Ethu spread his arms, "Only da good may enter here!"

Then, Kody saw the skull hesitate. Eerily, it turned in the air and seemed to look up at the second-floor windows of the building that faced Royal Street. Kody followed its hollow gaze and saw that one of the windows had opened! He leaped to his feet to yell a warning, but Aunt Simone had seen it, too. She gestured, bringing a thunderous boom and a dazzling flash of brilliant blue light. A billow of smoke burst up around Ethu just as a gunshot popped. The skull dropped into the lap of a guest, a woman who let out a hair-raising scream.

Ethu vanished in the smoke, but Kody dashed to where he'd been standing. Newton was only a small gleaming shape, but still on his feet and seeming unhurt. Kody brought him down like a lion, crashing onto the moss-covered ground and tumbling into the tangle of ferns.

Newton let out a yelp of surprise, but Kody clapped a hand to his mouth and dragged him deep in the foliage. The smoke was starting to clear away. The guests were looking confused... had that been a shot, or just part of the show? Raney had whipped out the pistol, which he'd concealed in his loincloth. For a moment he aimed at the empty window, but saw the people looking around and hid the gun again.

Aunt Simone's eyes penetrated the ferns, where Kody waved an okay. She turned to Raney, who'd recovered the skull and was gently calming the frightened guest. Raney brought the skull to the table, and Aunt Simone resumed her role:

"There is no evil among us, children, but it must have been very near tonight."

"Stay here!" Kody whispered to Newton. "An' keep your ass down!"

He studied the open window above. Would they wait up there for another shot? That would have been stupid as hell, but, after all, they were only kids. And that was the danger of baby-bangers, they took foolish chances that older kids wouldn't. He wondered what he could do: should he take the gun and go after them? But, to get up now would spoil the show.

"I'm scared!" whispered Newton, clinging to Kody.

"Chill out," murmured Kody. "They're probably two blocks away by now, unless they're as dumb as you were today."

The ceremony was almost over. In previous summers they'd had a dancer, and Kody had played the drums for him; but traditional dancers were hard to find, and street kids mostly did tap routines.

Sometimes his aunt gave personal readings after a ceremony, and people often lingered to talk. The Trouts had wanted to take Kody's picture, which was usually good for extra green. The guests were beginning to leave, Raney bowing them out through the gate, until only the Trouts remained. Kody warned Newton to stay on the under, then emerged from his ferny concealment.

"Oh, there he is," said Mrs. Trout. "You promised us a picture, remember?"

"Sho', ma'am," said Kody, tugging his loincloth up a bit. "Take all you want. No extra charge."

Mr. Trout winked. "How's your 'grave?'"

Kody grinned. "You know how that is." He posed between the man and woman while Aunt Simone snapped a picture.

Mrs. Trout asked, "Don't we get to meet Ethu?"

"Um," said Kody. "He done gone back to da spirit world."

The Trouts traded smiles, but the man gave Kody a five-dollar bill, and his wife thanked Aunt Simone. "Tell Ethu I think he's very cute."

They walked hand-in-hand to the gate like kids, then the man turned around and called back, "This is our second honeymoon, and we've really been enjoying ourselves. Tomorrow we're taking the graveyard tour."

Aunt Simone called, "Ethu's blessings upon you, children!"

"'Member to axe fo' da discount," said Kody.

Raney locked the gate and trotted over, toting his long heavy spear.

"Is the child all right?" asked Aunt Simone.

"Yeah," said Kody. "I told him to chill."

Raney growled, "Want me to go out an' track down them weasels?"

Aunt Simone frowned. "You will do no such thing, Raney Tanner! Take that child in the house!" She turned to Kody. "It seems you have something to tell me. I will be in when I clear the table." She saw Kody's eyes flick up to the window. "They have gone. All four of them."

"You seen 'em?" asked Raney.

"I did not need to see them to know there were four, and the eldest is fourteen-years-old. I had our guests to think about or else I would have discovered their names." Aunt Simone faced Kody again. "And *you* would have known they were up there, had you been paying attention!"

"I was!" Kody snapped.

"Only with your eyes. Have I not taught you to see with your spirit?"

"Voodoo ain't helpin' a lot right now."

"Only because you don't practice enough." Aunt Simone looked up at the window. "Little boys playing with guns! Thinking that makes them manly! They should be spanked and sent to bed!"

X X X

"Think you got Newton?" panted Terrel as he reached the top of a dim-lit staircase. He was a honey-brown boy of thirteen with a soft chubby body now dripping sweat from the gang's frantic getaway run. He toted an Olde English forty-ounce and paused for a few thirsty gulps. Like the other three boys he wore big sagger jeans that were dragging the drawers off his bottom, while a black bandanna adorned his short hair.

"Maybe," puffed Rick, fourteen and dusky, his body defined by small kid-muscles below an angular snub-nosed face. He shook sweat drops from his wild bush of hair and cautiously scanned the third-floor hallway, seeming relieved to find it deserted. He'd been packing a cheap little gun in one hand, but now shoved it into a pocket and tugged up his low-riding jeans. "With all that smoke it was hard to tell, but I think I seen Newton go down." He pushed up his slipping bandanna and led the way down the hall. "C'mon before somebody sees us."

"What was that place anyhow?" asked Matt, who was thirteen and so beautifully black a panther would have been jealous. His body was slender and graceful, his eyes as dark as a moonless night, his face more pretty than handsome, and his hair an ebony dandelion puff. A pair of leopard bikini briefs were more than revealed by his dangerous jeans as he padded along after Rick. He touched Rick's shoulder and added, "That was some kinda Voodoo thing! An' them ain't no folk to be messin' with!"

Rick stopped at a door and listened a moment, then dug a key from his pocket. "It was phony-ass shit for marks, fool!"

"I was scared!" whispered Devon. "Did you see that skull? It was floatin' around in the air by itself!" Devon, twelve, was dark-coffee brown with a featureless little-boy's body. His hair was an old-fashioned Afro that shadowed his childish wide-nosed face beneath the bill of a battered Saints cap.

"Everything scares you, nigger," Rick muttered, slipping the key in the lock. "An' that skull was probably on a string with a LED inside. Now, shut the fuck up or you wake up my mom."

Terrel snickered softly. "That would take a astro blast."

Rick spun around and slammed Terrel's chest, knocking him into the opposite wall. "Shut up, nigger!"

"Sorry, man," said Terrel, as Rick opened the door and peered cautiously in.

"Watch your mouth... boy," muttered Rick.

The small living room was messily kept, its battered old furniture bleeding cotton. An ancient console TV was on, pimping cheap junk on the Shopping Network. Rick's mom lay asleep on a tattered sofa, a worn-looking woman as dark as her son and clad in a shabby blue bathrobe. A Night Train bottle was clutched in a hand, and another lay dead on the floor.

"Go on in my room," Rick ordered his posse. He scanned their faces, alert for smirks, as they filed in from the hall. Rick locked the door, turned off the TV, then gently shook his mother's shoulder. "Mom? ...Mom. ...C'mon now, wake up."

The woman stirred and half opened her eyes. "What time is it?"

"'Round about ten. C'mon an' get ready for bed."

"You make any money today?"

"A little, mom."

The woman rubbed her forehead as if trying to press away pain. "The rent's overdue an' the check didn't come. Your father don't pay your support like he should."

Rick sighed. "I got it covered."

A minute later Rick entered his room, which was small and a total disaster. Terrel lay atop the disheveled bed, sharing the forty with Devon and Matt, who were sitting on the floor. Matt was smoking a cigarette, and the air was already hazy. Old comic book covers adorned the walls, mostly of classic superheroes, and a few dusty toys lay scattered around as if forgotten a long time ago. A human skull sat on a beat-up dresser surveying the boys with a sardonic smile, and though obviously old looked new to the room. Surrounding it was some tourist-trap *gris-gris* -- feathers, fake charms, and "spell-casting candles" -- along with the usual kinds of things a young teenage boy would have in his crib -- rap CDs, an old boom-box, and a pile of hip-hop magazines -- though space had been recently cleared for the skull.

Rick snagged a cigarette from Matt, and Devon flicked a lighter for him. Then Rick took the lighter and fired the candles, their glow reflecting from a mirror that hung above the dresser. Finally, he went to an open window that overlooked the cemetery.

Terrel took the bottle from Matt and swigged. "I don't think you got him, Rick. We woulda heard sirens by now."

"Axe me, that's good," said Matt, blowing smoke. "We don't need that kinda trouble."

Rick stood scanning the graveyard, its labyrinth of pale white tombs surrounded by a masonry wall. "I didn't axe you. That nigger ain't worthy, so he's gotta die like all the other niggers who ain't."

"Man, you learn a new word?" asked Terrel. "That 'nigger' shit startin' to wear on me, 'specially out no A."

"Shut up," growled Rick.

"I don't like this gang shit," said Matt. "We was better off dancin' an' sellin' charms."

Rick's eyes remained on the city of death. "Shut the fuck up, stupid nigger! We finally raisin' us power, an' all you doin' is holdin' us down!"

SIX

The three boys sat in the musty parlor, their bodies still slick and shiny with oil in the dim greenish glow of the flickering gas. The skeletal Baron watched from his corner with shadowed eye-sockets and glittering smile, while Ethu grinned at his own living image, who sat on the couch looking scared despite the fierce horns on his bushy-maned head.

"Want a cigar, little man?" asked Kody.

"Fuck yeah," said Newton. "I need doin' somethin'. ...An' another forty."

"Ain't no more, you drank the last one." Kody borrowed a cigar from Ethu and lit it from one of the lamps. He took a puff and sighed out smoke before handing it to Newton, who sucked it like a blunt. Like Raney, who lounged in a nearby chair, Kody was still in his loin-cloth, while Newton still barely wore feathers. There was silence except for the whisper of gas, the slow stately tick of a skeleton clock beneath a glass dome on the mantelpiece, and a sensuous throbbing from Bourbon Street, a sound almost more felt than heard. A carriage rattled past outside accompanied by the clopping of hooves. It might have been 1860 and the boys were slaves awaiting their master while taking liberties with his things.

Kody sat down on the couch beside Newton as Aunt Simone came in from the kitchen. She carried a tray with a bottle and glasses, and looked very stern in her bracelets and beads like the powerful *mambo* she was. She placed the tray on a coffee table and poured seven glasses of Barbancourt rum. It was the good stuff, Kody noted, two years older than him... which usually meant serious shit.

Aunt Simone set a glass at the Baron's feet and another at Ethu's toes. Finally she served the trio of boys, then settled herself in a plush velvet chair while raising an eyebrow at Kody. "I believe you have something to tell me?"

Kody and Raney sipped their rum, while Newton took a gulp from his glass. The boys exchanged glances, then Raney spoke: "Y'all find out any more about 'em?"

Aunt Simone shook her head. "It is hard to follow the mind of a child. Like a shadow in sunlight, a leaf in the wind, it is always elusive and seldom at rest. Children often act before thinking... but the eldest boy thinks, and I don't like his thoughts."

She turned to Newton. "Only *he* wants to kill you, child. I felt only fear from the others. They did not want to come there tonight, but he bends them to his will. He finds it exciting to play with death, yet he has never killed before." She watched Newton's face. "That surprises you?"

"Yeah," said Newton. "He tole me he capped a lotta marks."

Aunt Simone sighed. "The boasting of boys is not unique, though it saddens me what they boast about. But, he *will* murder you if he can. To fail is to lose his followers, and without them he would be nothing. He fears this more than the consequences should he be captured for killing you, and this makes him very dangerous."

She paused to sip from her glass. "If only I had something of his." She paused again to look at Raney. "Take that gun from under your bottom. It can't be very comfortable there. ...No, I do not want to touch it. It screams its hate and fury at me. It was made in 1942 and once belonged to a soldier. It has taken three lives on a battlefield, and thus may have served its purpose. But, it has stolen many more in mindless rage and senseless violence. In fear, greed, and robbery. It almost took *yours*, Kody Carver... I know what that cloth on your arm conceals, though Raney has tended it well. That gun has become an object of evil. Instead of serving, it will be served. You have already felt its corruption."

"Well," said Kody. "I felt a lot safer packin' it. But that's only natural, ain't it? When somebody's tryin' to kill you."

"That is how it begins. At first it makes you feel safe, protected. But

42

then it whispers that you have power... you hold death in your very own hands. And what a seduction that is for a child! You think you do not have to fear anyone. What does it matter if they are bigger, older, or stronger than you?" Aunt Simone shrugged. "But, all of you have handled it now, and little remains of its former possessor except the feelings of power it gave him. Newton was afraid of the thing. He sensed the evil that haunts it."

"Um?" asked Newton. "I thought only houses was haunted."

"Anything may be haunted, child. Or possessed, if you prefer. And that includes yourself."

"Woah!"

Aunt Simone regarded the gun, which Raney had lain on the coffee table. "It has no power on you, Raney Tanner. To you guns are tools and no more. But that other boy...!" She turned to Newton. "It excited him much, did it not?"

"...Yeah," said Newton. "He liked ta... um, never mind."

Aunt Simone smiled. "I know the symbolism, child. ...Just as it did a few minutes ago when he tried to murder you with another. It gives him the power of the powerless, and that will destroy him very soon. The boy is not evil but only confused. Why not? He is only fourteen, a terrible age to be in this land! Already a man in many cultures, but here he is forced to act like a child... to play the part of a child, at least... until he is punished as an adult. Like many others he could be saved, but no one cares to try." She turned to Kody. "I know what you thought about 'solving' the problem. But you would not do it, your heart is too strong."

Kody looked at the gun. "I could if I had to."

"Do not put yourself in that position or you will regret it the rest of your life... and possibly long afterward." Aunt Simone glanced again at the gun. "But, only his feelings about it remain. There is nothing more I can learn of him."

"We know where they live," said Kody. "In the Projects by the graveyard. An' Newton knows their names."

Aunt Simone sighed. "Have I taught you nothing? Or have you not paid attention? That is what *anyone* would know. I am sure the police are aware of this 'gang.' But, the law cannot save, it can only destroy them. We are not on this earth to destroy one-another." She sipped from her glass and smiled at Newton. "Come to me, child, and tell me your story."

It was hard to believe this fat little kid had tried to murder Kody today... not now, cuddled in Aunt Simone's arms. With the baby goat horns poking out of his hair, it looked as if she was comforting Ethu who'd made some ungodly mistake.

"There," said Aunt Simone to Kody after listening to Newton. "He will not need to be chained anymore, or locked in 'that coffin' again." She glanced at the skeleton clock. "We will decide what to do in the morning. For now take showers and go to bed."

"What about the gun?" asked Kody.

"That is another evil of guns. To possess one is often to *be* possessed, just as that boy has become. It is not unlike what you felt about Newton once you had taken him into your life. You are obligated, responsible. As to the gun, you cannot simply throw such an object away and leave it for others to find. And you must never use it yourself, for then it will surely enslave you. And yet it will demand to kill, plead to kill, and lie to kill. One might almost pity the thing; its only purpose in life is death. For now take it out of my sight."

The boys drank their rum as Aunt Simone left, then went to the bathroom to shower. Newton glanced at the cabinet mirror. "Is dis one cool?"

"Pretty much," said Kody. "But watch your back with the one in my room."

"What can it do?"

"Wanna see your face fall off?"

"Or maggots come out your eyes?" added Raney, stepping into the claw-footed tub and turning on the water.

"Fuck no!" Newton hesitated a moment, then cautiously studied himself in the glass. "I like havin' horns. Dey look cool."

Kody laughed. "You'll wish they were yours on the real in a minute. They don't come off very easy."

"Yeah," added Raney. "An' the longer you wear 'em the harder it get."

"Is it Super Glue?" asked Newton, giving one of his horns a tug.

"I never been sure what it is," said Kody. He took an old rum bottle off a shelf, half full of something that looked like blood. "Aunt Simone makes it with bone dust an' plants, an' also this stuff to dissolve it again."

"Like da magic stuff in da Voodoo store? All dem bottles of potions an' lotions?"

"Ain't nothin' magic in that phony place. It's only for tourists an' wannabe vamps." Kody poured some of the ruby liquid around the roots of Newton's horns. "Takes a few minutes to work."

"Somebody do my back," said Raney.

"Me," said Newton, grabbing a washcloth.

"Don't get your hair wet," warned Kody. "That stuff will set up like cement if you do."

Newton scrubbed Raney's wedge-shaped back as if he were rubbing down a horse. "It was cool bein' Ethu. Like, I was really somebody for once."

"I know what you sayin'," said Kody. "It made me feel like that, too. An' you were a really cool Ethu."

"Tanks," said Newton, smiling. He stretched up to reach Raney's shoulder, but his belly plunged over the rim of the tub and pulled him in along with it.

"Dammit, man!" yelled Kody. "You're getting' your hair all wet!"

"Sorry," said Newton as Kody helped him scramble out.

"Let's get those horns off now."

"Ow!" cried Newton as Kody pulled. "Dat fuckin' hurts!"

"I said it was gonna. An' now you're all wet so it's gonna hurt more."

"Ow, motherfucker!" yelled Newton as Kody pulled harder.

"Let me try," said Raney. He got a grip on both Newton's horns and almost lifted the boy off his feet.

"Be careful, man!" pleaded Newton. "...OW! Stop it, goddammit! You pullin' my fuckin' skull out my head!"

"Easy, cousin," said Kody.

Raney let go. "They really stuck! Like that time you got rained on last summer. Try some more of that horn remover."

"Nah," said Kody. "Wet like he is, that'll just make it worse. His hair should be dry in the mornin'."

The boys washed the oil from each other's backs, then went into Kody's room. Newton wouldn't look at the mirror and stayed away from the clothes-press. "So, you ain't gonna chain me up again?"

"Aunt Simone said you're cool," said Kody. "An' she's never wrong about people."

"Could she put a curse on da Skeleyton Crew?"

"Easy as pickin' a tick," said Raney.

"But, she probably won't," said Kody. "Cursin' is like shootin' people, once you done it you can't take it back."

"I sorry I shot you."

"I know you are, but bein' sorry don't change what's done, an' you can't go back an' fix the past."

"Den why your aunt wanna know more about 'em?"

Raney said, "For the future. It the same as tryin' to help somebody... like workin' with kids at the children's center. First you gotta find out what's wrong, an' most the time they dont know themselves. She wants to help them fools get better. ...Like, show 'em the light, what I sayin'. You can't help people by cursin' 'em, no more'n you can by shootin' 'em."

"Why she wanna help people?"

"'Cause that what good people do."

"Guess dat why she ain't rich."

Raney and Newton got into bed, but Kody put on his jeans and took the gun from atop the dresser.

"What's up?" asked Raney.

"I wanna feel this thing some more, now I know it's evil."

"Like Voodoo homework?" asked Newton.

"Yeah." Kody parted the curtains and stepped through a gallery window, going out to the rail. The sultry night air was like a steam bath, and sweat soon sheened his body again. Thunder rumbled distantly as a storm drifted slowly upriver. It was getting close to midnight: a few people strolled on Decatur Street and down near the levee not far away, but Ursulines was deserted. A woman came out on the gallery of another house a few doors down and dropped a garbage bag onto the sidewalk for pickup in the morning. A gang of rats investigated. Drums were throbbing in Congo Square, and a ship hooted out on the river. Kody tried to open his mind and ignore the strange warmth of the gun in his hand. Had the Skeleton Crew returned to the Projects? Or, were they still lurking around?

He tried to remember their faces, wishing he'd paid more attention. Aunt Simone knew the oldest boy's age, and the youngest had looked about twelve. The others were probably thirteen or so, and one was amazingly black. None were very muscular, so they wouldn't be much of a physical threat unless they fought together. He thought about defenses... he could make a ring of protection, but it wouldn't be easy to bust the house even without a magic defense; like most ancient dwellings in the Quarter the courtyard gate was savagely spiked, as well as the crowns of the gallery posts to guard against assassins and thieves... though most tourists thought they were ornaments.

And the Skeleton Crew were only kids, they still got tired and had to sleep. They might be at home and sleeping right now, while he was awake and worrying. *Damn those little niggers!*

He cradled the gun in both hands but only felt its strange steely heat. He pressed it to his chest, but nothing came into his mind. It whispered to him of power, but now he knew its sucker game. He scanned the opposite sidewalk again. Had the boys left something there he could use, a wad of gum, a curl of hair, maybe a piece of fingernail? But, those would be hard to find in the dark.

A small shape seemed to materialize... a shirtless boy in jeans! Kody tensed and aimed the gun! But then he saw the boy was white -- an almost luminous shade of pale -- while his silky hair rippled over his shoulders, flowing down his chest and back as glossy black as a raven's wing.

Kody jerked the gun down to his side, sure he felt it fighting him, though a shiver traced his spine... the dude was just so *white!* For a moment he thought he was seeing a ghost; but if so it was recently deceased, clad in loose jeans clinging low on its hips displaying six inches of crimson silk shorts, and shod in a new pair of big-footed Nikes almost concealed by its dragging cuffs. And, it was toting a skateboard.

Kody had never encountered a spirit who looked so fresh to the ghostly game, and decided the boy was still physical. It was hard to see his face in the dark, shadowed by all that shimmering hair, but his build was boyishly muscular with high-jutting pecs, pert biceps, and smoothly-sculpted six-pack abs; and Kody guessed him around thirteen.

The boy looked up as if sensing Kody, his teeth gleaming huge and child-star bright in a winsomely disarming smile. "Good evening," he said in a choir-boy voice, then seemed to amend with, "Hi."

"S'up?" asked Kody, hiding the gun behind his back while leaning over the rail.

The boy crossed the street to stand looking up and indicated his board. "Going down by the river to practice."

"I never tried skatin'," said Kody, and patted his belly with his free hand. "An' now I guess I'm too fat."

"You look very cool," said the boy. "A gentleman of substance."

Kody thought about asking the dude if he'd seen the gang-kids anywhere near, but that might have taken an explanation. "You visitin' here?" he asked instead.

The boy smiled again. His two upper front teeth were as big as chisels and probably always on display; but while another boy might have looked goofy, they only seemed to somehow enhance his youthful male attractiveness. "I lived here all my life down on Barracks Street. I saw you a couple of times last year, late at night at an ice cream parlor." He bowed a bit. "Arlan Comté, at your service."

"Kody Carver," said Kody, and smiled. "At your service. I'm down for the summer again. You oughta come over sometime."

"Are you inviting me in?" asked Arlan, almost coquettishly cocking his head.

"Hey, ya think."

"Sweet." Arlan yawned and stretched, leaning far back and raising his arms to lithe full extension, his hair cascading over his shoulders to more than midway down his back, his jeans and boxers slipping lower to just on the verge of changing his rating from E to X without passing T, and looking alluringly sensuous in a dangerously innocent way.

"Kinda late for skatin'," said Kody.

Arlan yawned again. "I just woke up so it's early for me."

"You party all day?" asked Kody.

Arlan hesitated a moment. "I... just like the night."

Kody studied the snowy-white boy: it wasn't a shade that looked unhealthy, just more like he'd never been out in the sun. Arlan smiled as if guessing his thoughts. "Wish I had a tan like yours. I've tried the moon but it doesn't work."

Kody laughed. "Well, you ain't got a cloak so you can't be a vampire."

Arlan laughed, too, his hair almost a natural cloak. "Who'd wanna dress in their grandfather's clothes?"

A drop of sweat fell from Kody's cheek to Arlan's upturned face. "Sorry man," said Kody.

Arlan only licked his lips around his rather fearsome teeth. "Blood, sweat and tears are the same composition... kinda like somebody's essence."

"Yeah," said Kody. "It was a part of Voodoo long before science figured it out."

"Can you come out?" asked Arlan. "We could get some ice cream. Or something stronger, if you prefer."

"Not tonight, man, sorry. But, I'll be here all summer."

"See you around," said Arlan. "If you stay up late."

"Most of the time," said Kody. "Come over some night for the ceremony... free for you, of course."

"Sweet. See you, man."

"Later." Then Kody added. "Be careful down by the levee, it's a real haunted place."

Arlan grinned. "Depends on who's doing the haunting."

SEVEN

Kodi watched Arlan pad away with a confident stride down the shadowy street. Then he returned to his room and carefully locked the windows. The bed had plenty of space for three, but Newton lay cuddled to Raney.

"He wants to sleep in the middle," said Raney. "'Cause he still scared of our ghost."

"No prob," said Kody, laying the gun on the bedside table and peeling off his jeans.

"Who was you talkin' to?" asked Raney.

"Just some dude. He seemed pretty cool."

"Can you cover da mirror?" asked Newton. "So da ghost can't see me naked."

"No," said Kody. "He don't like that."

"Not seein' me naked?"

"Covering the mirror."

"Is da coffin locked wit' da skeleyton in it?"

"It's just a skull, an' yeah it's locked. Now go to sleep."

"Can I have another glass of rum?"

"You drink too much."

"It keep ghosts out my skull."

"It don't keep 'em out, you just think it does."

"Den it work just as good."

"Go to sleep, man. There's more to worry about than ghosts."

"Who was da other glass for? Your aunt filled seven, 'member? She gave one ta Ethu an' Baron Samedi, but da last one still on da table."

"That's for our ghost," said Raney. "Sometimes it's gone in the

51

mornin'."

"Can he see us now all naked?"

"Guess he could if he wanted to," said Kody, "but he probably ain't into boys."

Raney added, "An' even a ghost couldn't see yours."

"It all dere," said Newton, gathering up two handfuls of belly. "Just don't stick out much, see?"

"We see," chuckled Raney, "but you still can't."

"I don't need ta see, it work fine, 'cept I still too young ta…" He made a hand gesture. "You know."

"You could look in the mirror to see it," said Kody.

"…NO!" Newton let go of his blubber, which cascaded over his lap again, then said wistfully, "Dere still some pie in da fridge."

"Help yourself," yawned Kody.

"I can't go alone, it dark out dere."

"You scared of the dark?" asked Raney.

"No, of da ghost."

Kody got up, went to the kitchen and brought back the last of the pie, which vanished like a ghost into Newton.

Raney asked, "Want a spooky bedtime story?"

"NO!"

Kody turned off the lights and slipped under the sheet. The glow of a street lamp shone in though the drapes, which he'd left partly open. The mirror looked like an ebony window, but Kody watched the real ones. Despite the spikes on the gallery posts, a kid who was strong and determined enough might be able reach the rail and pull himself up without getting gored. He thought again about making a circle, but picked up the gun instead. "Did he hold it a lot?"

"Rick?" said Newton sleepily. "Like he never wanted ta let it go. An' sometimes… guess your aunt know."

"That's pretty much standard symbolism."

"Wuttup, cousin?" asked Raney.

"Just thinkin'," said Kody. He put the gun back on the table, then relaxed and closed his eyes.

An hour passed as the three boys slept to the tick of the skeleton clock in the parlor. The storm had been slowly approaching, and flashes of lightning razored the sky, followed by booming rumbles of thunder. Lightning flickered closer now, glaring in through the windows and striking blue sparks in the ebony mirror. The sky opened up and rain pounded the roof, pouring off the gallery to splash the street below, but the boys slept through it undisturbed. Another flash glared in the mirror... and now a pale shape was beginning to form!

Newton stirred and sat up. His eyes were half closed, yet he groped for the gun on the bedside table, leaning over Kody's chest. Clumsily he cocked the hammer and pressed the muzzle to Kody's head!

Lightning stabbed above the house, and thunder roared like a cannon blast. Raney woke up.

"Newton!" He grabbed the gun before Newton could fire. "You dirty little weasel!"

Kody opened his eyes. "What...?"

"Shit!" yelled Raney. "Look at the mirror!"

Newton turned to look and screamed. A skull had appeared in the ebony window seeming about to burst into the room!

Newton burrowed under the sheet, but Kody cursed and leaped from the bed. "Get the hell outta here!" he yelled, facing the thing, which now filled the whole frame, his arm thrust toward its fleshless face and aiming two fingers and thumb. It seemed to retreat a little; and he tore a blanket off the bed and flung it over the mirror.

X X X

"Shit!" cried Rick as thunder crashed with a battering blast and lightning ripped the sky outside, flaring over the cemetery and tinting the tombs a ghoulish blue. His room was dark except for candles that flickered on the dresser. He held the grinning skull in his hands while gazing into the mirror.

"Now what the matter?" asked Matt drunkenly. He lay on his back on the rumpled bed, while Terrel, even drunker, was crouching above him holding the gun to Matt's forehead. Devon lay curled on the floor asleep.

"I don't know," said Rick, his eyes still searching the mirror. "I almost saw somethin', but then it went black."

Terrel looked at the gun still pressed to Matt's head. "I wouldn't of had to shoot him... would I?"

"'Course not," said Rick. "*He* would have done that in the other mirror."

"Who's he?" asked Terrel.

"You find out when you worthy."

"This gettin' strange," said Matt, and pushed the gun away.

"No stranger than you, pretty-boy," said Rick. He turned to the mirror again.

"Maybe Matt right," said Terrel, laying the gun on the bedside table beside a new box of .32 caps. "These 'ceremonies' are wack, man." He snagged a forty and drank.

"Shut up," said Rick, gazing into the glass. "I think I almost got him."

X   X   X

"The hell was that?" bawled Raney, then... "Newton almost kill you!"

"I couldn't help it!" cried Newton, peeping from under the sheet. "It was like I was dreamin'. ...Da ghost made me do it!"

"Our ghost?" asked Raney, his mouth dropping open.

"No," panted Kody, now dripping sweat as if facing the thing had tested his strength. "The skull in the mirror was different... never seen nothin' like it before. ...I shoulda expected somethin' bad an' made us a circle to sleep in."

"What you mean?" asked Raney.

"I been gettin' creepy feelings all day. ...Dammit, I should have been more careful!"

"Y'all better do some more homework, cousin."

Kody returned to the bed and sat down. "Thanks, Raney, you saved my butt."

Raney glared at the mirror. "But what the hell was that?"

"Mean, it wasn't your ghost?" asked Newton.

"No," said Kody. "Our ghost would never do nothin' like that."

Newton emerged from hiding. "But, I thought he used ta be bad?"

"Scary bad yeah," said Kody. "But, he never killed or hurt anybody, even before my aunt moved in, an' he's been in this house at least two-hundred years."

Raney got up and opened the press, ignoring the smiling skull inside. He put the gun on a shelf and locked the door again. "I keep the key, y'all don't mind." He slipped it under his pillow and gave Newton a scowl. "You try an' get that, I bust *your* skull."

Kody looked at the mirror again. "Ain't Newton we need to worry about. ...I think I know what the danger is now, so I know what to guard us against."

"The mirror, you sayin'?" asked Raney. He went over and cautiously lifted the blanket, his other hand cocked in a solid bronze fist to punch anything that might have flown out. "Whatever the hell it was, it gone."

"It's a window to somewhere," said Kody. "Any mirror can be a window, but you gotta know how to open it."

Raney glared at the empty glass. "Seem like somebody did."

"Or somethin'." Kody turned to Newton. "Those gang dudes been messin' with somethin' nasty. No wonder they actin' so weird."

Raney peered into the murky glass, his fist still ready to swing. "So, what the hell was it?"

"You said that already," said Kody.

"Cute, but no cigar."

Kody considered. "Maybe the gun."

"Huh?" said Newton, his eyes wide again.

Raney frowned, still searching the mirror. "A gun's only metal. A little machine."

Kody glanced at the coffin-like press. "But that one's soaked full of evil from all the bad it's been used for. Aunt Simone could feel it, remember? She said it was haunted... possessed. It got that kid; the wannabe thug."

"Rick," said Newton.

"Yeah, it possessed him, an' now he's haunted. An' it almost got me twice today... maybe even three times."

"What you mean, three?" asked Raney. "Newton shot you once already..." He gave the kid a sour look. "An' he try again just now. That only make two where I go to school."

Kody turned to the gallery windows. The storm was slowly passing, the lightning and thunder fading away, and the rain had softened to merely a drizzle cat-footing over the roof. "I almost shot that dude on the street... the one I was talkin' to. At first I couldn't even see he wasn't one of the gang. Somethin' just told me to kill him before he got a chance to kill me."

Raney grabbed the clothes-press key. "We best get rid of that thing right now!"

"But, what if dey come back?" said Newton. "Da Skeleyton Crew. We *need* dat gun ta cap dem niggers or dey gonna cap us!"

Kody shook his head. "That's the gun talkin', Newt, an' you're speakin' its language."

"...Mean it got in my skull?"

"There's a lot of empty space in there."

"Da fuck I do about dat?"

"Fill it up with good stuff," said Raney, and jiggled Newton's belly. "Same's you done with that."

Newton giggled. "Den I get a big fat brain."

"Better'n bein' a little dumb-ass." Raney turned to Kody. "We should give the gun to Aunt Simone. It won't have no power on her."

Kody thought for a moment. "She didn't have to leave it with us, an' she never does nothin' that don't have a reason."

EIGHT

"Just do it, Kody," growled Raney.

It was just before dawn and the air was cooler... which wasn't much for a New Orleans June. The sky was turning rose in the east, but clouds hovered low on the southern horizon and promised more thunderstorms later that day.

The narrow streets of the slow-rising Quarter were shadowy canyons at this early hour, deserted except for a few sleepy cats and a shopkeeper hosing his sidewalk. The homeless still slumbered in Jackson Square, lying on benches or curled in doorways, and the only sound was a lone garbage truck as it rumbled over the cobblestones. A handful of tourists were strolling Decatur, enjoying the cool of the wakening day, though almost nothing was open yet; most of the restaurants still shuttered and barred, though cooking aromas ghosted about and hauntingly hinted of good things to come.

Raney had played the chef again when the boys had risen to plan their next move, building a breakfast of gravy and grits, along with a monster Cajun omelet stuffed with peppers and succulent shrimp. There had also been toast and blueberry jelly, with plenty of milk and orange juice; and Newton had polished-off more than his share.

Kody had tried to remove Newton's horns, but he'd hollered enough to wake the dead so Kody had given up. Aunt Simone could have taken them off, but she'd already left for the children's center, so Newton was wearing a ragged black beanie, an old one of Kody's that covered his spikes.

The boys, in only jeans and sneaks, now stood on the riverbank levee watching the freighters and slow-moving tows. There were ships from ports all around the world, and barges filled with gravel, grain, corn, coal, and lofty stacks of cargo containers that towered over their churning tugboats. Seagulls circled and soared overhead, blending their cries with the bellowing tugs and hoots and honks of river traffic. The steamboat, *Natchez*, blew her own mellow whistle, a sound that echoed throughout Quarter with bittersweet notes of a long-vanished age. An old wooden trolley car trundled past on rails along the base of the levee: they were called Red Ladies because of their color, ancient and creaky but mostly on time. Another track followed the Red Lady line, and a freight train was slowly approaching.

Raney nudged Kody's rolly side where a thinner boy's ribs would have been. "Best get it over with, cousin."

But, Kody was feeling uncertain. He'd pulled the clip from the old .45, yet his mind was suddenly filled with reasons why he shouldn't throw it away. "Maybe just the bullets?" he murmured, almost as if to himself.

Raney scowled. "Y'all gonna put the gun on the tracks, so what difference it make?"

"An' here come a train," added Newton.

"It... seems like a waste," said Kody.

"Of what?" growled Raney. "That thing try an' *kill* you a few hours ago!"

"Yeah!" piped Newton. "It haunted my skull!"

Kody almost said he'd changed his mind: there were four little niggers trying to kill him so it would be stupid to give up the gun! Yet, another part of him realized the thing was trying to trick him. ...No, he thought, not the gun itself, a mass of metal, a little machine, but only the evil that haunted it. But what did that matter? It couldn't be cleansed of the blood it had spilled, the lives it had taken, the pain it had caused, or the hate and fear it had once inspired. Just like Aunt Simone had said, its only purpose in life was death.

But, this wasn't the place to be thinking of death: the levee itself was haunted! Beneath his feet were countless bones forgotten over the centuries, of native people massacred by those who came to steal their land, of men and women murdered here by thieves and river pirates. Slaves had died to build this wall, and now their bones were part of it. Suicides had happened here; that muddy water closing over lonely deaths of poverty, loveless lives and fortunes lost, broken dreams and sad mistakes. Or just unbearable despair. The levee was alive with death, and here the gun was strong.

He forced himself to remember last night... how Newton's childish face had looked when he'd tried to pull the trigger. For an instant it, too, had become a skull, rotten, grinning, oozing evil, just like the one in the mirror.

Kody threw the clip away, which seemed to take every ounce of his strength as if it weighed a ton.

"Fuck yeah!" cheered Newton, thrusting a fist at the lightening sky while making a clumsy leap in the air and almost losing his jeans.

"C'mon, hurry up," prodded Raney.

Kody was scanning the dark murky water, where ripples had spread from the splash, but Raney took his arm. The boys went down to the railroad tracks to face the slowly approaching train, which blew its whistle in warning.

"Hurry up, dammit!" said Raney again. "Or give it to me an' I do it."

"No!" Kody broke loose from Raney's hand. Voices were whispering deep in his mind, but they *understood* his confusion. After all, he was only thirteen, and anyone could make a mistake. He'd thrown the clip and bullets away, but he could get others. Easily. It wasn't too late to save the gun.

"Go to hell!" he muttered, then added when Raney stared at him, "Wasn't talkin' to you."

"Da train gettin' close," prompted Newton.

The engine blew its whistle again as the boys remained in its path. Its headlamp glared like an angry eye, and Kody could feel its heat on his face.

"Do it, Kody!" yelled Raney.

"*NO!*" cried a voice in Kody's mind, louder than all the others. "*I can save you, boy! I'm the ONLY thing that can save you in a hateful world that hates your kind! I can make them respect you, boy... all of them, no matter what color! I can make them afraid of you! I can make them give you things... all the things you'll never get by being a good little nigger!"*

"Please, Ethu," Kody whispered. "Help me."

"Huh?" said Newton.

The engine blew its whistle again, less than a hundred yards away... little boys played childish games and it wasn't going to stop for them! Kody lay the gun on a rail, and pain ripped through his wounded arm! For a second he almost recovered the thing, but Raney and Newton grabbed his shoulders and pulled him off the tracks. The engine speeded up a little, billowing smoke against the sky, its headlamp stabbing the morning dusk as it rumbled closer. The squeal and clanking of steel upon steel echoed and battered at Kody's ears; but his eyes stayed fixed on the gun... a beautiful object... a work of art! The massive wheels were ten feet away...

"*NOOOOOOOOOOOOOOOOOOOOOO!"* screamed the voice in his mind.

Kody tore free and dashed for the tracks!

Newton tackled his legs and they crashed to the ground in gravel and dirt. The train whistle shrieked a furious blast as Kody fought and kicked at Newton, dragging the smaller boy with him. His hands reached out... six more inches!

Then something else ripped through his mind: a hellish, hateful, raging scream...

And the steel wheels ran over the gun.

Kody lay there gasping for breath with Newton still clutching his ankles. The long, slow train went rumbling past. Oily heat washed over his body, while smoke and dust invaded his lungs and made him choke and cough. The last car finally went clanking by, its tail lamp glowing the color of blood. He couldn't see the remains of the gun, and didn't want to look. Raney crouched beside him. "How you feelin', cousin?"

Kody rose up on his elbows. His jeans had tumbled around his knees, and morning breeze played over his butt. Newton's jeans were in similar shape, and the beanie completely covered his eyes, though one of his horns poked up through a hole.

"Like I just met a real nasty dead thing." Kody sat up, raised Newton's beanie and gave the boy a hug. "Thanks, Ethu. I couldn't of done it without you."

"…Um… no prob," said Newton.

"Glad that's over!" said Raney. "Damn!"

Kody got up, hoisted his jeans and gave his cousin a hug. "So am I, man. An' thanks to you, too."

"…Oh," said Raney, squirming with Kody's arms around him. He awkwardly patted Kody's back. "Uh… anytime, cousin."

Kody brushed gravel and dirt from his chest, helped Newton get to his feet, then turned to scan the quiet Quarter… the narrow brick and plastered buildings that seemed to lean over the cobbled sidewalks, the shadowy streets and dark alleyways. For a moment he felt the age of the place settling onto his shoulders. He could dimly picture the cemetery, and the Projects overlooking it. They seemed to be *connected* somehow… those four young boys and the ancient dead. "But, it ain't over yet… whatever it is."

"Guess you right," said Raney. "Them gang-babies still wanna kill us."

"No," said Kody, shedding more dirt like a wakening zombie. "There's only one who wants to kill us. The others don't know what they want. They're only sick of what they got, which don't seem much of nothin'." He glanced at Newton again. "Guess you figured that out."

"I sorta doin' it now," said Newton. "Like puttin' somethin' good in my skull ta fill up da empty space."

"But, that other dude…" said Raney. "The leader…"

"Rick," said Newton, hoisting his jeans.

"Yeah," said Kody. "Rick. He's been messin' with somethin' nasty an' dead, an' New Orleans ain't the place for that. It's way too old, there's too many ghosts, an' he lives too close to the graveyard. Somethin's been listenin' to his thoughts… or maybe to his prayers." Kody tried to open his mind, but only got a creepy feeling. "He woke up somethin' in a grave, an' you never call up what you can't put down."

"How you know that?" asked Raney.

"'Cause the gun is dead, but the evil ain't. I can still feel it, an' just as strong. An' I know where it's comin' from now 'cause the gun ain't distracting me no more." Kody faced Newton again. "You been hangin' around in that graveyard."

Newton looked uneasy. "Yeah."

"Trying to dance with that train?" asked a charming young voice. "There's a lot less painful ways to die."

Kody turned to see Arlan, still shirtless in dangerously low-slipping jeans, toting his skateboard under an arm as if he'd been cruising all night, his body so pale it seemed to glow in the slowly growing light of near dawn. He was far from being as massive as Raney, but every muscle was tightly defined, while his snowy-white face was drop-dead handsome, his large and long-lashed winsome eyes as dark as a moonless midnight and shadowed by all his long silky hair.

"Hey," said Kody. "This's my cousin Raney, an' our friend Newton. ...This's Arlan, guys; the dude I was talkin' to last night."

"At your service, sirs," said Arlan, with a courtly bow.

"Woah!" exclaimed Newton. "Are you ever white!"

"Shush," said Raney, and offered a hand to shake with Arlan. "Hi, man."

"Hi." Arlan studied Newton. "Awesome horns! I've never seen those for sale anywhere."

"My aunt made 'em up for our show," said Kody.

"She ought to sell 'em. They look way cooler than vampire teeth." Then Arlan grinned, showing long gleaming fangs!

Newton yelped and backed away. Kody and Raney were startled, too, but Arlan removed the plastic fangs, though his real front teeth looked just as wicked, glittering white and big as chisels framed by cherubically full, rosy lips.

"Damn!" said Raney. "You almost gimmie a fit, man! ...Why y'all wearin' them silly ol' things?"

"Tourists want to take my picture. I make a few bucks as an undead boy."

Newton ventured back. "I can see why; you white as a ghost!"

"Some people ask where my seven dwarves are."

Raney laughed. "You could do with a tan... no offense."

"None taken, sir, I'm accustomed to that." Arlan glanced toward the eastern sky, now shading softly to lavender. "But sunlight would kill me."

"...Huh?" said Raney.

"It's an ancestral thing... 'genetic' in current terms. They call us children of the night."

"I read about that," said Kody. "You can't go out in the daytime, huh?"

"Daylight for me is deadly." Arlan glanced eastward again. "And I must get home or I'm toast."

"Come to the ceremony tonight."

Arlan presented a hand, softly-palmed though deceptively strong as Kody gripped it warmly, sensing, it seemed, an offer of friendship as Arlan met his eyes and smiled. "I accept your gracious invitation with the utmost pleasure, sir. Until then, I bid you all a good day; and with no ironic intent despite the fact I'll never have one. ...See ya." Arlan crossed the Red Lady tracks, mounting his board and gliding away as soon as he reached the street.

Raney stood looking after him. "Um, y'all think he a... you-know?"

"A you know what?" said Kody.

Raney frowned. "You know what."

"What?" asked Newton.

Raney looked uncomfortable, something he seldom did. "You know what I sayin', Kody. I seen the way he was lookin' at you."

"Huh?" said Newton.

"Like a raccoon at a big silver moon."

"Oh." Kody laughed. "Guess I should be flattered."

"Ooooooo," said Newton, and giggled.

Raney cleared his throat. "Arlan ain't the only one who shouldn't be out in the day. We best get Newton home. Them weasel boys still got a gun."

"It cool," said Newton. "Rick an' his posse get drunk every night so dey don't wake up till noon."

Raney turned to Kody. "So, what about Rick's other gun? Y'all suppose it evil, too, an' that what you been feelin'?"

Kody was quiet a moment, opening his mind. "I don't know... but maybe it ain't had time to get evil."

Newton said, "It kinda cheap, but almost new."

Kody nodded. "So, maybe it never killed anybody."

"An' dat why Rick wanna kill me? For losin' his evil ol' steel?"

"It's deeper than that," said Kody. He faced the unseen cemetery beyond the shadowed Quarter. "The gun only started this thing… this occurrence. It gave Rick somethin' to focus on, so it opened his mind like a window. An' things come in through open windows."

"Like in ta empty skulls?" asked Newton.

"'Specially when you invite 'em," said Raney. "An' speakin' of guns…" He snagged the mangled lump of metal and flung it over the levee. "So, Newton safe outside for a while?"

"Yeah," said Newton. "Rick an' his posse still asleep. Den dey get breakfast at da Flatboat… dat joint for workin' folks… or Rick make somethin' at home. Den dey go score some forties. We was stayin' buzzed ever day."

"Which give you the balls to shoot my cousin."

"Fuck no, man! I was possessed!"

"Don't blame all your bad on evil spirits. …Or your stupid, neither."

Newton shrugged. "Dey used ta sell charms an' dance, but den Rick got dat ol' gun."

"The gun got him," said Kody. "Where'd he get it anyway?"

"Boost it out a pawnshop. Said it da first thing he ever stole."

Kody nodded. "Big evils start with little ones. Like, if you open a window a little, somethin' bigger opens it wider. …What's he doin' for money now?"

"We jack us a mark a few days ago… some guy in da graveyard alone. He axe if we show him Marie Laveau's tomb, an' we took him way back in a corner an' Rick pull da gun on him. Scored almost two-hundred bucks."

"Damn!" said Raney. "Y'all didn't shoot him, did you?"

"Nah, he was scared an' give us his wallet."

"Shit!" muttered Kody, shaking his head. "You took somethin' old an' full of evil into a place of the dead. Then you used it for evil. There's things in graveyards waitin' for fools." He thought for a moment. "Then Rick told you to cap somebody?"

" Yeah, a few days later. He said it would make me worthy… whatever da fuck dat mean. We done a ceremony first… like, ta get me ready. Why I never had lunch yesterday."

Kody shook his head again. "Ceremonies! This keeps gettin' worse! Dammit, I need somethin' of Rick's!"

"You gonna make a doll?" asked Newton, "an' stick it fulla pins?"

"We don't play with dolls. But, I know a spell an' it's easy to do, so we can know if they're close. You can stay away from a lotta trouble by knowin' where to find it."

"Didn't work with that girl last summer," said Raney. "The one you was hot an' bothered about."

"Sure it worked. I knew where she was, but she didn't like me. Said I should go on a diet."

Raney laughed. "My mom done that once, but she normal again." Then he considered. "Y'all think Rick might give up on us? They's plenty of people who can't fight back."

"Could happen," said Kody. "But we can't risk him bangin' our ceremonies; one of the guests might get shot. An' if he keeps messin' with dead nasty things, one's gonna get him for sure."

Newton gave Kody a curious look. "Sayin' you worried 'bout *him*?"

"We're all supposed to be brothers."

"Thought dat stuff was ol'-school."

"That's part of what's wrong with new-school."

"Your arm bleedin', cousin," said Raney. "Maybe we best go home."

"I'm okay." Kody pictured what remained of the gun sinking into the river mud with all those long-forgotten bones. "It just tried to get me one last time."

The boys moved aside as a Red Lady passed. It was partially filled with tourists now as the Quarter began to wake up. Several cameras were aimed at the boys, and Kody straightened Newton's beanie to cover his little horns. The sun was beginning to rise, and breakfast aromas were ghosting the air.

"I'm hungry," said Newton.

"C'mon," said Kody. "Let's go get a snack, then make some magic."

"Hope you been doin' your homework," said Raney. "Got a feelin' there might be a test comin' up."

NINE

The early sun was blazing brightly. Decatur Street was coming to life as stores and shops were opening, their owners unlocking shutters and bars, and cranking awnings over the sidewalks, while hungry tourists prowled about in search of supernatural breakfasts. Jazz rhythms bumped from Jackson Square as street musicians tuned up for the day, and a smoky haze was settling in -- it was never called smog in New Orleans -- as the boys crossed over the Red Lady tracks and walked to the old French Market. This was a sprawling open-air place where you could buy just about anything from stuffed alligators to Zydeco disks. There were two-hundred brands of hot pepper sauces, tons of assorted souvenir junk, and stakes to pound through vampires' hearts, along with plastic skulls and bones. A few kids were also available: they didn't have signs or price tags, or stand naked on blocks like old-time slaves, but they were still for sale, and there seemed to be more every year.

A chubby chocolate-colored girl of possibly thirteen was opening an ice cream shop, and gave Kody a cute dimpled smile. She was clad in a 'beater and faded jeans; and Kody eyed her wistfully while order-ing Cokes and double-scoop cones. It would have been cool to spit some game, but he had ghostly things on his mind. The boys took their cones to a table outside beneath a shady awning, and Newton plopped wearily into a chair, his bottom half bare on the seat, and pulled off the beanie to mop his face.

"Ain't walked dis much in a year," he puffed.

"How's your cold today?" asked Kody.

"Better, I think. Ain't sneezed once."

"Maybe you were allergic to stupid-ass gang-bangin' fools."

"Damn," said Raney. "His hair lookin' like he done fell in the swamp. Them horns really stuck on him now!"

Kody took a swallow of Coke and a bite of his ice cream cone. "Aunt Simone can get 'em off. We got dead things to deal with."

Newton asked, "Can I be Ethu again tonight?" He guzzled his Coke like a forty-ounce and blasted a thunderous burp, then attacked his ice cream cone like a movie zombie eating brains.

"That's gonna depend on what happens today," said Kody, licking his cone. "We can't put you out in a spotlight if Rick's gonna try an' cap you."

Raney scanned around, and Kody followed his eyes. There were already quite a few people, but only the tourists appeared in a hurry. "Should he be out in the open now? Showin' off his horns?"

"This's 'Nawlins, cousin." Kody glanced to a souvenir stand, where a pair of vampires, boy and girl, complete with fangs and black silk capes, were checking out some "Voodoo dolls."

"...Oh yeah," said Raney. "So, what we do next?"

"Eat your ice cream an' scope the girls... like the fox in the shop."

"Cool," said Newton, slurping more Coke. "I never noticed 'em much before, but I like chubby ones, too."

"Yeah," agreed Raney. "She be a darlin' all right. I like the way she wearin' her hair, kinda long an' natural. An' them jeans fittin' real nice, too. ...But, you know what I sayin', 'bout what we do next."

Kody shrugged. "Like I said, we need somethin' of Rick's, so that's gotta be our next move."

Somebody laughed. "Well, look who came back from the grave."

Kody tensed, but quickly relaxed, turning to face the Trouts, who'd just come out of the ice cream shop. They looked like kids on a date again with strawberry sundaes and sodas in hand.

"And here's little Ethu," Mrs. Trout added.

"And our mighty guardian," said Mr. Trout, patting Raney's shoulder. "May we join you?"

"Sure," said Kody, rising politely along with Raney, who yanked Newton to his feet.

Mrs. Trout smiled. "I hope we can take your pictures. It's not every day you meet a god, especially eating an ice cream cone."

Newton giggled. "Sure."

The boys were posed and the camera clicked, then the Trouts sat down at the table, and Mr. Trout studied Newton. "If it wouldn't be disrespectful, may I look at your horns?"

Mrs. Trout added, "They're very cute on you."

"Sure," said Newton. "But don't pull 'em please."

"Hmmm," said Mr. Trout, parting Newton's bushy curls. "I was raised on a farm and we had a few goats, but I've never seen anything like these. They seem very real. ...And firmly attached."

"Got dat right!" said Newton.

Mr. Trout turned to Kody. "Trade secret?"

"Kinda, sir." Kody was gazing across the street as four boys emerged from a liquor store. The youngest might have been eleven, the oldest about fourteen. All were shirtless in jeans and sneaks, but carried Cokes and tap-dancing shoes. Kody eyed them a few moments more, but they weren't the Skeleton Crew.

Mr. Trout asked, "Would you guys like a cigar? I'm sure Ethu would. I just bought a box of genuine Cubans."

"Sure," said Kody. "Thank you, sir."

Mr. Trout winked as he passed the box. "Not, 'sho' and 'suh?' You seem to have lost your plantation accent."

"You know how that is," said Kody, as Mr. Trout fired a lighter and distributed flame.

"Showmanship, yes. I worked in a traveling carnival when I about your age." Mr. Trout turned to smile at his wife. "That's where I met the girl of my dreams."

Mrs. Trout took her husband's hand. "He used to throw knives at me."

"Woah!" exclaimed Newton, puffing out smoke.

"No offense," said Kody. "But it seems funny to think that... well, older people did cool things."

Mr. Trout laughed. "I thought the same way when I was young. But, magic must be fascinating."

Mrs. Trout added, "Not to mention ghosts."

Kody shrugged. "When you been raised around ghosts they don't seem all that interesting."

Mrs. Trout raised an eyebrow. "You don't think ghosts are interesting?"

"Most of 'em are kinda boring unless they're takin' their faces off an' really tryin' to scare you. They do the same things over an' over like they're trapped in a movie."

Raney blew smoke and added, "You can't teach a dead dog new tricks. There a little-boy ghost in the swamp where I live. He only come out on foggy nights. I think he drowned a long time ago. I tried talkin' to him a few times, but all he do is cry."

"That sounds very sad," said Mrs. Trout.

"Guess I cry too if I drowned."

"Have you seen any other ghosts in your swamp?"

"My dad seen a skeleton rowin' a coffin, but I never got that lucky."

"I don't suppose you have any vampires? We heard on the news this morning that someone was bitten last night on the levee... bitten by something, anyway... but they couldn't remember how it happened."

Raney glanced at the vampire teens. "I never met a real one, but you probably wouldn't out in the swamp. They's mostly citified critters... need lots of people around for victims."

Kody smiled. "The Quarter is full of wannabe vamps, an' sometimes they do bite tourists." He laughed. "An' sometimes they get paid." Then he considered. "But, when a real one bites you, you usually don't remember much."

"Till you wake up undead," said Raney. "We got an ol' witch in a shanty boat. She 'mind me of somethin' undead... or oughta be buried, anyways."

"Thought you were dating her daughter?" said Kody.

"What difference that make? Her mom still a witch... an' a nosy one, too! ...Feel like puttin' a spell on her, somethin' like fillin' her boat with frogs, but she probably get me back double."

Mr. Trout asked, "You do Voodoo, too?"

"Just the bayou kind, ma'am. Gots more to do with fishin' an' huntin' an' gettin' along with animals than messin' with bones an' ol' dead things."

Mrs. Trout turned to Kody again. "But, what about your ghost? Doesn't he have a story? What keeps him in your house?"

"Like I said, I never met him. I think his son died in the house when he was only a little boy. About two-hundred years ago."

"So the father came back to look for his son? But a little boy would be in heaven."

"Ghosts get confused about time," said Kody. "To them there's no time an' nothin' changes. Like, if a house has been remodeled they still come through doorways that ain't there no more. They exist in a sort of shadow world where nothin's really clear. They're supposed to go to the light when they die... go on to the next thing, whatever it is. But some of 'em don't. Maybe they're scared of lettin' go of all the familiar shadows around 'em. Or maybe they just don't wanna let go. Then there's some with unfinished business."

"Like revenge?" asked Mr. Trout.

"That happens, too. When people been wronged, or think they been."

Mrs. Trout spooned a bite of her sundae. "We're taking the cemetery tour. The first one leaves the museum at ten."

"Y'all gots plenty of time," said Raney. "You could walk there in twenty minutes, or you could take a carriage."

Mrs. Trout glanced at the sky. "Do you think it will rain?"

Kody scanned the darkening clouds still low on the southern horizon. "Probably not for a few more hours. They're only thunderstorms anyhow an' don't last very long."

"Do they spoil your aunt's ceremonies?"

"Nah. The rain's warm, an' we furnish umbrellas. An' thunder an' lightning make good atmosphere."

Mr. Trout asked, "Are you guys doing anything now? If not, could you give us the tour?"

"That would be great!" agreed his wife. "Of course we'll pay for your time. It would really be an experience to see the tomb of Marie Laveau with a Voodoo god and magic boys."

Kody was about to decline, but then had an idea. "Sure," he said. "An' I can get us a deal on a carriage."

"Yay, no walkin'!" said Newton.

Raney kicked Kody under the table. "Buy me another Coke, cousin."

"Me too," added Newton.

"I'll get them," offered Mr. Trout.

"That's okay, sir," said Kody, and put his cigar in an ashtray. "We be right back."

"The hell up with you?" demanded Raney after they'd entered the ice cream shop, where a sign on a wall said

BE NICE OR LEAVE

He glanced at the chubby girl, who was scooping blood-red cherry cones for the pair of vampire teens, and lowered his voice to a growl. "The graveyard next to them Projects where Rick an' his posse live! You wanna make Newton a ghost?"

"'Course not," said Kody. "But, we need to get somethin' of Rick's."

"You gonna try an' hurt him?"

"I could kill him if I wanted to, an' I wouldn't need Voodoo to do it. So could you, an' probably Newton... just get a gun an' wait somewhere, like playin' hide 'n seek with death. That's what the thugger game's about, ignorant kids playin' with death 'cause they never learned respect for life."

Raney sighed. "I hear you, cousin. Like, why it so hard to help somebody but always so easy to hurt 'em? ...But, why you wanna bring Newton?"

"It should be safe enough. Rick an' his gang won't be out till noon, an' a tour won't take that long. An' I can look for somethin' of Rick's."

"In the graveyard?" asked Raney. "What you 'spect to find in there 'cept ol' bones an' a ghost or two what ain't had the sense to go to the light?"

"Newton said they hang out there, so they probably got some special spot or maybe a 'clubhouse' in one of the tombs, an' Newton would know where it is. They might of left somethin' we could use."

"Like, maybe Rick done a ceremony?"

Kody frowned. "He's *really* a fool if he done it in there! Dead things are always attracted to life. An' the fresher the life... like a kid's...

the more the dead wanna get near it." Kody's eyes flicked to the girl, but she was making change for the vampires. "We might find somethin' from all those dudes. Somethin' we could use to help 'em. Or at least protect ourselves till we figure out what's up. The younger ones gotta be getting' freaked. They know what they're doin' ain't right. An' they know there's somethin' wrong with Rick an' gettin' wronger all the time. Maybe we could give 'em a scare an' they'd stop this shit."

"What kinda scare?"

"Zombie dreams work pretty good."

"Just don't call up a real one again! Remember what happen last summer."

"It wasn't that bad... except for the dishes. Besides, I knew how to put it back down."

"Aight," said Raney. "But, what about tellin' Aunt Simone? She could scare 'em all shitless just by *thinkin'* boo."

"She'd still need somethin' of theirs to do it. An' we could get it for her."

Raney thought for a moment. "Y'all think Rick start gettin' better? Like, by himself, what I sayin'? 'Cause we got rid of that nasty ol' gun?"

"The gun only started it," said Kody. "It's what he woke up that's dangerous now. That's what I been feelin', an' that's what we gotta deal with."

Raney nodded. "Guess it be safe enough for Newton... 'long's we out that boneyard by noon."

TEN

"How's your aunt these days?" asked the coachman, who had bright amber eyes and coffee-brown skin, and looked like an old-fashioned undertaker in a black frock coat and top-hat. His horse also wore a topper, its ears sticking up through holes in the brim like Newton's horns had poked from his beanie.

Kody climbed down from the creaky old carriage, almost losing his jeans on the way, and turned to smile at the elderly man. "She's fine, Mr. Clay. She's workin' with kids at the center again."

"Glad to hear it, son. Thought I seen her on Saint Anne Street. So, how's the Voodoo business? Y'all branchin' into guide service now?"

Kody glanced at the Trouts, who'd gone to look at the graveyard gate, which was set in a white-washed masonry wall that surrounded the city block of grounds. The gate was standing open now, but someone would come to lock it at three... as many people had learned through the years after spending a frightening night inside. Sometimes nothing happened to them, but others had come out terrified, some had actually gone insane, and a few had been carried out dead.

The cops always blamed the latter on gangs -- by which they meant young black males -- and it *was* a good place to get jacked, but a lot of the bodies had no marks of violence except a frozen look of horror.

"It's always slow in the summer," said Kody. "Too hot for a lot of tourists. But, we get a few guests for the haunted house tour, an' the ceremonies been full every night. We're showin' these folks the grave-yard to make some extra green."

The coachman laughed. "We can all use that while we still wearin' skin. ...Y'all still playin' Nathan an' Tau?"

Kody nodded. "I got too old for bein' Ethu, an' I never been able to dance very good."

The man studied Newton, who stood with the Trouts, while Raney was telling a ghostly tale. Newton wasn't wearing the beanie, which now hung out of his jeans' back pocket. "He's the best Ethu y'all ever had. No disrespect to you, son, but damn if he ain't the spittin' image packin' that bountiful belly. I might drop by myself some night to ask your aunt's advice. Troubles in love, what that all about."

"Ask Maman Brigette," said Kody. "Love is her department."

"I know," said the coachman. "But your aunt just as wise, an' just as pretty. An' she there in the skin if you know what I mean." He poked Kody's belly with the tip of his whip. "Speakin' of skin, y'all lookin' pretty prosperous, son. Them summers down here been doin' you good. Ain't nothin' fit to eat up north, an' nobody know how to cook anyway. An' these days they makin' they kids scared of food, an' ain't nothin' healthy 'bout that."

Kody laughed. "I think this is gonna be the summer I cross the line between chubby an' fat."

"Y'all got a foot on the fat side already. But they's a lot worse lines you could cross. I hear about all them gangs up north. Y'all keepin' clear of that trouble?"

"Pretty much," said Kody. "But, we got the same trouble down here."

"Lord, don't I know it!" The coachman glared at the Project buildings just across the street. "Gettin' so decent folks can't make a livin'. They's places I don't even go no more, leastways never at night. Ol' Marcus got hit by some punks last week when he had him a coach full of people. They lost every penny an' traveler's checks, even they watches an' cameras.'

"How old were they? The punks, I mean?"

"Ol' enough to be actin' like men 'stead of bad little boys playin' bang-bang you dead! Late teens an' twenties, accordin' to Marc."

"Oh," said Kody.

The coachman eyed the graveyard. "Y'all be careful in there, son. I warn them tourists every day, but some of 'em still wanna see it alone."

A Fed-Ex truck rolled to a stop at the curb. Its driver got out with an overnight letter and walked in through the gate.

"They's another for Miz Laveau." The coachman respectfully tipped his hat.

Kody nodded. "Probably somebody wantin' somethin'. She gotta get pretty tired of that." He glanced at the Project buildings... made of brick and supposed to look nice, but somehow you always knew what they were. "Seen any gang-boys hangin' 'round here?"

The coachman considered. "Hard to tell bad kids from good 'uns no more. All of 'em wearin' them baggy jeans... no offense to you, son. Lot of 'em got them rags on they heads. ...Used to be like a insult, them rags. Wouldn't be caught in a coffin with one! My daddy, he'd put a lump on your stump if he seen you walkin' around like that. 'Rag-headed niggers,' he'd call 'em, showin' off they ignorance an' lack of decent raisin'."

The man considered again. "Few of them Project kids 'round here, sellin' beads an' Voodoo charms or doin' a little dancin'. Some of 'em only beggin' for money. A few of 'em sayin' they's tour guides, but don't know nothin' 'bout history. An' a few just sellin' theyselves. Oughta be somewhere they could go... no disrespect to the children's center... but someplace where they's real men to show 'em what bein' a man's all about. Who our kids got to look up to these days? Fools who can't sing to save they own lives, yowlin' 'bout disrespectin' our women, shootin' they brothers like fish in a barrel, an' rollin' around in fancy cars made in places they can't even spell! More gold in they mouths than there be in Fort Knox, an' kids goin' hungry to buy they CDs. Or stealin' 'em an' goin' to jail. Ain't no wonder we losin' ground, son. Every good thing my daddy fought for, along with Martin Luther King, Malcolm X, Huey Newton, an' your grandaddy, too!"

Clay studied Newton once more. "Been some new ones 'round here lately... when they ain't over there at the liquor store beggin' folks to buy 'em beer."

"Is the oldest about fourteen?"

Clay's bright eyes returned to Kody. "Y'all knowin' somethin' I should?"

"Just be careful is all."

"Don't y'all worry 'bout that, son. 'Careful Clay' they call me.

75

Careful of things without they skin, an' just as careful with them still got it." He thought for a moment. "I might know who you talkin' about. They used to be pretty decent young men... poor as dump dogs but proud as princes. One of 'em a hell of a dancer... stopped to watch him myself a few times. Even brung some business his way. ...Y'all ain't gettin' mixed up in gang stuff?"

"I'm tryin' not to," said Kody. "But it's kinda like takin' a walk through a swamp an' tryin' not to get muddy."

"Y'all be out that boneyard by noon. Even trouble sleep late in this town." Clay handed Kody a business card. "Give me a call if y'all need a ride... got me a wireless now. An' give my respects to Miz Laveau, along with your aunt a'course."

"Thanks, Mr. Clay. I will."

Raney had kept the Trouts entertained by telling spooky stories, but now Mr. Trout came up to the carriage. "How much do I owe you, sir?"

The coachman tipped his hat, decorated with feathers and beads. "Not a single picayune, suh. Friends of Kody's is friends of mine."

Mr. Trout smiled. "Maybe your horse could use a new hat?" He gave the coachman a twenty.

"He thank y'all, suh." The carriage went creaking away.

"Sorry for takin' so long," said Kody. "Ain't seen him since I was down here last summer."

"We're not in a hurry," said Mr. Trout. "And your cousin's been telling some hair-raising tales."

"Like the one about the ghost steamboat that still leaves at dawn every morning?"

"Along with several others. We're certainly in a haunted mood and ready to meet Marie Laveau." Mr. Trout watched as the Fed-Ex driver got back in his truck and rolled off. "I wasn't sure I believed she got mail, but now I'd believe almost anything."

"Well then," said Kody. "Right this way, folks."

ELEVEN

The cemetery wasn't huge, but it did seem like an endless maze of ancient tombs and crumbling crypts, a separate city within a city, a silent stone necropolis where living voices sounded unwelcome as if they troubled the sleeping dead. Kody led along narrow paths that twisted and turned like a labyrinth. Weeds were tall, but dry and withered, and seemed to resent being brushed aside. The paving stones were cracked and broken, patched with gravel here and there. Its crunching sounded hideous, like breaking bones beneath your feet, or crushing brittle skulls.

Kody let the silence rule until the gate was far behind. Then he began with history... built in 1789, but filled up pretty fast. Yellow fever had helped with that. Every grave was above the ground because of the high water level. Coffins buried under the earth would only come rising up again... which probably wasn't a pleasant sight.

Raney added that deep in the swamp was an old abandoned graveyard. The land was sinking all around, the water slowly creeping in, and rotted coffins would often appear, occasionally open like grisly boats in which their occupants drifted away beneath the somber cypress trees. He added that he and his dad gave tours, and slipped Mr. Trout a business card.

The tombs were almost eerily white beneath the blazing mid-morning sun. Most were made of plastered brick, though some had marble facings. The smallest were simple rectangular shapes that only contained a coffin or two, while others were more elaborate. These ranged in size from small stone houses without any trim or decoration, all the way up to ornate little temples with stately columns and domes.

But the scale was all in miniature, like a children's village designed by Death.

Many tombs had iron doors, and some had windows heavily barred. A few of the doors stood slightly open, held in place by rusty chains. Kody explained this had once been a fashion... never to fully lock the doors in case somebody was buried alive.

There had also been "resurrection bells" with ropes going down in the coffins, so anyone who woke up in the dark could pull the rope and ring the bell. There were rumors that some of these bells had rung a *long* time after burials... so long, in fact, they'd been removed without investigation.

He explained the meaning of "oven tombs;" they resembled the old plantation ovens when slaves had done the cooking outdoors. But they did get hellishly hot in the sun, and a few had even exploded, their contents steaming and stewing within and building up a ghastly pressure that finally blew the bricks apart.

That probably hadn't been nice to see... and even worse to smell.

Some of the crypts had been leased, and evictions had once been common. Many tombs had a shaft in back that burrowed into the earth. If the rent wasn't paid, the occupant's bones were simply tumbled into the shaft and another coffin inserted above... which might have been the original meaning of people getting the shaft.

Kody went to the rear of a larger tomb that resembled a miniature castle. Like many, there were cracks and holes like grinning gaps of darkness. He reached into one clear up to his shoulder and drew out a long yellow bone. "I think it's called a femur."

The Trouts looked horrified, but were holding hands like kids again.

"Y'all wouldn't see that on a tour," added Raney.

"Cool!" said Newton. "Can I hold it?"

"I want a picture of this!" said Mrs. Trout. She posed the boys against the tomb, black and brown to glaring white, with Newton holding the bone. "Priceless!" she said as her camera clicked.

Mr. Trout laughed. "Wait till the Johnsons see this one! It beats their week in Mexico for the Day Of The Dead celebration."

Kody returned the bone to its rest after whispering thanks to its former owner, then led the way deeper among the graves. Besides the vault of Marie Laveau -- which he was saving for last -- he showed the crypts of Albert Blanchard, a general in the Confederate Army, and Homer Plessy who'd been the cause of Separate But Equal segregation... which in no way was equal. There was the crypt of Ben Latrobe, an architect, who'd worked on the U.S. Capitol Building and argued with Thomas Jefferson about the design of its columns. There was also the tomb of Paul Morphy, a master chess player who'd learned the game at ten-years-old: there was still a tournament held in his honor.

At last they came to Marie Laveau's crypt, a simple, small, rectangular shape of plastered red brick with a gray marble front. It was showing its age and needed paint like many others all around. As always, there were offerings... coins, flowers, charms and such, and scraps of paper stuck in the cracks. Sun-faded faded envelopes lay here and there bearing stamps from all over the world, and the overnight letter was wedged in a gap.

The man and woman regarded the structure. "I thought it would be a lot bigger," said Mr. Trout. "Fancier, anyhow."

"She wasn't a showtime," said Kody. "Even though she was beautiful, an' a really cool dancer."

"Yeah," added Raney. "But, she was a simple person. Kinda like bayou folks. Her family come from Haiti, they say. Lived most of her life in a little cottage over on Saint Anne Street. The fancy place they tell tourists was hers was really her one of her daughters' houses."

Mrs. Trout smiled. "What would she think of these plastic roses?"

"She probably say they was practical, ma'am. Bein' a practical person herself."

"You think a lot of her, don't you?"

Kody nodded. "Remember, we were slaves in her day. An' women didn't have any rights. Even white ones didn't. But, she was respected an' powerful here."

"Yeah," added Raney. "They say she wasn't educated, but she fought for people in court an' won... innocent people 'cused of crimes. An' it didn't matter what color they was."

"An' she had fifteen kids," said Kody. "So she musta liked children."

Mr. Trout smiled. "Or something else."

"I don't think she had to have 'em," said Kody. "Remember, she knew about stuff like that 'cause she was a healer, too. Voodoo is more about healing than hexing."

Mrs. Trout asked, "Why are these X's scratched on her tomb?"

"Some people believe it gets her attention. You always make 'em in three's like that. But, I think if she wanna hear you she will. If she don't, you can't make her listen."

Mr. Trout took his wife's hand. "I've noticed that about women."

Mrs. Trout asked, "Is it all right to look at these letters?"

"Sure. 'Cept I wouldn't open that new one."

Mr. Trout smiled again. "Because she hasn't read it yet."

"Kids take a lot of this stuff," added Raney. "Kids always lookin' for money."

Kody glanced at Mr. Trout's watch, noting the time was getting near ten, then gave Newton a nudge. "I'll show you a place to go. C'mon."

"Huh?"

"'S'cuse us, folks," said Kody. "Raney knows all about Miz Laveau, an' lots of history, too."

Mrs. Trout smiled. "A mind to match those handsome muscles."

"He also wrestles alligators." Kody took Newton's hand and led him away.

"But I don't gotta," said Newton.

"Shush," whispered Kody. He towed the boy down a lane of tombs. "I wanna see where your gang hung out. Like, when you were drinkin' an' stuff."

"Oh." Newton pointed. "Back dere in dat corner." Then he looked to the distant wall and the Project buildings looming beyond.

"Could Rick see us here from a window?" asked Kody.

"Not dis far back. ...I... was thinkin' about my mom."

"She be worried you didn't come home last night?"

"Nah. I been stayin' away a lot. It hard when your mom ain't dere for you."

"I hear you, little man," said Kody. "It makes you feel like you ain't worth nothin'. My mom ran off when I was a baby. But, lucky for me I

80

got a cool dad. ...Think Rick might try an' hurt her?"

"S'pose he could, but..." Newton looked down at the broken old stones. "I tole him I hate her... don't care about her."

"...Oh. But, you really do care?"

"'Course I do!" Newton wiped his eyes, then yanked up his slipping jeans. "C'mon." Puffing, at his shambling gait and holding the back of his jeans with a hand, he led the way down a narrow path between the silent rows of stone as heat waves shimmered against the sky as if the air was filled with ghosts. The gang's "clubhouse" was a small shabby crypt with an iron door and a stained-glass window. The lock had been broken for many years; and Newton tugged the door open. Its hinges screamed like tortured souls, and a blast of heat blew out in their faces, reeking of dust and ancient decay.

"Let me check it," said Kody, easing Newton back from the door. He scanned the gloomy chamber; about seven feet long and four feet wide. The window was at the opposite end, small, dirty, and heavily barred. It glowed bloody red like a furnace door glass in the brassy glare of the sun. Marble slabs lined the two longer walls, behind which skeletons lay in darkness. One of the slabs was shockingly cracked, and seemingly only spider webs were holding it together. Forties and beer bottles littered the floor amongst empty bags of cookies and chips. There were candy bar wrappers, cigarette butts, an old Bic lighter and other kid-trash. There was also a pair of ragged sneaks all shriveled and shrunk from the heat, and a grimy wife-beater balled up in a corner. Kody frowned at the stump of a candle stuck on the floor in a puddle of wax. Behind it was a small chunk of mirror propped against the wall. It wasn't a true altar yet, but the right *gris-gris* could make it one.

"You fools didn't come here at night?" asked Kody.

"I sure wouldn't!"

"Then what's the candle for?"

"Rick said it was cool."

"It ain't cool, dammit! A flame is a symbol of life, an' dead things are attracted to life. Did he have any 'ceremonies' in here?"

"He said weird things an' axed for stuff."

Kody's frown deepened. *"Who* did he ask? Did he say any names?"

"Nah. But he seem ta think somebody heard him, like when you prayin' in church. ...Mom used ta take me."

"Somethin' did hear him!" said Kody. "But it wasn't nothin' you'd pray to in church! An' that piece of mirror is like a window. Somethin' coulda seen us last night."

"But we never come here at night."

"I mean somethin' worse than your baby gang friends, an' it could see us anytime as long as that window is open." Kody glanced at the candle again. "When did he start askin' for stuff?"

"A few days ago. After we jack dat mark like I tole you."

Kody considered. "It ain't got him yet... whatever it is... not till he calls it up by its name. But it's gettin' close."

Newton's eyes widened. "Mean dere a ghost in dis tomb?"

Kody scanned around. There were names and dates carved into the slabs, but most were badly crumbled with age or buried in nets of spiderwebs. "There might not be a ghost in here, but we're in a grave-yard."

"Oh yeah."

Kody brushed away spiderwebs. "I need to find out who these people were."

"Like, doin' Voodoo homework?"

"Yeah. When did Rick have his last ceremony?"

"Yesterday mornin'. Why dere wasn't no time for lunch. Den I had ta go cap somebody. He say it was a sacrifice."

Kody shook his head again. "It's got him for sure if he makes one! An' it woulda got *you* if you'd killed anybody. Only evil things tell you to kill. ...It's not too late to stop this shit, but we don't got a lot of time."

Newton scratched behind one of his horns. "So, what we do?"

Kody pointed. "Where those old kicks come from?"

"Dey was Terrel's. Da chubby dude. He boost new ones at River-walk Mall."

"Did he wear these a lot without socks?"

"Yeah, he don't wear socks."

Kody snagged the tattered sneaks. Even dried out they smelled of kid-feet. He slipped them into an old cookie bag, a "family-size" of chocolate chip, then scoped around the other trash. "Who had the lighter?"

Newton came in. "Devon. He twelve."

"You all use it?"

"Devon lit everbody's smokes. ...Oh, I see what you sayin'. Dere some of him on it now, huh?"

"Gotta be some skin on the wheel." Kody dropped the lighter into the bag. "Ain't DNA like CSI stuff, but it's just as good for Voodoo. ...What about this 'beater?"

"Dat was Matt's. He thirteen."

Kody picked up and un-balled the shirt. "He the dark dude with long hair?"

"Yeah. Da blackest bro I ever seen."

"Me too." Kody pulled a hair from the cotton, an ebony spiral twelve inches long. "Aight, that's three." He started to toss the shirt away, then stopped and checked it again, sniffing at a grayish stain. "Is this what I think it is?"

"Yeah, it Rick's," said Newton. "He was playin' around wit' dat nasty ol' gun..." He made a hand gesture. "You know, like I said last night. An' da other dudes was doin' it, too. ...An' I was kinda tryin'. Rick said it would bring us some kinda power. But he got his... stuff... on Matt's shirt, so Matt left it here."

"Then we got Rick, too," said Kody. "Blood, sweat, tears an' this stuff are essences of people. An' hair, fingernail, or toenail pieces are almost as good for Voodoo."

He stuffed the shirt into the bag. "People in Haiti would burn all these things so nobody clse could get 'em."

He raised a foot to smash the mirror, but then had second thoughts. He didn't want Rick to know he'd been here... but he didn't want that window left open. He paused to think, his foot still poised -- anyone could have broken this mirror -- then crushed it to sparks on the floor.

There was a crash of falling stone as the cracked marble slab fell to pieces!

Newton yelped and lunged for the door, but Kody faced the grinning white thing as dust swirled up from the rubble. The skeleton's coffin had rotted away, and it lay on its side looking out.

"He turned in his grave," said Kody.

"W-what dat mean?" asked Newton, poised in the doorway to run.

"Sometimes nothin'," said Kody, now covered with dust so he looked like a zombie. "Corpse gas or maggots can do it. But they're just old bones like the one you was holdin' when the Trouts took your picture."

"But dey all *connected* in dere!"

"They ain't gettin' up... 'least not by themselves." Kody toed a chunk of marble. "That slab was ready to fall apart. Good thing you wasn't under it."

"Ain't never comin' in here again!"

"That's a cool idea, little man. You're way too alive to be hangin' with dead things.'

X X X

Rick's eyes flew open. Had that been a gunshot? He sat up in bed and listened, but there were only the usual sounds... stereos meat-punching gangster rap with a brutal, thudding, mind-numbing beat, babies crying, a man's voice yelling, all of which seemed to mix with the music, venomous, hateful and hopeless, like ignorant children cursing in rage at things they couldn't understand.

But, none of those normally woke him; he'd been hearing them all his life... including a lot of gunshots. He glanced at his clock: it was 10:13. Terrel's chubby body was sprawled against him on top of a grimy rat-colored sheet stained with a lot of stuff besides sweat, the boy snoring softly and reeking of beer, while Devon lay curled on the floor amongst empty forty-ounce bottles. Matt was nowhere in sight. Maybe he'd gone to the bathroom? Rick listened again and waited, but Matt had apparently skipped.

He rolled from the bed and went to the window, open as he'd left it last night, tugging up his boxers a bit. His head hurt a little from drinking, and the blazing sun dazzled his eyes, reflecting up from the stark white tombs in the silently shimmering cemetery. He saw a few figures here and there moving along the paths. A tour was gathering at the gate, after making a stop at the liquor store for bottled water and "healthy hydration." All were white except the guide.

He searched amongst the tombs again, wishing he could see *his* crypt, but it was concealed in a weedy corner. He wasn't sure what he was looking for, but had a feeling something was wrong. He glanced at the dresser: the yellowed skull grinned with its long ivory teeth, gazing at him with shadowy sockets. The candles had burned out during the night, leaving spiderweb dribbles of wax. He would have to get more today and keep them burning twenty-four-seven. That was important, *he* needed the flames. The cheap little gun lay next to the skull, and Rick went over to pick it up. It wasn't like the old one; it didn't promise anything, and Rick cursed Newton under his breath... *worthless little nigger!*

"I gonna kill him!" he whispered, gazing into the mirror. "I swear to you on my soul!"

There was a crash!

Rick darted first to the window, then realized it had come from inside. Had somebody busted the crib again? He cocked the gun and crept from his room, easing slowly down the hall, the weapon held out in both hands. He paused at the kitchen doorway, then peeped cautiously in. A broken plate littered the dusty floor, and his mother, barefoot and clad in her bathrobe, was shakily pouring a glass of wine. Rick stuck the pistol in back of his shorts and warily entered the room.

"Careful, mom, you'll cut yourself." Rick got a broom and dustpan as his mother sank down at the table.

"I'm not feelin' well this mornin'," she said. "Fix your own breakfast again... but don't be feedin' your no-count friends."

Rick dumped the remains of the plate in the trash. "Sure, mom."

"Your child support is late," said his mother, after taking a drink. "Don't know how I'ma pay the rent. I warn you about it last night... didn't I?"

Rick put the broom away. "It come last week. It always does. I seen the envelope."

"You got no business readin' my mail!"

"I didn't read it, I only seen it."

The woman took another drink. "Your father only sent half the money. He always shortin' me."

"Thought you said the check was late?"

His mother slapped him. "Don't you be sassin' me, nigger!"

Rick's mouth fell open. "Why you call me that?"

"'Cause that's what you are!" yelled his mother. "Nothin' but a worthless nigger!" She raised her hand and Rick dodged away. His own hand went for the gun, but his mother just reached for the bottle.

"I'm tellin' you that check is late, an' you better get us some money, boy! Or you gonna be sleepin' in Jackson Square with all the other no-count trash!"

Rick rubbed his cheek and sighed. "Sure, mom."

TWELVE

"Did you dig up some magic bones?" asked the man.

Kody glanced down at the cookie bag, which lay at his feet on the cobblestones. The Trouts had loved their graveyard tour, cheerfully paying him twenty dollars, along with an offer to buy the boys lunch. They had taken Clay's carriage to Jackson Square, and Raney had chosen a Cajun cafe with tables out front under big shady trees. The group now relaxed in the leaf-dappled light after downing huge platters of crawfish tails and *andouille* sausage with red beans and rice.

Street musicians were playing nearby, and the air was bumping with rhythms. An ice cream vendor was hawking his wares as if chanting a sweet incantation, while artists were sketching in charcoal and chalk, and fortune-tellers were casting cards or rattling shakers of bones. A bare-chested boy of maybe eleven was doing a tap-dance routine, his body gleaming like onyx with sweat, while other kids worked their way through the crowd offering beads and Voodoo charms... which were probably made in China. Cameras were clicking here and there as a trio of vampires made an appearance despite the deadly rays of the sun; and the dancing boy was being cammed, after pausing to cross his arms and demand five dollars before going on.

"...Oh," said Kody, sleepily stuffed. "I found an old pair of sneaks in the graveyard."

Mr. Trout laughed. "Not down a shaft like that leg bone, I hope?"

"Um, no."

"Are you poor?" asked Mrs. Trout.

Kody looked around at the kids at work, most of whom were

skeleton skinny... and not because it was "healthy." "I got more than ninety-percent of the world.. ...Maybe I give em' to some needy kid."

"You sound as practical as Marie Laveau."

Mr. Trout asked, "Would anyone like a cigar?"

The boys accepted graciously.

"Well," said Mr. Trout, after lighting everyone up. "We're going to be here one more day. Any suggestions on what we should see?"

Mrs. Trout added, "Hopefully a genuine ghost."

"...Huh?" said Kody. A girl stood watching the dancing boy, and Kody had been watching her. She was the fox from the ice cream shop, who filled her clothes as abundantly as she had packed the sugar cones and looked every ounce as sweet.

Mr. Trout followed Kody's eyes. "Besides the present sights, of course." He smiled at his wife. "Would you like to be their age again?"

Mrs. Trout pressed her husband's hand. "As long as I still meet you."

"...Oh," said Kody, returning to earth.

"We've been on the *Natchez*," said Mrs. Trout, watching the steamboat churn upriver. "And to the aquarium."

"Da Children's Museum is cool," said Newton, who sprawled in a chair with a hand on his belly as if to prevent an explosion. He puffed out a lazy ghost of smoke like Ethu after a feast. "Dey gots a skeleyton ridin' a bike."

"We were thinking of taking a plantation tour."

"Take the African tour," said Kody, reluctantly pulling his eyes from the girl. "White folks are always welcome. An' you get to hear how it *really* was instead of just a lot of Big Houses an' 'Noble Old Southern Style.'"

Raney nodded, relaxed in his chair, cigar in hand, his own stony stomach bulging a bit. "An' guides who say the slaves was 'servants' an' don't wanna talk about that."

"Yeah," agreed Kody. "Like slavery never existed to bankroll all that 'nobility.' ...Tell 'em you been to our ceremony an' they'll give you a discount."

"An' 'member my card," added Raney, "if y'all want a bayou tour." He leaned to Kody and murmured, "I gotta go home in two more days;

hope this nasty stuff over by then."

"We certainly will," said Mrs. Trout. "But it will have to be next time we're here."

Kody smiled. "Folks always come back to New Orleans."

"We'd love to see that flooded graveyard. And alligators, of course."

"We got tons of 'em," said Raney. "Even one you can pet. He sleep in my room in the wintertime. We got him a 'lectric blanket."

"And you wrestle them, too?"

"Ever since I was six, ma'am. An' we give a night tour of the ol' graveyard that guaranteed to curl your hair." He laughed. "Just look at mine!"

Mr. Trout patted his middle. "I could do with a nap right now. I must have gained five pounds this week. This city has such wonderful food."

"Don't I know it!" Kody agreed. "'As delicious as the less criminal forms of sin'... Mark Twain said that." He watched the girl disappear in the crowd. Did she live in the Quarter, he wondered?

Mrs. Trout and her husband got up. "I hope we'll see you again."

Kody also rose. "We do, too; an' thanks for lunch."

"Thank you for the tour," said Mr. Trout. "We've gained a whole new perspective on Voodoo."

Mrs. Trout said, "I'd really like to meet a vampire... but not on bitey terms."

"Try the Vampire Vault on Bourbon Street. Got the best bloody-marys in the Quarter." Kody glanced at the gunmetal clouds drifting slowly upriver. A dagger of lightning stabbed the sky, but the thunder was only a distant drum. "Might be a good night for huntin' undeads."

Mr. Trout shook hands with the boys, then added a wink for Kody. "Good hunting yourself."

"She went up Saint Anne Street," said Raney, after the Trouts had departed. "The girl from the ice cream shop."

"I seen her before," added Newton, gulping the last of a root beer float and blasting a monster burp.

"She live around here?" asked Kody.

"Somewhere's past da graveyard, I think."

A white family passed with a little blond girl. "Look, he's got horns!" exclaimed the girl.

"Yes, honey," said her father. "And the vampire boy last night had fangs."

"Take his picture, mommy! With me!"

The woman smiled at Newton. "May I?"

"Sure, ma'am," said Newton, and struggled valiantly to his feet. The kids were posed, the camera clicked, and the family moved cheerfully on.

Kody said, "I charged a dollar when I was Ethu. Five if I posed with somebody."

Newton reached to touch his horns. "I keep forgettin' I worth somethin' now."

"You were always worth somethin', you just didn't know it."

Raney yawned. "I could use a nap like Mr. Trout, but guess we got Voodoo need doin'?"

"Yeah," said Kody, tugging his jeans a bit higher. "An' we better get Newton off the street 'cause it's gettin' close to noon."

"Can you feel the gang with that stuff you found?"

"We gotta do a blessing first."

"I axed Miz Laveau if she help us," said Raney. "While you an' Newton was gone. I scratched three X's on her tomb. Y'all think that was cool?"

"I wouldn't of bothered her," said Kody. "It's just a nasty ghost after Rick an' we can probably put it down after we get all seven, but it's cool if she knows about it." He scanned the crowded square: it was easy to spot the homeless kids and the others who lived on the scraps of life, so plainly poor among the rich... at least to Kody's eyes. They were tortured daily by all this food, and the money parading in front of their faces. Some, like the gleaming dancer boy, were sweating buckets to earn their green, while others were only begging for bones or offering themselves for sale. A girl of twelve with childish makeup was trying to look at least thirteen, and a shirtless boy of maybe fourteen was advertising in half buttoned jeans. A few kids lurked in doorways and alleys, eying purses and prominent wallets while trying to calculate risks. But if Kody could spot them, so could the cops.

"Don't," Kody murmured, walking past a skinny boy who was scoping a fat man in tourist attire whose wallet peeked partly out of a pocket. "He's N.O.P.D., an' you're *his* mark."

The boy looked surprised but nodded a thanks.

At the corner of Chartres and Saint Anne Streets they were stopped by tourists with German accents, who wanted to take Newton's picture and smilingly paid him a dollar. Kody gave them Aunt Simone's card and told them about the ceremony where Ethu would be appearing tonight.

"Put on the beanie," said Kody, after the people had gone. "We shouldn't be gettin' attention like that. It's good for business, but not today."

"Damn!" said Newton, patting his pockets. "Musta fell out somewheres."

"Y'all had it in the graveyard," said Raney. "I seen it when you was goin' with Kody."

"Maybe I lost it in da carriage. Or when we was eatin' lunch."

"Ain't important," said Kody. "I had it so long it was fallin' apart. Now let's get you on the under." He started to lead down Chartres Street, but Raney touched his shoulder and pointed. "There she is, cousin."

THIRTEEN

Kodi turned around. A crowd had gathered on Saint Anne Street, and the chubby girl stood amongst it. The pulse of drums throbbed in the hot, steamy air, and someone seemed to be dancing. "Damn!" said Kody. "I don't have time! We got the gang to worry about."

"Just go up an' say hi," said Raney. "A few more minutes ain't gonna matter... 'less you don't figure she worth some time?"

Kody sighed. "If you got eyes, you know she's worth time. ...'Least I can see if she's interested an' maybe find out where she lives. But, don't stay out in the open... wait in that ice cream shop over there."

"Can I have a cone?" asked Newton.

Kody gave Newton the twenty dollars, handed the cookie bag to Raney, then trotted up the sidewalk. His chest and belly jiggled and bobbed, and his jeans were slipping to hazardous lows as he neared the circle of mostly tourists gathered under a gallery.

The girl was a *lot* more than just worth his time. Her white 'beater made a cool contrast to the warm chocolate shade of her skin, clinging enticingly tight to her body and baring the charming roll of her tummy. She was intently observing the show, and Kody made the most of his view. Her jeans fit as fly as the tight-clinging shirt, while her natural hair was a halo of curls that sparkled a little with oil. Kody paused to catch his breath...

But lost it again when he saw the dancer.

He wouldn't have thought it possible, but he almost forgot about the girl... at least for a couple of seconds. But anyone would, he told himself; the dancer was just so...

Kody wasn't sure what... a glistening shadow impossibly black, a graceful, midnight, seductive seducer; a slender, feral, prowling panther symbolically stalking invisible prey. For a minute he could only watch. The dancer's moves were shyly enticing, making him think for a moment of Arlan's innocent danger; the throbbing music so primal and deep his own pulse quickened to join it. He felt his throat tighten as if he would cry. His chest even hurt with the effort of breath... or maybe it was the ache of his heart, something he'd never believed could happen.

Dimly, he wondered if this was illegal, even in the tolerant Quarter: the dancing figure was nearly naked except for a wisp of leopardskin, slightly less than next to nothing. Yet, she couldn't have been much over thirteen, and her shape was only suggestive of... something. Her skin was like polished obsidian, gleamingly sheened with silvery sweat; her hair like an ebony dandelion puff, scattering sparkling jewels as she spun, creating a circle of magic around her that none of the watchers could penetrate. Dollar bills were thrown at her feet, and yet she seemed to ignore the money as if the dance itself was enough.

But then the enchantment was shattered... at least it was for Kody. He'd burrowed his way to the front of the crowd, completely forgetting the ice cream girl, but now he froze in shock... the dancer was a *boy!*

At least he was *almost* sure of that.

For a moment he didn't want to believe it; and then he felt guilty, even ashamed, of the sudden heat that had flared in his loins to strain the sweaty confines of his jeans. The boy's "leopard-skin" was bikini briefs, and his beautiful face was hauntingly male, though his lips were full in a natural pout, and his long-lashed eyes like starless night. His body was hard to describe, his proportions slenderly masculine, his shoulders too wide and hips too narrow for anything but a boy, yet he seemed to suggest a whole new creation. He must have had muscles to move like that, but his chest was only gently defined and the rest of his body was supple and smooth.

A backpack lay on the cobblestones and probably held his shoes and clothes, while a cheap little blaster provided the pulse. The boy knew how to work his crowd -- Kody's professionalism conceded -- steaming the air with pheromones, though maybe unintentionally, enrapt in himself in his sensuous dance. His briefs were almost agonizing... you wanted to see what they hardly concealed, if only to prove what you might have imagined. The boy would lunge to the edge of his circle as if to offer himself, but then he'd leap away again when money was thrust or a hand tried to touch. There weren't any whistles or calls from the crowd that might have attracted a cop... the boy was too good at his magic. There was nothing dirty in what he was doing, except his age and alluring beauty; but there was too little of one of those, and way too much of the other.

Kody's own body was gleaming with sweat, but a chill ran suddenly down his spine and his loins were dashed with ice. The boy was one of the Skeleton Crew! ...Matt, who'd left his shirt in the tomb!

Kody hadn't recognized him, nearly naked and casting his spell, but he'd stood on the sidewalk yesterday and waited for Kody to die. And he'd been in that crypt for the ceremony when Newton was sent out to kill.

Kody edged away from the circle before the boy could spot him. He scanned the doorways and sidewalks, expecting to find the rest of the gang -- who should have been watching their brother's back since people were throwing a lot of money -- but didn't see any of them.

Then he remembered the girl. *Damn!* He looked around but she wasn't there. Had she seen him watching the dance? Maybe she hadn't noticed him? ...But what if she had? She probably knew the "girl" was a boy, but what would she think of Kody? Kody had either been watching a girl -- *another* girl -- while panting like a pubescent puppy, or else he'd been peeping a pretty young boy while probably all-too obviously on the verge of creaming his jeans.

"There goes the summer!" he muttered.

Raney and Newton stood in a doorway eating chocolate ice cream cones, as Kody came puffing back down the street. Newton offered another cone. "I licked it a little 'cause it was meltin'."

"How's fishin'?" asked Raney.

Kody didn't want Newton to freak at hearing one of the gang was near, so he didn't say anything about Matt. "She got away."

"How you let that happen?" asked Raney. "You always been good at that kinda Voodoo... fair to middlin' anyways."

"Guess I was thinkin' about bustin' ghosts." Kody looked over his shoulder after taking the cone from Newton: the crowd up the street was dispersing, which meant the dance must have ended. He wondered again if Matt was alone. Was it worth the risk of trying to catch him? The dude was a deadly dancer, but he probably wouldn't be much of a fighter... assuming he wasn't packing steel. "C'mon," he said, "we should get home."

"'Least y'all know she like dancers," said Raney.

"Which takes me out of her game," sighed Kody, smooshing a bite of ice cream.

The afternoon heat was like blistering steam as the boys reached the corner of Ursulines, and Newton was puffing and panting again, his jeans so sodden and droopy with sweat he had to hold them up with a hand.

"Wait!" he finally gasped, slumping against a street light pole, the cave of his navel dribbling like a leaky faucet. "Way too much walkin' ta-day!"

"Think you could run if you had to?" asked Raney.

"…What you sayin'? Run from what? …Like a zombie after my brain?"

Raney laughed. "Up till you put on them horns yesterday, a zombie wouldn't of known you had one."

"Real zombies don't eat brains," said Kody. "An' runnin' wouldn't save you, 'cause it would just keep comin' no matter where you went."

"Might take a while," said Raney, "but it get you sooner or later."

Newton shuddered. "Den what it do?"

"Just 'cause they don't eat brains don't mean they don't get messy."

"I hope you kiddin'," said Newton. "I couldn't even get a head-start."

Raney knelt. "Climb on my back."

"Chill a minute," said Kody, who'd paused to scan around. A few people passed up on Royal Street, maybe to check out the Voodoo shop, while others were strolling down on Decatur, but the blocks in between were deserted. The air itself seemed to hold its breath as the thunderstorm slowly approached.

"They could be in our alley," said Raney. "Waitin' on us to come home."

"We shouldn't of taken the time for lunch." Kody glanced at the cookie bag in his hand. "An' we shoulda done the blessin' already so we could be feelin' 'em now."

"Let me try," said Newton.

"But, you don't know nothin' about Voodoo."

Raney looked thoughtful. "He know them dudes a lot better than us. Maybe that count for somethin'."

"Guess it can't hurt." Kody handed the bag to Newton. "Don't touch no more than you gotta."

But, Newton just closed his eyes for a moment while pressing the bag to his chest. He made a constipated face. "I can almost..." Then he blew out a breath. "Dat hard ta do."

"Yeah," said Kody. "Takes lots of practice. ...Guess you didn't feel nothin'?"

"Did so! ...Sorta. Dey ain't all ta-gether right now. I don't know where, but none of 'em close."

"Well," said Kody. "I trust you, but I ain't sure I trust your feelin's. Took me years to learn that stuff."

"Mean I done some magic?"

Kody ruffled Newton's hair. "Most kids your age got natural magic. The world just tells you not to use it, an' after a while you forget you had it."

"I used ta know when da phone gonna ring... before it did, what I sayin'. But mom told me not ta do dat."

"What I mean," said Kody. "Kid-magic makes adults nervous."

Newton climbed onto Raney's back, his sodden jeans slipping off his bottom to hang halfway down his thighs. "Let me go in da alley first. It me dey wanna kill."

"That was yesterday," said Kody. "Whatever Rick woke up in the graveyard, it's gotta be pissed 'cause I busted its window. Ain't none of us safe anymore. But, no sense in all of us riskin' our butts. You two wait here an' I'll check it out."

Kody went cautiously up the street and stopped at the alley entrance. He snagged a beer bottle out of the gutter and tossed it into the passage. He winced when it clattered but didn't break. Air-conditioners hummed overhead; the courtyard fountain trickled softly; a boom of thunder rattled windows, but there was no other sound. Finally, he peeked around the corner. The empty alley yawned at him. He signaled to Raney and Newton.

"What now?" asked Raney, a few minutes later, kicked-back in a chair in the steamy courtyard while Newton sprawled in another. Clouds were gathering rapidly, but the sweltering air had grown even hotter and felt as thick as Cajun stew. A spear of lightning stabbed the sky, and thunder crashed like cannon fire. Raney waited until it died. "We gonna do it in your room?"

"We can't take a chance with the mirror," said Kody. "Even if we cover it up, somethin' could be listenin'. We need to ask Ethu for blessings 'cause this thing is all about kids, but I don't even want *our* ghost watchin' us."

"Y'all think it might tell the one in the graveyard? Like, ghosts got a gang of they own?"

"I'm just bein' careful," said Kody. "It's hard enough trustin' people with skin."

"Should I bring Ethu down?"

"Hey," said Newton, thumbing his chest. "*I'm* Ethu, 'member."

"Yeah, you can represent," said Kody. "I'ma go up an' get the *gris-gris.* You gotta get naked, aight?"

Newton laughed. "Even naked I only E rated."

"Your rating don't matter, it's about purity."

"You sayin' I pure… like good?"

Raney said, "'Least a tad more than you was yesterday."

Kody added, "Ethu's like a real boy, does naughty things sometimes, not some little angel so smarmy sweet you wanna slap it."

"Guess dat me." Newton pointed. "But, what about dat window? Like, what if da Skeleyton Crew come back?"

Kody glanced up at the still-open window in the Voodoo shop. "Even Rick couldn't be that stupid. Not with the store full of people now."

Raney asked, "But, what if that ghost, or whatever it is, is makin' him wanna kill us so bad he just ain't usin' no sense?"

Newton shivered despite dripping sweat. "You talkin' 'bout dat skeleyton? Da one dat turned in its grave?"

Kody shook his head. "I told you they were just old bones. They ain't gonna get up an' come after us. It's a ghost we gotta deal with. But, it still ain't got Rick all the way in its power… not till he calls it up by name."

"But, what if it knows what we doin'?" asked Raney. "Tryin' to help them dumb-ass fools?"

"It can't see us without a window. An' even if it could see us, it might not know what we're doin'. If it didn't know nothin' about Voodoo alive, it can't know any more dead."

Newton glanced at the cookie bag. "Den it can't tell Rick we got dis stuff?"

Lightning slashed the sky again, and Kody paused for the thunder. "It could tell him we got it, but maybe not why. But, it's gettin' enough of a hold on him to look out his eyes, an' feel through his body, an' know what he's thinkin' about."

"Like, Rick a window, too?" asked Newton.

"He could be," said Kody. "An' so could his posse. The longer you hang with evil things the more they can use you for evil."

FOURTEEN

"**G**immie your money, boy!"

For a moment the young man stood frozen. He felt like he'd just met the boogeyman his mother used to warn him about, the monster who came after bad little boys who didn't eat their broccoli. But she'd warned him about a lot of things, like playing in puddles and getting obese.

The young man wasn't obese: in fact his BMI was perfect according to what he'd been taught. He was twenty-three, white, and a medical student who lived in Iola, Wisconsin; and though he'd grown up in a "nice little town," he was still well aware that shit happened.

But, shit always happened to somebody else!

Of course he'd known he was taking a risk, but you risked your life when crossing a street, or even just stepping into a shower. Sure, he'd suspected black kids were "bad." You heard about it all the time; they hijacked cars, robbed liquor stores, and shot and killed each other.

But he hadn't considered *these* kids.

For a moment he almost wanted to laugh... these little dudes had to be putting him on! The oldest boy was maybe fourteen, while the youngest was no more than twelve. All were shirtless in big-jeans and sneaks, their sweaty underwear on display as if proud of showing the world their asses. The middle boy's body was all baby-chub -- more than acceptable BMI -- the little one's childish and sway-backed, while a Saints cap almost covered his eyes. The elder boy had a few kid-muscles -- his BMI just about right -- but the gun was rock-steady in ebony hands as he aimed at the young student's chest.

The boy snarled, "Don't dally with me!"

"Dally" seemed a strange word to use – "fuck" would have seem-ed more in character -- but thunder rumbled ominously as if to back the boy's threat.

The man couldn't read those obsidian eyes, except to see they were narrow and glazed. The boy almost seemed to be *listening* to something as the rumbling echoes of thunder died.

The man cursed himself for being so stupid: he'd met these kids only minutes ago outside on the street at the graveyard gate. He'd suspected they might be on something -- at least he'd smelled beer on their breaths -- but that had made them seem vulnerable, as if he was taking advantage of them. Besides, they were *kids* not video thugs! Yes, they were all wearing black bandannas, but the dangerous colors were red and blue... what he'd been taught by TV. Sure, he'd been warned not to come here alone by a taxi driver, a hotel clerk, and even an elderly coachman; but he'd wanted to see Marie Laveau's tomb and these kids had offered to show him... and for only a dollar. Tours were for senior citizens in Bermuda shorts and black gartered socks; this had seemed like a cool thing to do, like hiring native safari guides.

The young man studied the younger kids' faces: they seemed uncertain and maybe scared, but that might have been from drinking or drugs. The elder boy was breathing hard and scenting the air with alcohol fumes. All the kids were shiny with sweat, and their black and brown bodies looked somehow surreal in this sweltering maze of eerie white tombs.

But, the whole cemetery was somehow surreal, a silent stone city within its own walls, its crypts and vaults so strangely shaped, with iron doors and rusty bars, miniature columns and weird architecture, like spectral things from another dimension where Death was the master designer.

Clouds were gathering heavy and dark, but only seemed to increase the heat, and the man was sweating more than the kids despite being physically fit, clad in jeans and a Packers tank-top. He told himself not to do anything stupid... more than he already had. People bragged about what they would do if someone stuck a gun in their face, but of course that had never *happened* to them. He remembered reading an old ghost story: *Only a fool would boast of courage in situations he'd never encountered.*

He had about fifty dollars in cash, the price of a frugal French Quarter evening, and the rest of his wealth was safe in plastic. A phone call would get him a new card, and his parents could wire him money. For a moment he almost smiled: he'd wanted adventure and now he had it! Fifty bucks was a bargain price for a tale he could tell for years to come... jacked by gangsters in New Orleans.

"NOW!" bawled the boy, jabbing the gun muzzle viciously.

Reality-check, the man told himself; dead men didn't tell any tales! The boy's sweaty scent seemed to burn in his nose, that sharp bitter bite of young adolescence, mingled with denim and dirty old sneaks. This wasn't a kid to be messing with; a fiery furnace of rage and frustration, fueled by emotion and boiling hormones, possessed by the lusts of his own desperate body.

"All right," said the man, while thinking, *boy!* "Just stay cool, okay?" He didn't know much about gunshot wounds, but he *was* a medical student and had his anatomy down. The gun wasn't quite to his heart, but a shattered sternum was serious trauma, not to mention a punctured lung. Besides, he'd studied psychology, and this kid was more than a little disturbed.

Yet, he discovered he wasn't afraid, which gave him a little satisfaction. He even managed to feel annoyed, like being security searched in an airport, or stopped by a cop for a broken tail light. Careful not to make any fast moves, he slowly pulled out his wallet, a high-school graduation gift of genuine alligator skin. The chubby boy snatched it away. In seconds it was thoroughly raped, including the condom he carried. The youngest boy giggled at this.

Now that the worst was over it seemed important to salvage some pride. Naturally he'd embellish this tale, but he wasn't a bold-faced liar: the kids would be older, bigger and badder... they didn't have to be any blacker. He also felt a little smug; he'd left his Rolex in the hotel safe. Maybe he wasn't a man of the world, but he wasn't a totally clueless fool. "Can I have it back?" he asked. "You can't use the card, you know?"

Big mistake! The boy jammed the gun even tighter, and now it *was* to his heart!

"Be tellin' me what I can do!" yelled the kid. He glanced at the Visa card. "What your PIN number, boy? ...An' don't you tell me it backwards!"

The young man hadn't expected that! He tried to force his mind to think: of course he could always make up a number, but there was an ATM at the liquor store across the street... the beautiful street with its cars and people that now seemed a light-year away! He'd gone in to buy a bottle of water, but actually for the experience of seeing a genuine ghetto store.

The clouds rolled in and the sun disappeared as if pulling a hoodie over its face and turning its back on the man. Lightning slashed across the sky as if ripping a gash with a razor. The crash of thunder was deafening and almost made him jump. He felt his pose beginning to crumble like rotten old bones in the crypts all around... this wasn't amusing anymore! ...But what the hell, he told himself, they could only get his daily limit, and he'd call the bank...

Assuming he managed to get out of here... and hopefully not in a body bag!

He had to swallow to make his voice work; and the kid seemed to smirk at the cowardly sound. Funny, he wasn't a bad-looking boy, with a small snub nose and full pouty lips that once might have smiled at *Little Bill*. Could the kid smell his fear, he wondered? The man's voice quavered reciting his code, the name of his dog, now long deceased, which really sounded stupid... Barfy! He'd buried old Barf in his mom's flower garden, complete with a crude little cross.

"Down on your knees!" yelled the kid.

The man had been thinking of pretty rose bushes and summer days on a Slip 'N Slide, but now there were only the bone-white tombs beneath a glowering gunmetal sky.

"DOWN!" bawled the boy. "Or I'll put a pistol ball through your skull!" He flicked his eyes to the chubby kid and his voice seemed to change, sounding younger. "Get busy, Terrel!"

The man sank to his knees in the graveyard dirt, and the boy jammed the gun to his forehead. *Cause of death was the loss of a mind.* About all he could see was the boy's sweaty belly. A few curls of hair showed down below, and he wanted to tell him to pull up his pants.

The chubby kid trotted away with the card, and the young man watched him go. Fear was flooding over him now, and the boy seemed to savor it. Worse, it seemed to excite him. The man was suddenly aware that he was kneeling before the boy in a very symbolic position. The younger kid was watching him, maybe uneasy but fascinated. The older one laughed. "Who's the master now?"

The smaller kid giggled nervously.

"That was over a long time ago," the young man said, though not sure why.

"I never forgot," said the boy.

Absurdly, the man said, "I'm from the north."

"I know," said the boy.

Lightning slashed the sky again, and the thunder was like an explosion. Iron doors rattled in crumbling crypts, and the man pictured skeletons shaken awake. "You got my money, and I won't tell."

The kid laughed again, but more like a kid. "'Course you won't. You come here alone. The cops laugh they asses off at you."

The man pictured that; the smirking cops and their sarcastic questions: *how old were these assailants... sir?* The crime report in their files forever to make him look like a brainless bumpkin who'd only gotten what he deserved.

"Please," said the man. He knew the boy had spoken the truth; he would take this secret into his grave.

Then he heard footsteps crunching gravel, a sound like the breaking of brittle old bones. Had the chubby kid returned already? Then he felt a flicker of hope... it was somebody else! For a moment he almost forgot the gun, amazed that a human could be so black! Most white people were beige at best, but this kid was living midnight. Was it a girl, he wondered? If so, she wasn't wearing a shirt... not that it might have mattered because she was gracefully slender and only about thirteen.

But, no, it had to be a boy... the man was *almost* sure of that despite the halo of thistledown hair. The boy was clad in baggy old jeans, about to fall off in "gangster style," and displaying a wisp of leopard-skin briefs. He toted a bottle of Olde English malt, yet seemed too fragile to be a thug. But the older boy didn't look surprised.

"The hell you been, Matt?" he demanded.

"Makin' some money, the hell you think?"

The older boy spat. "*This* the way to make money, fool!" He twisted the gun a little.

"Don't, Rick," said the midnight kid, who seemed a little drunk.

"Shut up, pretty-boy!" Rick snatched the bottle with one hand while keeping the gun under steady control. He sloppily guzzled amber brew, and trickles of foam ran down his chest and over his belly to soak his shorts. He downed about half, then came up for air. "Get any word about Newton?"

Lightning flashed and thunder roared. Big fat raindrops splattered down, hissing steam as they hit the tombs, but the kids ignored the downpour. The midnight boy had midnight eyes that studied the cowering man on the ground. "Nobody know what happen to him, but that probably mean he okay."

Rick's face twisted in sudden new rage. "I'ma kill that damn little nigger! Soon's I'm done with this dirty white trash!"

"Man, we gotta talk," said Matt. "This shit is gettin' really strange. An' you don't know who you messin' with."

Rick looked as if he was listening again, but there were only the echoes of thunder and roaring rush of pelting rain. He passed the brew to the youngest kid, who tilted it up with both little hands. "What you tellin' me?"

"That show we seen last night," said Matt. "Before you shot at Newton. I done some checkin' today. Y'all don't mess with that lady, Rick! She big-time Voodoo on the real!"

Rick glanced down at the kneeling man. "Tell me about it later. We doin' another ceremony."

"No," said Matt. "I don't wanna do that shit no more. There somethin' evil about it, man… like real old-school evil."

More rage flashed across Rick's face, and the young man's stomach twisted in fear. He was sure the boy would pull the trigger! The rain was pounding furiously, and mist was oozing out of the ground as if the earth was bleeding ghosts. *Please,* the young man prayed in his mind, though he'd never much believed in God.

But, finally Rick seemed to force a laugh and sounded more like a kid again. "So, how much you make, pretty-boy?"

"'Bout thirty dollars."

"I just made us a lot more'n that."

"Let him go," said Matt. "He ain't gonna tell nobody."

"He's right," said the man. "I promise."

"Shut up!" snarled Rick. He seemed to listen for something again. "I think we got a sacrifice."

The man felt a finger of ice on his spine. He gazed at the beautiful midnight boy, who stood with the rain streaming over his body and gleaming like polished onyx. Maybe an angel would look like that… assuming there were black ones. Was he going to find out soon?

"C'mon, Rick," Matt said gently, laying a hand on Rick's shoulder.

"I known you all my life, man. You never done shit like this before."

"'Cause I was a stupid nigger like you! Beggin' for bones off the master's table!"

"That crazy talk, Rick."

"Shut up, fool!" Rick glanced again at the man. "Who beggin' now, boy? ...Say it!"

"I am," said the man.

"Beg me for your life, boy!"

"There a tour goin' on," said Matt.

Rick shrugged. "They never come back this far." He paused again as if listening. "An' they won't hear the shot when it thunders."

The youngest boy moved close to Matt, and Matt lay a hand on his shoulder. "Let him go, Rick," said Matt again. "Or I'm outta here. ...I *mean* it, Rick. 'Less you wanna 'sacrifice' me."

For a moment Rick's eyes seemed to flame with hate, then his lips pulled back in a skullish smile and he pressed the gun muzzle to Matt's slender chest. "I *could*, an' don't never forget it." He hesitated another moment, then finally stepped away from the man. "This your lucky day... boy! Now, begone 'fore I change my mind!"

The man got slowly to his feet, afraid to make any fast moves. He wanted to thank the midnight kid, but he didn't know what to say to an angel.

"Run, fool!" the black angel yelled.

The young man did, with no thought of pride, fleeing down the narrow paths twisting and turning between the tombs, and losing his sense of direction. It amazed him to find he was crying. He burst around a plastered vault into the midst of a small group of people, all white -- thank God! -- except for the guide, a young black woman who stopped in mid-sentence describing the life of Marie Laveau.

Some of the group were elderly, and there was a handful of kids. Most of the people were holding umbrellas. The young man halted, gasping for breath, while everyone turned to stare at him. Then a pair of enormously fat little boys with curly mops of red hair giggled:

"He looks like he's just seen a ghost," said one, around a mouthful of Milky Way.

"Musta got lucky," snickered the other, appropriately munching a

Snickers.

The young man wiped his face, thankful the rain camouflaged his tears. "...Uh... Which way is the gate?"

The guide pointed. "Follow that path and turn right."

The man mumbled thanks and hurried away.

FIFTEEN

"Can you feel 'em yet?" asked Newton, sprawled on his back on the courtyard table, his arms flung out and legs spread wide, his belly ballooning between the latter as Raney fed him the last offering, a piece of pecan pie with whipped cream. A pair of candles flanked Newton's shoulders, flickering pale in the steamy sunlight, while his bushy hair sparkled with rainwater jewels and his body glistened like newly-made chocolate, his funnel-like navel a miniature pond.

The thunderstorm had passed away but its coolness hadn't lingered. The lush foliage trickled and dripped, and puddles had formed like glimmering lakes, covering some of the flagstones.

"One thing at a time, little man," said Kody. "Do a spell wrong an' you get somethin' nasty."

"Like that zombie you call up last summer," said Raney.

"I did the spell right," said Kody. "It just didn't know how to do dishes."

"Maybe it didn't wanna."

"What happen?" asked Newton, through a mouthful of pie.

Raney chuckled. "It pitched a fit an' busted 'em. Dishes flyin' everywhere! Lucky they wasn't the Sunday set."

"...Oh," said Newton, after a moment of seemingly trying to picture that. "But, we da good guys."

"Try tellin' that to a zombie."

"Yeah," agreed Kody, corking the last of four little bottles -- three inches tall and of different colors -- red, blue, amber and green. "Just bein' good don't always count. It's like that fool up the block last year... the one I was tellin' the Trouts about. He might have been a good person, but he called up somethin' he couldn't put down, an' just bein' good couldn't save him."

Raney added, "Good ain't much good if you stupid."

X X X

Steam thickly shrouded the cemetery, swirling about in spectral shapes as rainwater dripped from glistening tombs. The air was growing hot once more as Rick, trailed by Devon and Matt, searched in the mist for their clubhouse crypt. Rick was packing the gun in one hand and pausing often to listen, yet only silence surrounded the boys, except for the sucking and splash of their sneakers though slimy puddles and graveyard mud.

"You lost?" asked Matt.

"Shut up," muttered Rick.

Then he tensed as footsteps crunched gravel ahead. He dropped to a crouch and aimed the gun, but Terrel came puffing out of the mist. He was toting another forty, which was sweating as much as himself. Rick shoved the gun in a pocket. "'Bout time, boy! How much you get?"

Terrel swigged from the bottle. "His limit was three-hundred, but I still gots the card."

"Won't be no good no more," said Matt.

"Yeah," agreed Rick. "Throw it away. ...Down that crack in the tomb over there. An' gimmie the green."

"We s'posed to share," said Terrel.

"Yeah!" squeaked Devon, shoving the Saints cap out of his eyes. "*We* been doin' all the work! You just point the gun an' talk bad!"

"I'm the one gettin' us power, fool!" Rick snarled. But then he forced a shrug. "I gotta pay the rent. We split the next one, aight?"

"Whatever," sighed Terrel, handing over a wet wad of bills.

"There better not be a next one," said Matt. "That's twice in a week we jack somebody. You gonna get us busted, Rick, an' I don't wanna be locked in a cage."

Rick shoved the bills in a pocket. "You in one already, pretty-boy, you just too stupid to know it. ...Besides, like you said, that fool won't tell. Now c'mon, we got stuff to do."

"I don't like none of this shit," said Matt. "Hangin' in graveyards an' prayin' to mirrors. Playin' with skulls, an' 'ceremonies.' What it gettin' us, man?"

"*Power!*" snapped Rick. "How many times I gotta say that?"

"So, how much power it take shootin' people? Give Devon a gun an' he could do it."

"Yeah?" snorted Rick. "I give Newton a gun... the *best* gun... an' the little nigger lost it! An' he got caught by them Voodoo boys. ...Now, c'mon, an' do what I say."

Matt sighed. "Let's get this shit over an' get outta here. I'm sick of hangin' with dead things."

The mist was slowly burning off, and Rick found the way to the tomb. The door hinges let out a hair-raising scream, and even he winced as he dragged it open. Then he froze. "The fuck...!"

"Now what the matter?" asked Matt. He looked over Rick's shoulder into the crypt. Terrel and Devon also peered in, but then recoiled in horror.

"That skeleton's tryin' to get up!" cried Terrel, backing away in the mud.

"Shut up, fool!" yelled Rick. "Them bones ain't goin' nowhere."

"Fuck if I goin' in there!" shrilled Devon, hurriedly joining Terrel.

"Stop bein' ignorant niggers!" bawled Rick, spinning around to face his crew. Then he turned back to scope the tomb, where the skeleton lay in its dusty niche and rubble now covered the floor. "Somebody come here an' done this!"

"Maybe not," said Matt. "That slab was all cracked anyways. Thunder coulda done it."

Rick entered the crypt and scanned around, the broken stone clattering under his sneaks and wraiths of dust rising around him. "Somebody busted the mirror!"

Terrel and Devon joined Matt at the door. Terrel took a gulp from the forty and doubtfully studied the skeleton. "Prob'ly one of them chunks of rock."

Matt laughed. "Or maybe a ghost."

Rick spun around and grabbed Matt by the throat, slamming him into the rusty door. "Don't sass me, nigger!"

For a moment the boys locked eyes, chest-to-chest and tensed to fight. Rick had a lot more muscle, though Matt's slender body was strong. But, Rick released Matt and turned back around, surveying the tomb in the bloody red glow filtering through the dusty window. Then he snatched something off the floor. "Do ghosts wear these?" he demanded, thrusting a ragged black beanie at Matt.

Matt shrugged. "So, somebody come in here messin' around. Don't mean they tryin' to get you, Rick."

Rick scowled. "Power draws enemies, an' somebody always wants what you got." He studied the beanie a moment. "I need some more stuff from the Voodoo store."

"Aw, fuck," said Terrel, after drinking again. "Ain't you got enough of that shit?"

"You an' Devon start cleanin' this up."

Devon squeaked, "Ain't touchin' no nasty-ass skeleton bones!"

"Nobody touch 'em!" Rick pulled the money out of his pocket and peeled two twenties off the roll. "Matt, you go to the store. ...An' move your ass so we don't get locked in!" He studied the rubble again, then picked up a jagged piece of marble and brushed the dust from a chiseled name.

X   X   X

"Gots any more?" asked Newton, pleasurably patting his bulging belly, a look of pure bliss on his cherub-imp face.

Raney laughed. "You already ate everything in the fridge." Snagging the can of whipped cream, he stuck the nozzle in Newton's mouth and puffed the boy's cheeks like a chipmunk's.

Newton swallowed. "Gots any more?"

Kody laughed. "Better not, Raney, he'll have an orgasm."

An amazed look came over Newton's face. He gathered his belly fat with both hands and struggled to half sit up while trying to look at himself. "Check it out! Is it...?"

"Well, damn," said Raney, "sure is."

"COOL!" exclaimed Newton. One hand going to grasp himself.

"Mean I can…?"

"Not now," said Kody, tagging each bottle with a stick-on label and printing a name with a Magic Marker.

"Ain't you s'prised?" asked Raney.

Kody shrugged. "He's wearin' Ethu's horns."

"That a pun?"

"He is a kid."

"I wanna see it!" said Newton.

"Use Kody's mirror," said Raney.

"…NO!"

"Hang onto your belly." Raney picked Newton up and held him face-forward over a puddle.

"COOL!"

Kody laughed. "Mine's bigger."

"I only eight!" snapped Newton.

Raney set Newton back on the table, his belly rating him E again, and Newton burrowed a hand underneath.

"Save it for later," said Kody.

"But, won't it go away?"

"Trust me, it'll be back… an' lots of times when you don't want it."

Reluctantly Newton withdrew his hand, then cocked his head and asked, "Why you writin' dere names?"

Kody held up the amber bottle. "We know this hair belongs to Matt, but it's hard to tell the others apart."

"So, what I do now?"

Kody placed bottles at Newton's feet. "Bless our good endeavor."

"What a endeavor?"

"Like a mission," said Raney.

"How I bless it?"

"You're Ethu," said Kody, "use your magic."

"…Um…" Newton waved a hand. "Poof, we blessed."

"Think that worked?" asked Raney.

Kody picked up the amber bottle again. "It's somethin' smart-ass like Ethu would say."

"Feed me some more," said Newton.

"Ceremony's over," said Raney. "Y'all back to bein' a punkin again... just don't be a punkin head." He ruffled Newton's hair, scattering silver sparks. "They's nothin' wrong with bein' you... 'least not since you come back to you."

"I didn't like who I wasn't." Newton laughed. "An' dere somethin' more ta me now!"

Raney rolled his eyes. "Don't be Mr. Pecker the party wrecker."

"Got one! It worked!" said Kody, pressing the bottle to his forehead.

"Woah!" said Newton. "Which one?"

"Matt," said Kody.

Raney looked up at the open window in the Voodoo shop. "Where is he?"

"Close," murmured Kody, closing his eyes. "But it ain't like a GPS, an' kinda fuzzy an' blurred." Kody was silent for several moments. "Never did this much before... s'posed to practice, but it's kinda borin'. ...Don't feel like he's comin' closer."

"What about the others?" asked Raney.

"I can only do one at a time."

"Can I try?" asked Newton.

"Sure."

Newton scanned the other three bottles. "Which one who?"

"Devon's the green one, Terrel is blue."

"Gimmie da red one, Rick's." Newton held it to his forehead. For a minute there was only silence except for the dripping of leaves and ferns and the trickling splash of the fountain. At last he said, "Can't see nothin'."

Raney turned to Kody. "Gettin' anymore from Matt?"

"He... might be over on Bourbon Street. I'm seein' flashes of that."

"Dat make sense," said Newton. "We been scorin' brew from a store over dere; twice da price, but dey sell ta kids."

"'Spect money wasn't no problem," said Raney, "jackin' people like you was. ...So, Matt ain't comin' for us?"

"He was thinkin' about Newton," said Kody. "But then I lost him."

"Mean ta kill me?" asked Newton.

"No, he don't *wanna* hurt you. But he's real scared of somethin'. ...Let me try Rick."

114

Newton handed the ruby bottle to Kody. "What about 'em hurtin' my mom?"

"I don't think Matt would… or 'least wouldn't wanna. He don't feel like a bad kinda dude. An' maybe Rick ain't thought about that for a way of bringin' you out."

"What you mean, bringin' me out? Like I was a you-know?"

"Got nothin' to do with you-knows," growled Raney.

"It's a thing you do in magic," said Kody. "Bring your enemy out in the open after you choose the time an' place. Then he's unprotected. Or 'least on equal ground."

Raney added, "Like, Rick might try an' bring you out… make you go home where he could get you… if you thought he was gonna hurt your mom."

Kody nodded. "But, you told him you hated your mom, so maybe he won't try."

"But I don't hate her! I was lyin'!"

"I know," said Kody. "But he thinks you do, an' it's good he does. We can't do much to protect her."

"But I can, and I have," said a woman's voice.

The boys turned to see Aunt Simone. For a lady of her impressive size, she had entered the courtyard quiet as cats and now stood in bracelets, beads and blue dress, her onyx eyes appraising the scene.

"I am not pleased that you chose to go out before we were able to talk, though you seem to have spent the morning well. Destroying the gun was the right thing to do, and I know that took courage and strength."

"That why you left it with us?" asked Raney.

"It was better that you chose to destroy it, for now you know how such objects can tempt and have felt the power of things possessed." Aunt Simone smiled at Kody and indicated the bottles. "I see that my lessons were not all in vain."

She took the red bottle from him. "Rick is your greatest danger now. As I told you last night, he is only a child but very confused and searching for power. There has been little love in his life, and if you never receive any love it is very hard to give it. Or even recognize it." She closed her hand on the bottle and frowned. "He has awakened an evil thing. But you know that."

"You know where he is?" asked Kody.

"He is in the graveyard with blue and green... Terrel and Devon. He rages because you have broken his mirror."

"I had to, it was a window."

"Very good. But we should have spoken about these things before you left the house this morning. I had many thoughts about him last night. There was a shape that hovered behind him, but I thought it was only the gun."

"What I thought, too, but it wasn't." said Kody. "Does he know it was me who busted the mirror?"

"I would guess he suspects it. He has already made you his enemy because you have 'stolen' his weapon." Aunt Simone touched Newton's shoulder. "And one of his followers. It is good that he no longer has the gun because now he is free of its evil, at least... though of course he does not realize that."

She regarded the ruby bottle again. "The gun gave him feelings of power, which took the place of love in his life. It also bound the other boys to him, which again substituted for love. But, something *else* has promised him power, and unlike the gun it can reason and scheme. You were right to destroy the mirror, but Rick will soon rebuild his altar, and this time perhaps it will be complete."

"In da tomb?" asked Newton. "Wit' dat ol' skeleyton?"

Aunt Simone frowned. "What skeleton?"

Kody explained what had happened.

Aunt Simone shook her head. "I do not like that occurrence. It might have been only chance... many tombs are falling apart. But we must learn more about that one. Can you draw me a map of its location? I will search the burial records." She picked up the amber bottle. "This child is near... and has been drinking."

Kody nodded. "Why everything looked blurry."

"Just feel," warned his aunt. "Do not try to see through this boy's eyes, because something else is trying."

"Does Matt got a gun?" asked Raney.

"I cannot tell. But, a gun is only physical danger. Nor do I think Matt is dangerous on more than the physical level. He is afraid, and very confused by what is trying to see through his eyes."

"Mean somethin' got in his skull?" asked Newton.

"Something is trying," said Aunt Simone. "But, the real danger is what Rick awakened… rage and hatred from deep in the past. That is why it remains in the tomb. It cannot, or will not, go to the light. The burial records will give us its name, and then we may learn more about it."

Aunt Simone shook her head again. "It has waited long for someone like Rick, lonely, confused and powerless… searching for what he has never known and therefore does not recognize. It will not let go of him easily."

"Does it know anything about Voodoo?" asked Raney.

"Many people knew something of Voodoo back in the days when this thing was alive. But, to most whites it was just superstition, only the tales of ignorant slaves, or parlor games to frighten the ladies. It knows it needs an altar to gather and focus its followers, to lure them away from the light and into its web of darkness. It will give them earthy pleasures… or rather make them think it does, because any pleasures they find in its presence are only what they bring themselves. It has learned how to see through a window, and so it will try to find another."

She clasped the ruby bottle, glowing like blood in the steamy sunlight. "It has demanded a sacrifice to enslave this boy to its will… which could have been you, Kody Carver, if Newton had taken more careful aim. But, it will compel Rick to try again, if not to kill you, then someone else. Then, when Rick is enslaved, it will use him and his younger companions."

"For what?" asked Newton.

"Not for anything good, child. But that is what we must discover. What *is* this thing's evil purpose? Much more, I am sure, than enslaving young boys for its entertainment. Learning who it was in life will probably give us the answer, and for now that is all we can do."

Aunt Simone faced Kody again. "You *must* know your enemy, child. Then *you* must choose the battle ground. You must not fight this thing where it dwells."

"Mean in da graveyard?" asked Newton. "Like, dat where it strong?"

Aunt Simone nodded. "It is strongest close to its bones. But there are other levels of power and it is learning to use them."

"Like in video games?"

"Crude but correct, my child. For the moment it can only compel... only whisper, tempt and trick. It cannot force its will on the living. But, for the lonely and confused, even a whisper can be a command."

"Um?" asked Newton. "You said somethin' about my mom?"

"I have been to see her, and she is very concerned about you. She is now in a drug-recovery house, but it is best you do not know where until this occurrence is settled."

"'Cause somethin' nasty got in my skull?"

"Only for a moment last night, but it may try again, so beware of thoughts that are not your own."

"How I know what ain't my own thinkin'?"

Aunt Simone pressed a palm to his chest. "Your heart is good, so you will know... if you listen to it. Rick cannot find or harm your mother, and she has entrusted your care to me. ...Why do you still wear the horns of Ethu?"

Kody explained, and Aunt Simone laughed. "I will have them off in a moment."

Newton turned to Kody. "Dat mean I can't... you know?"

Kody smiled. "Ethu won't take his blessing back."

"Cool! ...So, can I be him again ta-night?"

"Certainly, child," said Aunt Simone.

"Den you can just leave 'em on."

Aunt Simone smiled. "You wear them well."

"I a real kid now!"

"As with any power, child, use it with kindness and care."

"What about that?" asked Raney, pointing to the open window. "What if they come back tonight?"

"I will speak with the store's proprietor. We are not friends, as you may imagine, because of the nonsense he sells. But, I doubt he wants his shop invaded by foolish little boys with guns. Your greatest danger is out in the streets. Do not leave this house again today."

"Can't you just fix dere minds?" asked Newton. "Like, do a good spell on Rick an' da gang?"

"To make someone love instead of hate? What a wonderful power that would be! You can only show someone why they should love by offering them your own. To love or to hate is a choice of free will, and thus we create or destroy our own lives." Aunt Simone glanced at Kody again. "Do you now see the danger in acting too quickly before you understand what you face?"

"Yeah. I thought it was just baby-bangers at first."

"But now you know it is deeper than that. Deeper and far more dangerous. We must learn who is inside that tomb. Please draw the map. And be precise. More than your life may depend upon it." She opened her brightly-beaded tote and brought out a notebook and pen.

"We could take you there," said Kody.

"But Rick is there now with the two younger boys. I do not fear him or what he awakened, but I fear for you, Newton and Raney."

Raney watched Kody draw the map, then turned to Aunt Simone. "Can't you tell the graveyard people? Get 'em to lock up the tomb again so Rick can't build another altar?"

"I could say that a tomb has been desecrated, but no one will rush to repair it." Aunt Simone studied what Kody had drawn. "That is a desolate section. Most of those families have long since died out, which is why no one cares for the tomb." She glanced at her watch. "It is after one o'clock, and no doubt those children will leave the grounds before the gate is locked at three. For now be at peace, you have done all you can. I will be back for the ceremony. ...I warn you again to stay in the house, and do not go out on the gallery."

"What about guests?" asked Kody.

"Just be careful who you admit. It saddens me to say it, but beware of young black men. That is also evil, making us fear one-another." Aunt Simone left and the gate clanked shut.

"I hate this gang shit!" growled Raney.

"It's more than that," said Kody.

"But it come down to the same damn thing. Now we locked in 'cause we scared of somebody, but they can go wherever they want!"

Newton picked up the amber bottle and held it to his forehead.

"Matt still close?" asked Raney. "We know them others in the graveyard."

"I... think he a little closer," said Newton. "Don't know how ta work dis yet... but I think he gettin' really drunk. ...An' he real scared of somethin'. Keeps lookin' over his shoulder."

"You see that?" asked Kody.

"It more of a feelin'... like, when I knew a phone gonna ring."

Raney asked, "Y'all thinkin' what I thinkin', cousin?"

"Matt don't wanna play Rick's games, an' maybe he ran away?" said Kody. "But, Rick might of sent him to watch us. ...Or *it* might of sent him an' Matt don't know it. Like Aunt Simone said, he's scared an' confused; an' a whisper might make him do anything."

He took the bottle from Newton and pressed it to his forehead. "...I think you're right, Matt's really drunk. An' he can't be more than a few blocks away."

"He got a gun?" asked Raney.

"...Can't tell," said Kody. "I'ma try an' see where he is."

"Yo!" said Newton. "Your aunt say not ta!"

"Ain't gonna get caught by no ghost." Kody closed his eyes. "Matt's so drunk he can barely see. ...He's down on Barracks Street... off Royal. Back in a little alley. ...I can see an old house with its shutters all closed. ...Let's go get him!"

"What you mean?" asked Newton.

"Like we got you. Make him our friend instead of an enemy."

"Cool!"

Raney frowned. "Aunt Simone told us to stay here."

"It's okay," said Kody. "It's like when we got rid of the gun... like an endeavor. There were five little thuggers yesterday, an' now there's only four. Be cool if we could make it three."

Newton sighed. "More damn walkin'."

SIXTEEN

Clouds were re-gathering over the Quarter, and thunder rumbled distantly as the boys turned the corner of Ursulines and headed down Royal Street. Water trickled along the gutters and dripped from roofs and galleries, and puddles glimmered here and there on cobblestones and brick sidewalks, while steam rose up like awakening ghosts to mistily haunt the humid air.

Kody was holding the amber bottle as if he was tracking a compass, while Raney carried the red and green, and Newton packed the blue. The boys approached the Voodoo shop, its window filled with useless dolls and powerless *gris-gris* of feathers and beads. There were also piles of *Mardi Gras* trinkets, vampire capes and plastic fangs, along with other assorted junk like "magic candles," plaster skulls, and back-scratchers shaped like skeleton hands.

Newton, already sweaty and puffing and on the verge of losing his jeans, stopped to study the dolls, which were made of white cloth, about six inches tall, and looked like naked Raggedy-Anns though were ambiguous as to sex. Each was entombed in a cardboard coffin complete with pins and "secret knowledge for putting a curse on your enemy."

"So, you can't use dem for nothin'?" he asked, pressing his little snub nose to the glass.

"A doll's gotta look like somebody," said Kody. "An' it's gotta be made with stuff from that person, some essence of them like we got in these bottles."

Raney snorted. "Them things 'bout as magic as Barbie dolls, 'less you wanna try puttin' a spell on Ken."

Newton regarded his reflection superimposed on the dolls. "What if Rick got some essence of me?"

"Don't think about stuff like that," said Kody, "even if they're your own thoughts."

"'Cause da ghost might hear me?"

"Ain't only that," said Kody. "Worry an' fear attracts evil things an' lets 'em know what you scared of."

"Mean, good people don't get haunted?"

"Not all ghosts are bad," said Raney. "Folks usually get the ghosts they deserve."

"Why Rick got a bad one?"

"Pretty much," said Kody. "Love makes you strong an' resistant to evil; hate makes you weak an' vulnerable… like bein' sick, which it is. Love draws power from all good things, but hate only feeds on the hater. Kids are born knowin' how to love, but they gotta to be taught how to hate."

"What Rick shoulda been doin'," said Raney. "Practicin' what come natural 'stead of schoolin' himself in what ain't."

Kody nodded. "An' we gotta stop him before he ends up in a grave. Or worse."

"What worse den a grave?" asked Newton.

"Bein' awake when you're in it… not alive, just awake."

"Aunt Simone can help him," said Raney. "Once she find out what he woke up."

"Or maybe is gonna call up," said Kody. "If he finds out its name."

"In da graveyard, you sayin'?" asked Newton.

"Yeah," said Kody. "But, now we're tryin' to help Matt."

"He still on Barracks Street?" asked Raney.

Kody fingered the amber bottle. "Don't feel like he's moved since we left the house."

"What if he gots a gun?" asked Newton.

"We worry about that when we get there."

"More damn walkin'," sighed Newton, tugging up his jeans.

The boys moved on, crossing Nicholas Street and leaving the tourists behind. This part of the Quarter was mostly houses with only a few little shops and stores that mainly served the residents. A lot of the buildings needed paint, and many were shuttered and empty now because of the summer heat. They passed a tiny market, and two shirtless boys stepped out of its doorway. Kody tensed, but they weren't Rick's dawgs... nine or ten with ice cream bars.

"Kickin' horns, bro," said one boy to Newton.

"Cooler than vampire teeth," said the other.

"Tanks," said Newton.

The kids walked away up the street.

"'Beware of young black men'," said Raney.

Kody nodded. "That's another kind of evil hateful things are tryin' to teach us."

Clouds were still rolling in, and thunder rumbled ominously, but the sun still ruled in a patch of blue as the boys reached the corner of Royal and Barracks and stopped to scan around. This wasn't a picturesque part of the Quarter, and tourists were often advised to avoid it... mostly because of young black men. Nothing moved on Barracks Street along the rows of ancient houses, and the only sounds were air-conditioners humming in windows here and there. Some of the homes had little front yards where steam ghosted up from weedy lawns to drift across the sidewalks.

Kody pressed the bottle to his forehead. "Can't see nothin' now." He pointed up the street. "But, there's the house with its shutters all closed. An' there's the alley across the from it like I seen through Matt's eyes. ...He's in there, I can feel him. ...C'mon, an' stay quiet."

The boys moved up the sidewalk, Newton trying to muffle his panting while holding on to his jeans.

"Climb on my back," whispered Raney, kneeling, and Newton gratefully did.

A ship hooted out on the river but here it was eerily still. Even the distant thunder had ceased, though clouds continued to gather. It was hard to believe that a few blocks away were crowds of people and bustling life.

Newton whispered, "It creepy, man! Dere any ghosts around here?"

Raney murmured, "More ghosts in the Quarter than livin' folks, but most of 'em don't bother nobody 'less somebody bother 'em first."

"Yeah," agreed Kody. "To most of 'em this is all in the past, an' we're the ghosts hauntin' their world."

Newton eyed the shuttered house, almost paintless and looking deserted. "Bet dere a ghost in dat spooky ol' joint!"

Kody glanced at the rusty mailbox. "If there is, it buy books from Amazon."

"An' it ain't gonna haunt us now," chuckled Raney, pointing to a little placard on the dwelling's front door:

DAY SLEEPER
DO NOT DISTURB

They crossed the street to the alley; like most, it was only a few feet wide, a brick-lined passage between two houses that led to a little courtyard. An iron gate of bars and spikes defended its opposite end. Near the gate was a garbage can. A pair of sneaks stuck out from behind it, and there was a glimpse of faded jeans, their cuffs in tatters like zombie rags.

"Got him!" whispered Kody.

"Hold up, cousin," said Raney, gripping Kody's shoulder. "Might be three new ghosts in the Quarter if Matt gots a gun an' we try an' catch him."

"We chose the battle ground," said Kody. "We know his name an' he's out in the open. Besides, he's drunk. I'll check him out, but you better hide in case he is packin'." He pointed to the shuttered house. "By the porch over there."

Raney carried Newton away, while Kody crept up the alley. He heard the clunk of a forty-ounce set drunkenly down on the paving stones, and pressed himself to a baking brick wall for what little cover it gave, but there was no other sign of life. He waited a minute, then moved on. His sweat-soaked jeans slipped awkwardly low, but he didn't dare stop to recover them. He hugged the wall, which broiled his body like being in an oven tomb, though the sun was growing dimmer as clouds continued massing above. Lightning flashed and thunder boomed. The iron gate rattled like chattering teeth. Kody eased up to the garbage can, scaring a few bloated flies. The sneakers still hadn't moved. Kody sucked a breath and leaped.

Matt lay sprawled with his back to the wall, his shirtless body black as night as if he was only a shadow. He was tilting the bottle to his lips when Kody landed on top of him. Matt let out a hair-raising scream, but Kody grabbed his upper arms, slamming him back against the bricks and pinning him under his weight. Matt kicked and struggled to throw him off, but Kody weighed a lot more. Finally, Matt gave up and went limp.

"Who are you?" he panted, trying to focus on Kody's face, their noses just inches apart.

"A friend," puffed Kody. "Chill out. You packin'?"

"...No."

"Sorry for jumpin' you, man, but you gotta know how that is."

The slender boy looked scared. Kody remembered seeing him dance, performing those graceful panther-like moves and casting his magic spell, and felt a little ashamed to be treating him like this.

"Don't got no friends," said Matt.

"You do now."

"...Why?"

Kody smiled. "If I said I wanted to cap your ass, you probably wouldn't ask why." He peered around the garbage can: Raney was coming for backup, with Newton puffing along behind. The clouds had snuffed the sun, dimming the daylight to gunmetal gray. There was a blinding lightning flash, followed by a thunder blast. He waited until the echoes died. "'Cause you need friends... 'specially now."

Matt only looked confused. He still held the neck of the bottle, though Kody was gripping his upper arms so it couldn't be used as a weapon. "Wanna drink?" he finally asked.

"Sure, Matt." Kody signaled to Raney and Newton to wait at the alley entrance. Another thunderclap rattled the gate. A few big raindrops splattered the ground, and spurts of hissing steam shot up.

"How you know my name?" asked Matt.

"Seen you around."

Matt tried to focus on Kody's face. "I seen you somewheres, too."

"I watched you dance," said Kody. "You're really Voodoo, dawg."

"Thanks," said Matt. "My gramma taught me them moves. She used to dance at the Vampire Vault back when it was on the real." He shrugged. "I make a few bucks."

"More than a few, from what I seen."

"It pay the rent."

"I figured you wasn't bad."

"Guess I weren't made for bein' bad."

"Nobody is." Kody let go of Matt and crouched between his wide-spread legs. A razor of lightning gutted the clouds and rain gushed out like sliver blood. In seconds the alley was shrouded in steam. Matt offered the bottle: there wasn't much left, hot and flat, and laced with spit, but Kody took a courtesy swig. "Thanks."

Matt gulped down the remains. "Can we get some more?"

"Looks like you had enough for today."

"Ain't enough, I can..." Matt's eyes seemed to clear for an instant, and fear flashed over his face.

"What?" asked Kody, leaning close as the rain pounded down.

Matt suddenly looked about to cry. "I hear whisperin', man! An' it evil!" He stared around in the swirling steam. "Where are we?"

"Barracks Street near Royal."

"We gotta get outta here before dark!"

"Chill out, Matt. It's still afternoon. It's just the rain makes it seem later."

Matt relaxed a little. "I wanted to get away from the graveyard. Far as I could."

"'Cause of what you been hearin'?"

"Yeah! Rick sent me out to get some stuff, but I kept on goin'. Then I started hearin' whispers! Tellin' me to come back to... him. ...An' him wasn't Rick!"

"Runnin' away won't help," said Kody. "But, I got a place you'll be safe."

"...Why you give a shit about me?"

"'Cause we're brothers. ...C'mon."

Matt struggled to rise like a drunken cat. Kody grasped him under the arms and helped him to his feet. Raney and Newton were still at the entrance, but Kody waved them out of sight. "It's cool," said Kody, steadying Matt by his shoulders. "Ain't even three o'clock yet."

"That when they lock up the graveyard."

"Think they might come after you? Rick an' his posse?"

"I don't know... but Rick crazy, man! He gonna kill somebody! ...Callin' it a sacrifice."

"It's not his idea," said Kody. "He woke up a ghost in that tomb an' it's been tellin' him what to do."

Matt nodded slowly. "That kinda make sense. It never felt right, what we was doin'. An' Rick was getting' different... actin' different, talkin' different."

"That was the ghost gettin' hold of him."

Matt shivered. "Let's get outta here!" He stumbled along at Kody's side with Kody's arm around his waist until they reached the alley mouth. But then he seemed to stiffen in shock, seeing the other boys.

"You damn little *nigger!*" he screamed at Newton. He tore loose from Kody and whipped out a knife, a big gleaming Buck with a six-inch blade, and lunged for the smaller boy. Kody grabbed him from behind, but Matt's slim body was slick with rain; he tore loose again and slashed at Newton.

Newton jumped back, slamming Raney, who shoved him aside and charged at Matt. But Matt was too fast. He dodged past Raney and went for Newton, his blade flashing deadly bright in the gloom. Kody grabbed Matt from behind again, trying to lock Matt's arms to his sides, but Matt seemed as strong as a panther now, backing Newton into the street, splashing through the deepening puddles while Kody struggled to bring him down.

Raney tried to grab Matt's arm, but dodged a savage slash of steel. Newton was backing farther away, almost onto the opposite sidewalk in front of the shuttered house, ankle-deep in gutter water foaming over his shoes. Kody yelled for Newton to run, desperately trying to drag Matt down. But Newton only closed his eyes.

Suddenly, Matt collapsed like a corpse! The knife slipped from his fragile fingers to clatter on the paving stones. An instant later he lay beside it.

Raney lurched to a halt. "The hell...?"

There was only the roaring rush of rain and gurgling of gutter drains. Kody dropped to his knees beside Matt and turned the boy on his back. "He ain't breathin'!"

He tried to remember a class in school... "Street Survival," they'd called it. He pressed his lips over Matt's, tasting sweat and rainwater. "Raney!" he yelled between desperate breaths. "Go get help! Call 911!" He pointed to the shuttered house.

But Newton stepped forward. "He ain't gonna die."

Kody looked up, shaking rain from his eyes. "What did you do?"

"I wanted him ta drop da knife."

"But, *how* you do that?" Raney demanded.

Newton shrugged. "I dunno... had ta do somethin' 'cause I can't run."

"Undo whatever you did!" snapped Kody.

Newton closed his eyes again, and Matt's fluttered open a moment later, confused at first, then filling with fear.

"Easy, man," said Kody. He stroked Matt's hair away from his face. "Nobody gonna hurt you."

Raney snatched up the knife, folded, and shoved it into a pocket. Then he glared down at Matt. "Why you try an' kill Newton?"

"...I... don't know," stammered Matt. "I couldn't help it." He sat up and stared at Kody and Raney. "You them Voodoo boys! I seen you last night."

"The first time you try an' kill Newton," said Raney, "from the Voodoo shop window. An' before that when you was out in the street waitin' for him to kill Kody."

"...I never wanted to do that shit! But Rick kept sayin' it would give us power... he almost made me believe him."

"We know," said Kody. "That thing's been inside Rick's skull for a while, whisperin' to him like it did to you. Probably since he stole the first gun an' took it into the graveyard."

"But it lyin'," said Newton. "It can't give you power, it *takin'* your power."

"It's feedin' on you," said Kody. "All of you. An' it's gettin' stronger while you're gettin' weaker."

"We don't know its name yet," said Raney. "But when we do we shut it up an' put it right back in its dirty ol' grave!"

"Can you really do that?" asked Matt.

"We got it goin' on," said Kody. "But you gotta help. Aight?"

"...Aight." Matt looked up at Newton. "Why you got horns?"

Newton crossed arms over his chest. "'Cause I da Voodoo god of kids."

Matt suddenly clamped his hands to his ears. "It's whisperin' again!"

Kody held on to the trembling boy. "Don't listen, Matt."

Tears squeezed out of Matt's eyes. "I can't make it stop!"

"Don't be scared," soothed Kody. "It feeds on fear as much as hate. Listen to us. When did it start? After Rick's ceremony today?"

"...I wasn't there. Like I said, Rick sent me out to get him stuff."

Newton asked, "After you seen da skeleyton?"

"How you know about that?"

"'Cause we found the tomb this morinin'," said Kody.

Raney asked, "When did the whisperin' start?"

"After I left the graveyard," said Matt. "When I decide to run away."

"What did Rick tell you to get?" asked Kody.

"Some candles from the Voodoo store. An' a book."

"What kinda book?"

"I can hear it!" said Newton, cocking his head.

"Don't say nothin' back," Kody warned.

"It talkin' ta Matt, not me."

"Does it know you can hear it?" asked Raney.

"Don't think so. ...But it tellin' Matt ta kill me 'cause if he don't I gonna kill him."

"Don't listen, Matt," said Kody. "Try an' think of somethin' good."

"I don't know much good."

"Think of dancin'. That's your power. I felt it today watchin' you." Kody smiled. "An', trust me, man, you got a lot." He patted Matt's shoulder. "That thing ain't as strong as you. It just knows how to lie a lot better." He looked up at Newton. "Be careful."

"I ain't scared of dat nasty ol' ghost."

"Don't try an' fight it now. We gotta choose the battle ground."

"We best get home," said Raney. "That ol' spook don't scare me neither, but there still them three dudes with a gun."

SEVENTEEN

The shadows were deep in Kody's room with the heavy drapes drawn on the windows. His boom-box sat on the dresser, and Zydeco music was capering out. Kody had covered the mirror again: the house's ghost didn't like that, but ghosts were territorial things and it might have resented the other ghost more for trying to invade its space. Besides, it had a real home to haunt instead of a crumbling old tomb.

The air-conditioner hummed -- this being a special occasion -- and the room was comfortably cool for a change. Raney lounged in the antique chair while the other boys lay on the bed. Raney and Kody had put on dry jeans, leaving their wet ones, along with their sneaks, to steam in the courtyard with Newton's and Matt's. Matt was clad in his brief wisp of briefs, while Newton wore only his horns. The massive slave collar was locked on Matt's neck, and its chain secured to a bedpost. Matt had agreed he shouldn't be trusted... not with the whispering ghost in his mind.

The Cajun accordion music stopped and a heavily-accented bayou voice predicted occasional thunderstorms for the rest of the day and into the night.

"Can it see out my eyes?" asked Matt, who lay between Kody and Newton. "Like I was a haunted camera?"

"It ain't got you dat bad," said Newton, who was eating a sandwich he'd made... sausage and crawfish with Crystal hot sauce on chewy slabs of French bread.

Raney turned to Kody. "Y'all think he right?"

"Probably," said Kody. "It's been focusing on Rick an' usin' him to control the gang. Rick got the gun, Rick woke it up, an' Rick's been feedin' it hate an' fear. It can live on those things... if you call that livin'... like maggots eatin' a corpse. But, it ain't strong enough to possess all those dudes. Not unless Rick calls it up by name an' gives it a sacrifice."

"What you mean call it up?" asked Matt.

"Did Rick ever say any names when he was doin' a ceremony?"

"He just sorta mumbled like prayin' in church. Axin' for 'power' an' shit like that." Matt touched the bandage on Kody's arm. "So, the sacrifice was s'posed to be you?"

"Coulda been anybody," said Kody. "It needs a life to get up."

"I almost can't hear it no more," said Matt. "Like a TV in another 'partment."

Newton finished his sandwich. "I can! An' now I know what evil sound like! It somethin' screamin' in pain all da time. It wanna come inta da light, but it scared of da light."

"Light is good," said Kody. "An' maybe a part of it still knows that. But it's scared to let go of its hate in the dark 'cause it thinks it wouldn't have nothin' without it. What's really sad is that ain't true. If it gave up its hate it could be free."

He turned back to Matt. "So, what was Rick plannin' to do if you'd got him that stuff from the Voodoo store?"

Matt sighed. "I don't know. He's changed so much in the last two weeks. We come up since kindergarten, but now he like somebody else... a real nasty somebody else! I know he want a sacrifice, but I guess, like you said, could be anybody."

Raney frowned. "But the ghost gotta know we after it now, so maybe it want us more?"

The colored bottles were on the night table, and Kody picked up the red one.

"Don't try ta see," Newton warned.

"I'm not, just feelin'."

"They 'round here?" asked Raney.

"...Don't think so," said Kody. "But it's gettin' near three an' they probably left the graveyard by now." He turned to Matt again. "Figure they try an' bust this house?"

131

"Rick talk about it last night," said Matt, "'fore he took us up in the Voodoo shop window. Be hard to climb your gallery with them spikes on the posts. Maybe Rick could do it, but Terrel's too fat, an' Devon's too little."

"You probably coulda done it," said Kody. "I seen those moves of yours."

"Lucky for me I didn't try, or I might be in a coffin now."

"Prob'ly," said Newton. "'Cause we had da evil gun an' it wanted ta kill anybody it could."

Kody added, "I don't think Rick can get back in that store. My aunt was gonna warn the owner."

Raney nodded. "So, like she said, we safe in the house."

The gate buzzer sounded and all the boys tensed.

"Check the bottles," said Raney.

"It's cool," said Kody, relaxing. "Probably people wantin' a tour."

Raney suggested, "Y'all could say it the ghost's day off."

"Aunt Simone needs the money," said Kody. "An' we can't let this gang shit rule our lives. That only makes us weaker." He got up and took off his jeans. "Put on your Voodoo stuff."

"Me too?" asked Newton.

"Yeah, little man, you one of us now."

"Cool! Like we's da Voodoo Dawgz."

"Should we hide Matt?" asked Raney.

"Not in dat coffin!" piped Newton.

"It's not..." said Kody. "Wait an' see who it is."

Raney glanced at the bottles again. "Y'all *sure* it ain't Rick an' his posse?"

"Just about sure." Kody put on his loincloth, slipped the bone necklace over his head and padded into the parlor. He descended the stairs to the courtyard, noting that someone had closed the store window, but crept warily up to the gate and called around the corner, "Who's there?"

"We saw your sign," said a woman's voice. "Are you giving haunted house tours today?"

"Sho', ma'am." Kody stepped to the gate. A white family stood in the alley... mother, father, pink and plump, and two red-haired boys who were twins, maybe ten and awesomely fat, far overflowing droopy jeans and spilling out of souvenir shirts with bootleg *Lestat The Vampire* graphics… probably from the Voodoo shop. Kody scanned the alley behind them before unlocking the gate. "Right dis way, folks. Ah hope y'all ain't scared of ghosts."

"Sweet!" said one of the boys.

"Are you a slave?" asked the other.

The parents looked uneasy, but Kody made a spooky smile. "Ah was in another life, dude."

"Is it very intense?" asked the man. "We've already seen the Voodoo Museum and taken the Cemetery Tour."

"No, suh," said Kody. "An' nothin' suggestive, neither."

"That means E-rated," said one of the boys, not enthusiastically.

The other one said, "The boneyard tour was kinda boring."

"Then we got rained on," added the first. "And we didn't see any ghosts."

"Can't promise y'all a ghost," said Kody, "but we got lots of scary stuff."

"Cool!" said the boys in chorus.

X   X   X

"Think them Voodoo-boys got Matt?" panted Terrel, who was stumbling drunk. He stopped to swig from a forty, leaning way back and almost falling.

"The fuck I know?" snarled Rick. "But *I* gonna kill him if they didn't! …Just like I gonna kill Newton… an' all them others!"

"What others?" asked Devon, also buzzed, the Saints cap slipping over his eyes as he snagged the bottle from Terrel.

"All the worthless niggers! A pestilence on the face of this earth! Ain't none of 'em worthy to serve him!"

"Serve who?" asked Devon.

"You find out when he get what he want." Rick grabbed the bottle and killed it, then flung it shattering into the gutter. "Now, c'mon, we wastin' time." He led the way down Royal Street to the Voodoo shop.

"Think it safe?" asked Terrel. "The owner seen us run out last night."

"We all look alike to them," said Rick, peering into the window. "An', the place is full of people. You get them candles like I said. Devon, you get the book. I snag the other stuff."

"You gonna pay?" asked Devon.

"I need all the money to pay the rent, just grab what I told you an' run."

X   X   X

Kody led his guests across the court, but his mind was only half on the tour: the gang must have left the graveyard by now, and the gate would be locked until morning. Rick was probably freaking... he'd lost a gun and two of his crew. How smart was he, Kody wondered? He'd survived the Projects all his life and started his own little gang, but now he was in a more dangerous game and at least one player was already dead.

Newton was down in the foyer, wearing feathers under his belly.

"Woah!" said one of the red-haired boys. "Are those real horns?"

"Got dat right," said Newton. "Cooler than vampire teeth, huh?"

"Def!" said the other boy.

Kody was good at adapting these tours to fit his guests' personalities. Some people came in with chips on their shoulders, not wanting to hear about slavery or even admit it had once existed. Others came only to scoff; and some were upset by these "pagan things" because only their own god was real.

Kids always wanted to see spooky stuff; and Newton was a good assistant because the boys could relate to him while Kody spoke with their parents. Newton captivated the twins by leading them into the shadowy parlor to show them the skeletal Baron.

"Hey, that's you!" cried one of the boys, spotting the idol of Ethu.

"Got dat right," said Newton.

"Cool!" said the other boy.

Kody escorted the parents around: they had an interest in "period houses" and what the style of life had been back in the days of Marie Laveau. Aunt Simone's room was a perfect example; you wouldn't have known it was actually used, with a four-poster bed and preserved furniture. The man and his wife took pictures like mad after learning there wasn't an extra charge. Then they inspected the kitchen, still mostly antique except for the fridge, and finally went into the parlor.

Newton had brought out a couple of skulls -- Aunt Simone had a huge supply, thanks to Raney's flooded graveyard -- and the boys were intently examining them. Kody explained they weren't for sale, but suggested a shop that sold skulls and bones... the parents looked nervous at this.

The door to Kody's room was closed, and he wondered what Raney had done with Matt. He wouldn't have dared the gallery, especially now with the graveyard locked and the Skeleton Crew on the streets, but Raney would have figured out something, so Kody turned his mind to the tour.

He spoke of the Baron, the god of graveyards, and then of Ethu the god of kids. Ethu loved jokes and was sometimes naughty, often playing tricks on people. He also loved snacks and gifts of food, which was how he'd gotten his titanic tummy. Rubbing his tummy could bring good luck as long as you also offered him something; and the twins gave Newton dollar bills, then giggled and patted his belly.

Kody went to the relics and chains on the wall, which instantly got the twins' attention; they left the skulls on the coffee table and joined their mother and father. The bedroom door opened and Raney came in, leading Matt on the traders chain and toting a long leather whip. Kody picked up on the cue, saying some slaves had been overseers and often hunted runaways. Raney cracked the whip a few times, which made a truly evil sound, and Kody took down a branding iron to press an R into Matt's slender back, where it stayed like a ghost on his skin for a moment. The camera flashed and the boys were posed, the red-haired kids with the runaway slave, the family together with little Ethu, Raney with a twin on each shoulder – a supernatural feat of strength -- then everyone standing with Baron Samedi, whose smile was always a terminal cheese.

Then Kody showed the guests his room and told the tale of Marie Laveau's bed. The man gave him a five dollar tip, and Kody touted the night ceremony. Then Newton escorted the guests to the gate while the other boys stayed in the parlor.

"You were cool, Matt," said Kody.

"So was you, man. Y'all know a lot about history, huh?" Matt studied the slavery relics and fingered the collar around his neck. "We think we got it bad today, but we only shittin' ourselves. It like we keepin' our ownselves down."

Raney nodded. "Playin' thug games an' actin' like fools ain't helpin' to bring us up none."

"It cool havin' friends again," said Matt.

"Rick an' the others are still your friends. They just don't know what they doin' right now."

"'Cause they possessed by that evil ol' ghost?"

"Not all the way," said Kody. "Or at least not yet. More like gettin' bad advice. Like, when you tried to kill Newton."

"But it said Newton would kill me if I didn't kill him first."

"I call that bad advice," said Raney.

Kody added, "Rick thought he was trapped with no way out, an' buried alive in the Projects; an' evil things wait for dudes like him with promises an' lies." He handed Matt the amber bottle. "Here, man, it's yours."

Matt studied it for a moment. "You caught me with this? Thought you needed a doll?"

"We didn't catch you with nothin', Matt. You chose to be free on your own after you left the graveyard."

"But I almost didn't make it."

"What friends are for," said Raney. "Good ones can help you get free of bad things."

"So, what I do with this?" asked Matt.

"Whatever you want," said Kody. "But if I were you, I'd bust it an' burn it."

Raney glanced at the skeleton clock. "Wonder when Aunt Simone be back?"

Kody shrugged. "She'll be here in time for the ceremony."

"Wish she was here right now. I gettin' creepy feelin's myself. Maybe y'all better check them bottles…"

Newton burst into the room. "Dey close!" he yelled. "I can feel 'em!"

A siren shattered the Quarter quiet, blasting fast up Ursulines, and tires screamed on the corner of Royal.

Raney ran to a window. "Maybe they tried gettin' back in that store?"

"Maybe they gonna get busted," said Matt.

"DAMN!" Kody dashed for the stairs.

"Don't go out there!" yelled Raney.

"All of you stay in the house!" Kody ordered over a shoulder. He leaped down the stairs three at a time, dashed from the doorway, raced through the courtyard, flung the gate open and ran down the alley. Another police car rocketed past, skidding around the corner of Royal as Kody burst onto the sidewalk. He stopped for a moment, panting, then he saw the Skeleton Crew.

Rick was leading, the gun in one hand, the other boys doing their best to keep up. They had doubled-back on the cops somehow, gotten past them on Royal Street, rounded the corner of Ursulines, and were headed straight for Kody! He scrambled back in the alley before the boys could spot him. What could he do? Could he tackle Rick as the boys ran by, grab the gun, catch them all, and get them out of this deadly game?

Tires squealed on Royal Street as the cops blasted off in pursuit. Kody heard panting breaths and the slapping of sneaks as the boys neared the alley. What could he *do*, he wondered again? If he stopped them now the cops would catch them!

He pressed his back to the wall. An instant later the boys flashed by. Kody tried to think... did they have a chance of getting away? The cops were only seconds behind. But, if they could reach Decatur Street, they might lose the cops in the tourist crowd.

He heard the cruisers rounding the corner, sirens screaming, engines roaring, tires crying on cobblestones. He dashed from the alley and stopped in the street -- just another young black male -- then spun around and ran for cover. Wheels locked and rubber shrieked. The first car skidded onto the sidewalk, the second slewing sideways beside it. The cops, all white, burst out and crouched, aiming their guns.

"DOWN ON YOUR FACE, BOY!... *NOW!*"

137

EIGHTEEN

"**B**est coffee I ever tasted, ma'am." The cop was a beer-bellied, ruddy-faced man whose shirt looked ready to pop several buttons. He lounged in a chair at the kitchen table, his clipboard open, a pen lying near. His walkie-talkie was turned down low and sputtered out sounds like an alley-cat fight.

"Thank you," said Aunt Simone. "Would you like another piece of pie?"

"I would," said the cop, "but ain't no rest for the wicked they say… 'least not on this side of the grave." He turned to Kody, who stood by the sink. "I know you was only curious, son, runnin' out in the street like that, but don't never do that again, hear?"

"Ah's sorry, suh," said Kody.

"Well, ain't like you done it a' purpose."

"'Spect dem bad boys got away, suh?"

The cop snapped his clipboard shut like a bite and cocked an ear to the walkie-talkie, which seemed to be speaking in tongues. "Looks like they did for now, but we'll catch 'em sooner or later. They always playin' them 'ghetto games,' an' once they get guns it's too late to save 'em. There's only prison ahead… or a graveyard. Y'all remember that, son."

"Sho' will, suh. …Was dey tryin' to rob dat Voodoo store?"

"Shopliftin'… 'boostin',' they call it nowadays. Ain't no hangin' offense, an' they mighta even got off with a warnin', but they had to pull a gun to show how 'bad' they was."

The cop got up with a creak of leather and clamped his cap on his head. "Thanks for the coffee an' pie, ma'am." He turned to Kody and offered a hand. "Sorry about the misunderstandin'."

"Ah's sorry, too, suh," said Kody.

The cop patted Kody's head. "Just stay away from the dark side, son, an' may the force be with you."

"Well," said Aunt Simone, after the cop had descended the stairs. "Just how angry with you should I be?"

She had returned about five o'clock, when the cops had Kody pinned to the wall, manacled like a runaway slave, and were rubber-glove searching his loincloth. They weren't happy at losing their prey, and only had Kody to blame; but Aunt Simone had taken charge without the cops even knowing. Three of them had roared off in their cars to try to catch the Skeleton Crew, while the fourth had stayed to write a report; and Aunt Simone, being Aunt Simone, had invited him up for coffee and pie. She had used her powers to solve a few crimes, and was often consulted by the police when "matters of the occult" were involved.

"Ain't like I called up a zombie," said Kody.

"That, at least, is a blessing." Aunt Simone considered. "Not fury at your foolishness then, but anger still at the chance you took by going out this afternoon."

"But we saved Matt."

"Yes, but at a very great risk."

"Sometimes you gotta risk your butt when somethin' good needs doin'."

"In this case it was more than your 'butt,' though I commend your courage."

Kody thought for a moment. "Why would Rick want anything from that store? Ain't nothin' in there but phony junk an' you can't do Voodoo with that."

"Perhaps he does not know that."

"That makes sense."

Aunt Simone raised an eyebrow. "I am happy to hear I make sense. But I doubt if they will get in there again, either for useless *gris-gris* or to shoot from the window. I warned the store's proprietor, which is probably why they were almost caught. But they have escaped, thanks to you. Escaped one fate which would have destroyed them, so perhaps it was for the best."

Raney and Newton, followed by Matt, filed into the kitchen. They had stayed on the under in Kody's room, which had probably simplified things with the cop. Aunt Simone smiled. "So this is Matt. How beautiful!"

Matt looked shy. "Thanks, ma'am."

"And a magical dancer. I have watched you often. ...I think we can do without the chain." The padlock fell open.

Matt's eyes flew wide. "How you do that?"

"Locks are easy to overcome when you realize you have the keys. Will you dance at our ceremony tonight? We would be honored to have you."

"I been drinkin' a lot today."

Aunt Simone nodded. "Because of the whispers. But that will only muffle them for a little while."

Raney asked, "Did you find out its name, Aunt Simone?"

"I believe so. Sit down and have coffee and pie."

"Yay!" said Newton, taking a chair.

Thunder rumbled over the house, shaking the Sunday plates on a shelf, but sunlight shone in through the window, casting a cheerful golden glow on the black and brown skins of the near-naked boys as they seated themselves at the table, while Aunt Simone filled cups with coffee and distributed slices of pie.

"The tomb belonged to the Stafford family," Aunt Simone said after sitting down. She glanced at Kody. "I believe you 'met' Mr. Raleigh Stafford during your graveyard visit this morning."

"Huh?" asked Newton, his mouth full of pie. "You sayin' dey still here in 'Nawlins?"

"Not in the corporeal sense, my child."

"Not with their skin on," clarified Kody.

"...Mean dat nasty ol' skeleyton?"

"Crude but correct," said Aunt Simone. "The Staffords died out within one generation after the end of the Civil War, and Raleigh was the last of his line."

"Was they evil?" asked Raney.

Aunt Simone took a sip from her cup. "Some would say no, even today. Some would say that to trade in slaves, to hunt and capture human beings... men, women, children, infants... to chain them like beasts in the hold of a ship and sell them like animals here at the market was simply a matter of business. In this case a family business. A long tradition of inhuman trade. The law said this was moral and right. A whole way of life had been built upon slaves, and those who wanted to end it were evil. So, to the Stafford family, there was nothing evil in what they did."

"But it was!" cried Matt.

"Yeah," agreed Kody. "Good people know when somethin' is evil. It's like you can feel it in your bones."

Aunt Simone nodded. "I would say, in your heart, my child."

Raney muttered, "So the Staffords was slavers. That make 'em evil enough for me!"

Aunt Simone nodded again. "I have not had time for much research, though I called a friend at the Historical Society, who is looking into this matter for me. But it seems the Staffords enjoyed their business... very much so from what I have learned... and were broken and bitter to lose it."

Matt cocked his head. "You sayin' they pissed 'cause they lost they business? ...Or they ghosts are pissed, what I mean."

"Crude but correct, my beautiful dancer. Although there appears to be only one ghost lurking in the Stafford tomb. But, many rich families lost all they owned after the end of the Civil War, yet they managed to rise again, and not upon the backs of slaves. Perhaps they learned from their mistakes. But the Staffords learned nothing and did not recover. Their fortune was built upon suffering, the buying and selling of human beings, and they knew no other trade."

Aunt Simone sipped more coffee. "A factory used for the making of weapons may just as profitably make plows. An ex-naval officer goes to sea in command of a merchant vessel. And a farmer will always grow food. But what is left for a dealer in slaves when slavery is no more? Some would call it Divine Retribution. Others, perhaps, simply lack of foresight. But the family fell and never recovered. Raleigh's father hanged himself in preference to living in poverty, and his mother died insane."

Aunt Simone fell silent. There was only the tick of the skeleton clock and a distant rumble of thunder. Finally she spoke again: "Evil always lingers in a land when men have enslaved other men. I feel intense hate from the past. There is no logic or reason in hate. It is useless to say that the hater was wrong... that history and government, that armies, war, and economics brought the Stafford family down. To him we caused his family's destruction, and he has never forgotten."

"We?" asked Raney. "Meanin' black folks?"

"That is how it appears, child. He hates us for having our freedom, and blames us for his suffering." Aunt Simone closed her eyes for a moment. "I see a broken old man alone... a crumbling mansion, empty rooms, and silent, lightless halls. Dark, decaying... stench of death."

Newton shivered. "I wanna sleep in da middle ta-night!"

Aunt Simone finished her coffee. "I will learn more about him." She faced Kody. "You *must* know your enemy, child; every strength and weakness, before you engage him in battle. The smallest detail may be important... which is something you tend to neglect. So far you have been very lucky. ...All of you have. But, I will settle this occurrence as soon as I have all the knowledge."

A cloud passed over the sun, dimming the light in the room. Matt looked uneasy, but Aunt Simone smiled. "You are safe in this house, which includes the courtyard."

"Like a magic circle?" asked Newton.

"I would call it a circle of love. And, to further strengthen it, let us join hands for a moment."

Everyone did, but then Kody said, "But, he can look in through a window."

"A window on love should always be open, for only love can light the world, and those who look in should see that light. Be sure you show it to them, for even the hateful long for love, even if they have forgotten they do."

There was a thud in Kody's room. Raney cocked his head. "Sound like your boomer fell off the dresser."

Aunt Simone laughed. "Fell... or was pushed?"

"Guess I should open the window," said Kody.

Aunt Simone turned to Matt again. "Will you dance for us?"

"You'll get tips," added Kody.

"I give it a try if you want," said Matt.

Aunt Simone asked, "May I call your grandmother and tell her you are safe with us?"

"Sure," said Matt. "...But, how you know...?"

Kody laughed. "Basic Voodoo."

Aunt Simone looked toward the graveyard. "I do not fear you, Raleigh Stafford! There will be no whispering in my house! You have only to go to the light to be free, and you are a fool if you don't."

"Woah!" said Newton.

"Ain't that callin' him up?" asked Matt. "Sayin' his name like that?"

"Not when you got the power," said Kody. "But it sure gonna put him down."

"Can you hear him now, Matt?" asked Raney.

"...No."

Newton closed his eyes.

"Don't even try!" snapped Kody.

"Yes," said Aunt Simone. "Do not listen to hateful things. He can only hurt you through those boys, and I will soon put an end to that."

Thunder rumbled overhead as if to challenge her words, but Aunt Simone only laughed. "I may have to perform an eviction."

"Mean, give him da shaft?" asked Newton.

"In a spiritual sense, my child." Aunt Simone turned to Kody. "We are having a guest to supper this evening, a friend who works at the children's center. A shower would not harm any of you."

"What we eatin'?" asked Newton, finishing the last of his pie.

"I do not know," said Aunt Simone. "There have been many distractions today... ghosts are often distracting. Our guest will be here at seven, and now it is after six. There is hardly time to cook anything."

"We could order pizza," said Raney.

"Yeah!" said Newton. "Cajun style."

"Do," said Aunt Simone. "And I will make a shrimp salad." She looked at Kody meaningfully. "Which means I will go to the market now."

"I know," said Kody. "Don't leave the house."

The telephone rang in a cupboard... like most modern things it was kept out of sight. Aunt Simone went to answer it. "Yes?"

She listened for several minutes. Kody couldn't read her expression, except to see it was thoughtful... but Aunt Simone would have looked thoughtful if a skull flew screaming into the room. Finally she thanked the caller and returned the phone to its place.

"That was my friend at the Historical Society. She has found a few things about Raleigh Stafford." She glanced at Kody again. "Details which may be important. It seems that he took an interest in Voodoo during his last years of life. This was a common thing in his time, but he only consulted the charlatans; the so-called 'black-magic' practitioners... most of whom were, ironically, white... and my friend has discovered a journal he kept."

"Mean, he learned ta make spells?" asked Newton.

"Possibly, child. Though I would suspect they are flawed."

"Mean they won't work right?" asked Matt.

"Spells which are flawed or incomplete may not work at all. Or they may be dangerous, producing unforeseen results, especially if evoked to do harm."

"Like, they can backfire," said Kody.

"Crude but correct. Will you conduct the ceremony?"

"Sure," said Kody. "But, how can I do it an' still play my part?"

"You will think of something... you usually do when you have to." Aunt Simone lay a hand on Matt's shoulder. "And we have our beautiful dancer to enchant our guests. I want to see that journal tonight to find out who Raleigh Stafford consulted and what he may have learned, so I will leave after supper."

"Can I call up a zombie to do the dishes?"

"Kody Carver...!"

"Just kiddin'."

A half an hour later in Kody's room, the boys were dressing for dinner. "Wonder who comin'?" said Raney.

Kody rummaged around in the clothes-press, pushing the smiling skull aside, then tossing white T-shirts to Newton and Matt from his meager wardrobe. "Probably some old lady. Ain't many men wanna work in those places."

Matt donned one of the XL tees, which draped him like a funeral shroud. "Seem like a lotta men don't like kids. My daddy run off. An' Rick's daddy, too."

"Don't even know if I got one," said Newton, putting on the other shirt, which hung past his knees like a kid's ghost costume.

"You wasn't no 'maculate 'ception," said Raney.

"So, what your aunt gonna do?" asked Matt, "after she get the 411?"

"I never seen her evict a ghost," said Kody, also donning a tee. "But I wouldn't wanna be a ghost if she ever got pissed at me."

"She never got rid of yours," said Newton, glancing at the mirror, from which Kody had taken the blanket.

Raney laughed. "Y'all can't have a haunted house 'less you got a haunt to haunt it."

"But, he shove Kody's boomer on da floor. Lucky he didn't bust it."

Kody shrugged. "He just got pissed 'cause I covered the window."

"But, he can leave anytime," said Raney. "Nobody keepin' him here but himself."

"Where dey go?" asked Newton.

"They're supposed to go to the light an' be free." Kody faced the shadowy glass. "What about 'go to the light' don't you understand, Raleigh Stafford?"

For an instant something seemed to flicker but didn't materialize.

Raney frowned. "Leave the ghost bustin' to Aunt Simone."

"Mean, they get forgiven?" asked Matt. "Even the ones was evil alive?"

"That's how it's supposed to work," said Kody. "But first they gotta go to the light."

"Don't seem right to me," said Matt. "Somebody evil should burn in hell."

Kody shrugged again. "He's been rottin' away in that dirty old tomb, layin' awake for all these years with only his hate for company. That's gotta be some kinda hell." He sat on the bed to tie his sneakers. "But, Aunt Simone's gonna put him down, so he ain't our problem no more. All we got to worry about are Rick an' what's left of his crew."

"An' the ceremony," said Raney.

"Matt will kill 'em with his dance." Kody ruffled Newton's hair. "An' we got little Ethu."

Newton's eyes flicked to the mirror. "Think da ghost can see us now? Dat nasty ol' one in da graveyard?"

Kody gave Newton a hug. "Let him see this. ...Ow!"

"Did I poke you wit' my horns? Sorry."

"Nah, it was my arm."

"It hurtin'?" asked Raney.

"Been hurtin' a little all day, but that's probably normal."

Raney came over and checked Kody's arm. "I know I cleaned it good... don't see no swellin', can't be infected."

"I just hugged Newton too hard."

The gate buzzer sounded.

"Yay pizza!" piped Newton.

"How you know?" asked Matt.

"Gots me natural magic. Just like you wit' your dancin'."

Raney went to a window. "I could look from the gallery."

"No," said Kody. "You heard Aunt Simone. But I don't think Rick's deliverin' pizza."

"Him an' his posse could still be out there."

"Why I don't want you out there."

"Um?" asked Matt. "What gonna happen after your aunt get rid of that ghost? Rick gonna start bein' good again?"

Kody smiled. "Are you?"

"I be as good as I can most the time, but I don't feel no gooder since you help me get free."

Raney said, "Nobody never get no gooder than they wanna be."

The buzzer sounded again.

"I'ma get the pizza," said Kody. He descended the stairs and crossed the court. Clouds were rolling in once more, and thunder rumbled distantly, but the evening sun was beaming bright and the puddles were giving up steam. The pizza guy was waiting, black and maybe seventeen, with a pair of jumbo-size boxes. Kody gave him a five-dollar tip and started to shut the gate, when a shadow appeared at the alley entrance. Kody tensed for a second, but then his eyes went wide... it was the girl from the ice cream shop!

146

He could only stand in stupid surprise as she came up to the gate after trading smiles with the pizza boy. She was wearing a newer pair of jeans and a plain white T-shirt, both of which were enchantingly snug. Her scent was something like rain on flowers, and her hair was freshly washed and oiled above a rounded, cheerful face with large almond eyes and a small snub nose.

"Hi," she said. "I'm Michelle Devereux."

"…Um, hi. …I'm Kody Carver."

"Hi, Kody. Your aunt invited me for dinner."

"Um, yeah, she told me." Kody displayed the pizza boxes. "An' this is dinner… part of it." *What a dorky thing to say!*

Michelle laughed. "I love Cajun pizza." She patted her tummy. "I guess it shows."

"I love just about anything. …Um… food, I mean." Kody patted his belly. "An' obviously that shows. ...But, I like other things, too. ...Lots of things. ...Um, good things."

Michelle smiled. "Like dancin'?"

"...Oh, you seen me? ...Um, Matt's a boy."

"I know. I watch him whenever I can."

"Um, I really wanted to talk to you. Why I came to watch."

"Really? I should have hung around longer. But, I had to get to the children's center. I work there in the afternoon reading to little kids."

"That's cool." Kody held the gate open. "I used to dance... believe it or not."

"Why wouldn't I believe it?"

"I dunno."

"Why did you stop?"

"I ain't very good. Not like Matt."

"That's nothing to be ashamed of. I've never seen anyone dance like him. It's like a magic spell."

"Yeah, it is. An' he's dancin' tonight at our ceremony."

"Cool. Are you?"

"Nah. ...Do you dance?"

"Not anywhere as good as Matt."

Kody smiled. "I'm sure you're magic, too."

NINETEEN

"Why are you cryin'?" asked Kody. He was "dressed" in his loincloth and baby oil, and had slipped away through the shadowy foliage after introducing Ethu – who'd appeared in a flash and a billow of smoke -- to where Michelle sat in the last row of chairs. There were only about twenty people tonight, including the red-haired twins and their parents – the boys commandeering two front row seats -- probably due to the threatening weather, so Michelle was alone near the fountain. All the guests had been given umbrellas, and the stars overhead were hidden by clouds, but despite an occasional flicker of lightning it hadn't yet started to rain.

Michelle wiped her eyes. "You were so sweet as Nathan and Tau. You made me remember a lot of things, and some of them were sad."

"Oh," said Kody, who'd managed to play his usual part while also directing the show. "I always cry, too, at the end."

"It's not over, is it?"

Kody glanced to the alley gate, where Raney stood guard with his spear, and then across the crackling fire where Newton was calling up a cigar. "I can shut up if you wanna hear this."

Michelle smiled. "I meant it's not over for us as a people. We've still got a long way to go before we'll really be free. We've got so much hate and anger now, and so much of it is toward ourselves. We say we're 'keeping it real,' but keeping it real is keeping us down."

"Yeah," agreed Kody. "We supposedly got equal rights back in my grandfather's day, but we're still keepin' ourselves apart by hatin' on each other."

"That's what I meant, and you made me remember." Michelle

149

smiled again and her chubby cheeks dimpled. "But, I got to meet Ethu at dinner, so maybe we could talk a while? There's a lot going on with you that don't show. ...It's a feeling I get. I can always come back another time to see what I missed tonight."

"Oh sure," said Kody. "Anytime."

"Can you sit down?"

Kody glanced at the people: all were intent upon Newton, who seemed at home in his god-boy role; and even a brilliant lightning flash didn't distract the astonished crowd when he floated the glowing skull in the air.

"I'd really like to," said Kody. "But Matt said he had an idea so I gotta talk to him." He paused for the rumbling thunder. "Did you get an umbrella?"

"It's under my chair," said Michelle. "But, I like the rain in the summer. And your show... a lot."

"Thanks, Michelle. I like havin' you here. But, it's better when my aunt's the M.C."

From beyond the fire came Newton's voice: "If dere is evil among us ta-night, let's bring it ta light an' banish it!" The skull began to cruise the crowd and peer into people's faces. As usual, there were different reactions -- disquiet, fright, uneasy laughter – though the twins looked delighted and tried to catch it until their parents nervously quelled them.

"That's off the hook!" exclaimed Michelle. "All of this is. It's nothing like I expected."

Kody smiled. "No dolls an' pins?"

"It's more like a history lesson."

"Voodoo is part of our history, an' it's somethin' to celebrate instead of bein' ashamed of." Kody smiled again. "Matt's gonna dance pretty soon, an' I know you're gonna like that."

The skull had reached the last row of chairs and floated past Kody to gaze at Michelle, but Kody shooed it away.

Michelle looked at her watch. "I have to be home by eleven."

Kody almost offered to walk her home, but caught himself before asking. He couldn't leave this place tonight with the gang and the ghost still dangerous. Did she want him to ask, he wondered? And what would she think if he didn't?

The skull was still hanging around, peering over Kody's shoulder, and Kody shooed it off again. "Um, maybe we could have lunch tomorrow? ...If that's cool with you?"

"Lunch is always cool with me."

"Cool," said Kody.

The ferns parted and Matt appeared. Kody felt charmed by the boy's slender beauty, especially stripped to his leopard briefs and glistening with oil in the firelight.

"Yo," whispered Matt. "I wanna do somethin' special tonight 'cause you an' your aunt been good to me."

"You'd be special no matter what," said Kody. "...Oh, this is Michelle. She seen you dance."

"Hi," said Michelle. "You're way past magic."

"Thanks," said Matt. "But I need a partner."

"Michelle?" asked Kody, wondering, maybe absurdly, if he would have to "share" her with this enchanting boy.

"Nah, you." Matt smiled at Michelle. "If that's cool?"

Michelle laughed. "We can share him."

"...Oh," said Kody. "But, I can't dance like you."

"I need somebody strong," said Matt. "An' all you do is follow my lead. I call it the Zombie Dance."

"But, I gotta play the drums for you."

"Raney gonna do that."

"But, who's gonna watch the gate?"

Matt leaned to Kody's ear. "Newton say he can't feel no evil."

Kody replied in a murmur, "Ain't worried about evil right now, just those three dudes an' their gun." He considered for a moment, about to refuse, but Michelle said:

"Please dance, Kody."

"...Um... aight." Kody turned to Matt. "But I hope I don't mess it up for you. My arm's still hurtin' a little."

"You be zombie-cool," said Matt. He signaled Raney, who went to the drums. Then Matt disappeared in the foliage.

"Good evening," said another voice.

Just as he'd been by Matt's midnight beauty, Kody was a little spellbound by Arlan's handsome pale figure seeming to glide from the shadows, his snowy-white skin almost luminous, which made his black hair look twice as dark to the point of having a silvery sheen. His eyes were winsomely innocent; and his boyishly muscular body needed no further enhancement, but he wore a black satin tank-top clinging like paint to the plates of his chest while showing six inches of stony six-pack, in addition to jeans at a dangerous level displaying more inches of crimson silk shorts at the absolute limit allowed by E; and Michelle also seemed enchanted.

Arlan smiled with his huge chisel teeth. "Thanks for inviting me in, Kody. Sorry I'm a little late, I overslept as usual."

"That's cool," said Kody, "there's more comin' up."

The skull came floating to gaze at Arlan, impolitely nothing-to-nose, who only smiled back at its empty sockets. The skull began to chatter its teeth…which wasn't a pleasant sound. Michelle shrank back a bit in her chair, but Kody whacked the skull away, sending it spinning across the courtyard. "Sorry. Guess it's havin' a mood. …Um, Michelle, this is Arlan."

Arlan bowed, and kissed Michelle's hand, and of course said something perfect, and Kody felt a little less charmed. It was natural for Arlan to sit by Michelle, but that was also less charming.

"Um, see you later, Michelle… Arlan." Kody returned to the fire-lit circle, where Raney now stood at the drums. Ethu vanished in swirling smoke to cue up the blaster concealed in ferns. There was silence except for the crackle of flame and the shivery splash of the fountain. Kody called back the flying skull, which had been misbehaving and swooping at Arlan, who nonchalantly fended it off like flicking a fly with a finger. Then Kody answered the usual questions about spirits, zombies, and Voodoo dolls… people always wanted those dolls. And – to the twins -- zombies didn't eat brains. He glanced across the fire several times to where Michelle and Arlan were sitting. Both were listening intently to him and seemed unaware of each other.

Kody introduced Matt as a spirit warrior. There was another swirl of smoke and Matt glided into the firelight, nearly naked, gleaming with oil, and black as a million midnights. There were murmurs and sighs from the crowd, male and female alike, while the twins looked mesmerized in childish open-mouthed wonder. Lightning flickered and thunder crashed, but no one seemed to think of umbrellas. Matt leaned to Kody and whispered:

"Yo! Am I seein' a ghost?"

"Huh?" said Kody. He looked across the flames again. "...Oh. That's Arlan. Met him last night."

"But, how'd he get in?"

"...What you mean?"

"I thought the gate was locked? An' Raney's at the drums."

"Sometimes it don't always lock by itself. Raney shoulda checked it." Kody signaled for Newton to do that.

Matt smiled. "I make you look hot for your lady-friend." He patted Kody's shoulder.

"Ow!"

"Sorry. What's up with your arm?"

"It only hurts once in a while. I should be okay for the dance."

"Can you pick me up?"

"No problem. Just don't make it complicated."

"Like I said, just follow my lead."

The echoes of thunder died away, and Raney began to beat the drums as Newton switched on the music... appropriately *Eye Of The Zombie*. At first Kody felt like a fool, his moves seeming comically clumsy as Matt wove around him with sensual grace, but then he remembered he was a zombie, nothing more than a walking corpse, and let himself slip into that role, which seemed to be one of pursuit and attack while Matt did magical battle with him.

Lightning glared and thunder roared, but only intensified the dance. Cameras were also flashing, and people stood up to see better. A few warm drops came pattering down, but the audience seemed oblivious to anything but the glistening boys. Matt ended the dance in Kody's arms and gave him a forgiving kiss, full and long on his lips. The people all stood up and applauded, and the twins eluded parental control to come and touch Matt as if to ascertain he wasn't a Disnyland hologram, while Ethu took tips in a topless skull.

The rain was still light but increasing, and the candles had all flickered out, leaving only the fire's glow. Kody stood panting next to

Matt, arms over each other's shoulders, after they'd bowed several times to the crowd, while Raney had taken the M.C. spot and was blessing the guests as they left. Ethu now stood at the open gate politely reclaiming umbrellas.

"Wanna do it again sometime?" asked Matt.

"Yeah," puffed Kody. "You're pure Voodoo, man."

"That was the E-rated version."

"If you got an X, it's gotta be triple."

"That's for at night on the street. Brings in the biggest bucks."

"I can see why. ...But who was your partner?"

"Rick used to be."

"Till he went thugger?"

Matt sighed. "Till he got worried about his image. Guess I ain't manly enough for him."

Kody shrugged. "There's all kinds of ways to be a man."

Matt gave Kody a nudge. "Go see your lady-friend, man."

Michelle and Arlan were talking together, not seeming to notice the rain. "That was awesome!" said Michelle as Kody came over.

"Yeah," agreed Arlan. "Super sweet!" He grinned. "But you're just about to lose something."

"...Oh." Kody yanked up his loincloth.

"I have to see that again," laughed Michelle. "The dance, I mean."

"Me too," said Arlan.

"Thanks," said Kody, then turned to Michelle. "So, we're on for lunch tomorrow?"

"Very, Voodoo boy."

Arlan asked, "Y'all wanna go get a soda now? Or something stronger, if you prefer? The three of us. I'll buy."

"I can't, man," said Kody. "Sorry. ...Gotta put the *gris-gris* away."

"Aw," said Arlan. He turned to Michelle. "May I have the pleasure of walking you home? The streets can be rather frightening at night."

Michelle smiled. "Why, thank you, sir."

Kody searched Arlan's enchanting face, though wasn't sure what he was looking for. "Take an umbrella."

"You're a gentleman, sir," said Arlan.

"Only when I gotta be."

Michelle pressed Kody's hand. "Thank you for dancing."

"Yeah," said Arlan. "You're really Voodoo." He looked across the fire at Matt and his eyes shone brighter. "So is he."

"I'll tell him," said Kody. He watched them walk through the gateway... Arlan looked very gentlemanly, taking an umbrella from Newton and gallantly sheltering Michelle.

Raney came over. "Normally I say you got worries, up against a dude like that."

Kody shrugged. "So he's got a few manners an' ain't bad-lookin'. He still has to pose as an undead boy to make enough green for a soda. ...What you sayin', 'normally?'"

"'Cause he gotta be a you-know, like Matt."

"How you know anybody's a you-know? You got you-know-dar?"

Raney went after the floating skull, which had followed Arlan to the gate. He grabbed for it, but missed, and it circled around past Kody chattering like a sepulchral snicker. "I just sorta figured, you know."

Kody made a snatch but the skull dodged away. "I didn't know you-knows bothered you."

Raney lunged for the skull but missed, and it snicker-chattered again. "It don't seem natural, you know."

"What ain't natural ta know?" asked Newton, appearing with a net on a pole and trying to snag the swooping skull.

"Bein' a you-know!" snapped Raney, making another grab.

"A you know, what?" asked Newton, finally netting the naughty death's head.

Raney looked ready to pitch a fit. "Like Matt!"

"Oh," said Newton. "I didn't know."

"You sayin' he ain't?" demanded Raney. He snatched the skull out of the net and stuffed it into a plastic bag as it tried to nip his fingers.

"I dunno," said Newton. "I always just thought he was cool. Like, gentle an' nice kinda cool."

"Till he try an' fillet you like a fish!"

"Dat wasn't his fault."

Kody gazed down the alley. "Only thing I know for sure is I wish I was walkin' her home."

Matt came over. "I wish I was walkin' Arlan home."

"I knew it!" said Raney.

"It don't rub off, you know," said Kody. Then he smiled at Matt. "I dance with you anytime, man."

"You cool," said Matt.

Newton giggled. "We know."

Kody glanced at the fire. The rain was still light and comfortably warm, but the flames were hissing and dying down. "Newton, you better go inside or you might catch another cold."

Newton hurried into the house as Raney went to the table to gather more skulls and other *gris-gris* and put them in another bag. Matt sighed. "Ain't been easy makin' friends. Why it so hard to lose 'em."

Kody touched Matt's shoulder. "You'll get your friends back; an' don't trip about Raney. It takes him a while to accept somethin' new. He can wrestle a ten-foot alligator, but he still freaks if I give him a hug."

"Sometimes I ain't sure I accept myself."

"Just *be* yourself, man. Everyone starts out bein' good, the hard part is stayin' that way."

"How come you ain't scared of me?"

"Why would I be scared of you?"

"Even Rick got scared of me. That why he stop dancin'."

Kody touched Matt's shoulder again and smiled. "I met a lot scarier things than you."

"Like that ghost in the graveyard?"

"Don't worry 'bout him," said Raney, returning. "Once Aunt Simone get her hands on that spook it'll wish it was dead!"

Kody clutched his arm. "Ow!"

"Let me check it again," said Raney.

Kody winced but shook his head. "Nah. I'm cool." He turned to Matt. "This a good time to bust your bottle. I hope your homies can do the same by this time tomorrow."

They gathered around the fire pit, and Matt flung the bottle into the flames, which flared ghostly blue as it shattered on bricks. Raney hesitated, then gently patted Matt's shoulder. "Best get out this rain, man. Y'all catch your death wearin' nothin'."

Matt offered a hand. "Thanks for savin' me today."

Raney took Matt's slender hand as if cautious of breaking a fragile thing. "See y'all upstairs."

"Still think he ain't natural?" asked Kody, as Matt went into the house.

"'Long's he don't try an' kiss me."

"I don't think you gotta worry 'bout that."

"…Why the hell not?"

Kody hugged Raney and kissed his cheek. "'Cause you're more my type."

"Stop that shit," Raney growled.

"Ain't we kissin' cousins?"

"Oh shut up."

Kody laughed. Go on in, I'll get the *gris-gris*."

Kody finished clearing the table and checked to be sure the gate was locked. The fire had subsided to glowing embers. There was silence except for the patter of rain, its whispering hiss on the smoldering coals, and the trickling splash of the fountain. Kody reached for the sack of skulls, then his eyes caught a shadow across the courtyard!

For a second he froze... had the Skeleton Crew gotten in? But, no, the figure was a man's. He was slender and looked well-dressed -- at least from what Kody could see in the dark -- and appeared to be white. A broad-brimmed hat overshadowed his face, but that was natural in the rain. Kody relaxed a little: he knew the gate was locked, so it whoever it was must have had a key.

"Hi," said Kody.

For a moment the figure said nothing. Kody suddenly thought of Raleigh Stafford! A skeleton finger traced his spine... but *he* could never have entered this place with Aunt Simone's magic around it. Kody tried to open his mind but didn't feel anything scary. Rain pattered down on the ferns, the fountain continued to gurgle and splash. Finally there came a gentle reply:

"Good evening, son."

"Are you from one of the houses?" asked Kody. "I thought they were closed for the summer."

Again there followed a moment of silence before the man replied. "I always seem to forget something here. I was watching your show. I hope you don't mind?"

"'Course not, sir. It's your courtyard, too."

"I never realized all the wrongs that were done to you by those of my race. We called ourselves civilized people, and yet we acted as savages. We claimed our religion was loving and kind, and yet we spread hatred and suffering."

The man's face was hidden in shadow, but Kody seemed to sense it was sad. "I guess the most important thing is when people learn from their mistakes. ...My name's Kody Carver. Simone Dubois is my aunt."

"Yes," said the man. "We're well acquainted. She speaks of you often during the winters and reads your letters aloud. I almost feel I know you. I'm Charles Whitney." The man chuckled softly. "No relation to Ely."

"Nice to meet you, sir."

"The pleasure is all mine, sir." The man touched the brim of his hat. "Goodnight, Master Carver."

"'Night, Mr. Whitney."

The man strode off into deeper shadow. Kody snagged the sack of skulls and carried them into the house.

TWENTY

Lightning slashed the nighted sky and thunder exploded over the Quarter, echoing down narrow alleys, rattling shutters and window glass. The rain was falling heavily now as Michelle and Arlan reached Bourbon Street at the corner of Ursulines.

"So you're a child of the night," said Michelle, raising her voice as the rain roared down and jazz rhythms throbbed in the hot steamy air.

"That's one thing they call us," said Arlan. "There's a big medical word."

Michelle smiled. "Child of the night sounds mysterious. And a little romantic."

"I used to keep it a secret, but it's something I've learned to live with." Then Arlan asked, "Where do you live?"

"About three blocks past the cemetery."

"Want to go up to Rampart Street then over to Basin?"

"I usually take Bourbon Street at night so I don't have to pass the graveyard."

"Are you afraid of ghosts?"

"Never had any reason to be. I'm a lot more scared of the Projects."

Arlan glanced up Bourbon Street, which was booming as always despite the storm. The glistening sidewalks were swarming with people; music blared from all the juke-joints; and many shop windows were luridly lit, displaying the kind of merchandise that usually came in plain brown wrappers with warnings to keep out of reach of children. Voices shouted, whooped and howled, and a few kids wove their way through the crowd touting trinkets, charms or drugs, and/or sometimes themselves. "But there's all those bars and porn parlors to pass, and weird people looking for weirder stuff. Besides, it's darker on Rampart Street, and bright lights hurt my eyes."

"Then let's go that way," said Michelle.

A man and woman came out of a club, a middle-aged white couple holding hands. "Excuse me a minute," said Arlan, and gave Michelle the umbrella.

"What's up?" asked Michelle.

"It's a living. Don't be afraid."

"Afraid of what?"

Arlan turned away for a moment, and when he turned back he had fangs!

"Yow!" cried Michelle, flinching back. But then she laughed. "You're a natural."

Arlan indicated the couple. "That's why they were in the Vampire Vault. I can always tell."

"All you need is a cloak," said Michelle.

Arlan laughed. "That's all there is in that place anymore."

"Must be a lot of fangs, too."

"If you were in Disneyland you'd be looking for Mickey Mouse ears. ...Be right back."

Michelle remained on the lamp-lit corner while Arlan sauntered up to the couple. In a minute he'd had his picture taken.

"Is it too late for a soda?" he asked, coming back and removing his fangs. "I made five dollars."

"You must be reading my mind," said Michelle. "But, mom wants me home by eleven, and there's just enough time to make it. Sorry."

"Maybe some other night?"

"Sure," said Michelle. "But..."

Arlan smiled. "With Kody, of course."

"You sure you can't read minds?"

"I'm just a good judge of people. I guess it's a survival skill." Arlan glanced at the man and woman walking away up the street. "I knew they were nice. No freaky or bitey."

"Do you do freaky and bitey?"

Arlan grinned with his chisel-like teeth, which looked every bit as fearsome as fangs. "It pays a lot better. And some people like the danger of being with a boy of my age. But, most victims want someone older. I guess it's more romantic and scary."

Michelle smiled. "You're romantic and scary enough for me."

Arlan cocked his head. "You don't want me to bite, do you?"

Michelle laughed. "I'm not into that kind of romance."

Arlan grinned again. "I saw the way you were looking at Kody, and he's very romantic, but I promise I won't get jealous."

"You're full of surprises," said Michelle. "But, don't you think Matt is romantic?"

Arlan's big eyes grew wistful. "To infinity and beyond. I watch him a lot when he's dancing at night. But he's just so…"

"What?" asked Michelle.

Arlan sighed. "*Beautiful.* I never thought he'd like me."

"You've never even said hi?"

"I'm too scared."

"It's hard to believe you'd be scared of anything."

Arlan sighed again. "Sometimes I scare myself. …We better be going so you won't be late." He took the umbrella and sheltered Michelle as they crossed the cobbles of Bourbon Street and headed up darker Ursulines, passing rows of ancient houses, most of them shuttered and barred for the night.

"Not to seem ungrateful," said Michelle in the rainy gloom and taking Arlan's hand. "But, in light of your revelations, may I ask why you're walking me home?"

"I was too scared to ask Matt. …I hope you're not offended."

"Only untruths offend me, sir."

Arlan's strong shoulders slumped a bit. "I don't have any real friends. Kids make most of their friends when they're little, and little kids go to bed early… usually when I was just waking up. And kids do stuff in the daytime. Sometimes I feel a hundred years old."

They reached the corner of Rampart Street. A few cars passed, swishing through puddles, their wipers slapping heartbeat rhythms, but otherwise the street was deserted beneath its dimly glimmering lights. They continued on toward the cemetery, and Michelle took Arlan's hand again. "Consider me a real friend."

X X X

"Fuck, this ain't workin'!" Rick stared into his dresser-top mirror while holding the red-covered "Bible of Voodoo" he'd boosted from the Voodoo shop. The room was in darkness except for candles that burned beside the grinning skull.

"I'm startin' to think you wack," said Terrel, shirtless like Rick and sprawled on the bed amongst the remains of take-out food, while Devon lay asleep beside him, a forty clutched like a teddy bear. "Maybe Matt was right."

Rick glared up from the book. "You don't think at all, you worthless nigger! That's why you don't got no power! An' Matt's a worthless nigger, too!" He re-read a spell titled, Bringing Your Enemy Out.

Terrel took a gulp from a forty. "Check *yourself* in that mirror... boy."

"Shut the fuck up! I can't concentrate!" Rick gazed into the mirror again, not seeming to see his own reflection behind the mouldering skull. Lightning stabbed the sky outside, and thunder shivered the building. Still holding the book, he went to the window and stood surveying the rain-flooded graveyard. "We gotta get closer. The power's in there."

Terrel snorted. "The hell you keep talkin' 'bout power? If there any 'power' it all in your mind."

The echoes of thunder died away, and Rick cocked his head as if listening. "Wake up Devon."

"Huh?" said Terrel, drinking again. "What you talkin' about, man? I ain't goin' into that boneyard at night!"

Rick suddenly whipped the gun from his jeans and jammed the muzzle against Terrel's chest. "Don't defy me, nigger!"

"...But, it rainin', man!"

"Ain't no soap in that water, boy, so you ain't gonna melt." Rick donned a black hoodie and zipped it halfway as Terrel shook Devon awake. Rick slipped the book in the front of the hoodie and picked up a little cardboard coffin. "We gonna need a ladder. Should be one in the janitor's room."

"S'up?" yawned Devon, rubbing his eyes.

Terrel got up unsteadily and put on his own black hoodie. "Fool wanna go in the graveyard now."

"No fuckin' way!" squeaked Devon.

Rick aimed the gun at the smaller boy. "You do what I say, little nigger!"

"Nigger yourself!" squalled Devon. "Had me enough of this freaky-ass shit!"

"Get him!" yelled Rick, as Devon leaped up and dashed for the door.

Terrel brought him down with a clumsy tackle, both boys crashing onto the floor. "Lemme go, fucker!" screamed Devon, kicking and punching. "HELP!"

Rick shoved the gun in Devon's face. "Shut up or I...!"

"Rick!" yelled his mother's slurred voice from the hall. "What the hell you doin' in there?"

Rick clapped a hand over Devon's mouth while Terrel held the struggling boy. "Nothin', mom. Just messin' around."

"Stop makin' all that goddamn noise! You gonna get us evicted!"

Devon bit Rick, who jerked back his hand. "I wanna go home!" Devon howled.

The door burst open, and Rick hid the gun as his mother glared in. She held a wine bottle and swayed on her feet. "The hell got into you lately, boy? You let him go home if he want!"

Something flickered pale in the mirror. Rick's hand almost went for the gun. But he muttered to Devon, "Keep your mouth shut or you dead!"

"What you say, boy?" demanded his mother.

"Nothin', mom."

Terrel let go of Devon, who scrambled to his feet and ran out.

Rick's mother pointed. "Put out them candles! You gonna burn the whole place down!" She focused her eyes on the mirror. "I want that skull outta here, too! Thing givin' me the creeps at night!"

"But..."

"Get your ass in bed, boy! It nearly 'leven o'clock!"

"Yeah, mom."

Rick's mom slammed the door, and Terrel snickered. "You so bad."

"Shut up, shithead!" Rick got to his feet and blew out the candles, then stuffed them into his pockets.

Terrel snagged a forty and drank. "Your 'power' ain't gettin' you nothin', Rick. Fact is, you losin' all your friends."

"'Cause I got enemies castin' spells! Doin' dirty Voodoo on me! We gotta do this thing tonight before they get any stronger!" Rick opened the door and checked the hall. "She gone to bed. C'mon."

A few minutes later Rick and Terrel were splashing across the flooded street to reach the graveyard wall. They toted a short aluminum ladder boosted from the maintenance room. It was still raining hard and the boys were soaked, their hoodies hanging sodden and heavy, their waterlogged jeans dragging low.

"I still think you wack," muttered Terrel, swigging again from the forty as Rick set up the ladder.

"Shut the fuck up an' get your ass over! We gotta do the ceremony."

"Thought 'he' needed a sacrifice?"

Rick pulled out the little coffin. "I get that Voodoo-boy with this! He the one been fuckin' things up!"

"*You* almost got us busted today!"

Rick gripped Terrel's shoulders and pulled him close. "Listen, man, it gonna work! I promise, man... swear on my soul! We just gotta do the ceremony."

Terrel sighed. "Aight, Rick. But, this *better* work... whatever the fuck it's s'posed to do... or I'm outta here, too." He gulped from the bottle again, then shoved it into his hoodie and clumsily mounted the ladder.

A dagger of lightning stabbed overhead, and Rick scanned around in its blazing blue glare. He grabbed Terrel's leg and pointed. "Yo! Check it out!"

Two figures were passing the front of the graveyard, a boy and girl beneath an umbrella.

"So what?" asked Terrel, shaking rain from his eyes.

Rick whipped out the gun. "We just got his sacrifice!"

X   X   X

Michelle paused at the curb to study the street, which looked like a rippling rain-pocked river, oily, black, and smelling of swamp. "I should have worn my old sneaks tonight."

"I'll carry you across," said Arlan.

Michelle laughed. "The 'Noble Old South' isn't totally dead."

"Hold the umbrella," said Arlan. He lifted the chubby girl effortlessly and started to wade through the ankle-deep water. "You're almost home, dear lady, and we got past the ghosts in the graveyard without so much as a boo."

"There's still the Project zombies ahead, but maybe they won't be out the rain."

Footsteps sounded, splashing water, and Rick came charging through the rain, his gun thrust out in both hands. "Put her down, boy! She ain't gonna melt."

"We don't have any money," said Michelle.

"Ain't your money I want, girl."

Arlan set Michelle gently down, then stepped between her and the gun. "What *do* you want?"

"Her," said Rick. "Take off, white-boy, an' I let you live."

Arlan seemed to hesitate, and Rick moved closer, the gun muzzle shifting back and forth as he tried to cover the two other kids.

"She ain't worth dyin' for, boy..." Rick began.

Arlan leaped! He grabbed Rick's arm and yanked it up as Rick swung the gun to target Michelle. Lighting slashed the clouds above, and the gun went off as thunder roared. Still clutching Rick's arm, the gun pointing skyward, Arlan slammed his chest into Rick's, driving him back toward the graveyard wall. They struggled and cursed, splashing up water, Arlan's long hair flinging glittering drops as the two boys battered each other. Rick fought to tear his gun hand free, while Arlan savagely twisted his wrist, trying to make him drop it. Rick jammed a knee between Arlan's legs, but only managed to trip him, and the boys crashed down in the flooded street.

"Run, Michelle!" yelled Arlan.

Instead, Michelle went for the gun, dropping beside the struggling boys, pinning Rick's arm under the water and trying to pry his fingers loose. But another figure burst from the rain.

"Arlan! Look out!" cried Michelle.

Terrel swung the forty-ounce bottle, bashing the side of Arlan's head and knocking him into the water.

"Get her!" yelled Rick, scrambling up.

Terrel made a drunken grab for Michelle, who punched him expertly on the jaw. Terrel stumbled back, almost falling. Rick shoved him aside and aimed the gun. "Don't move, girl!"

Arlan rose up on his hands and knees, his hair trailing down in the oily water, and dazedly shook his head.

"Take him, fool!" yelled Rick.

Terrel aimed a clumsy but savage kick, slamming his sneak into Arlan's ribs, and Arlan collapsed in the water again.

"Tie her hands!" ordered Rick. "Use your bandana! Get busy, fool!"

Arlan struggled to rise again as Terrel pulled off his black bandana and yanked Michelle's hands behind her back. Rick jammed the gun to Arlan's head.

"No!" cried Michelle.

"Don't, Rick!" panted Terrel. "He white, it trouble!"

Rick's finger twitched on the trigger. "White trash ain't no better than niggers!"

"There a car comin', Rick!"

Rick whipped the gun in an arc, slamming the butt against Arlan's head and dropping the boy in the water again. Then he spun to target Michelle. "Somebody waitin' to meet you, girl!"

Shoving Michelle at stumbling run, the boys splashed away up the street, leaving Arlan face down in the water.

X X X

Kody cried out and grabbed his arm as thunder blasted over the house. Rain pounded down on the gallery, and sheets of water poured off the roof with a rushing waterfall sound. All the boys had showered, washing off the baby oil. and now lay in their jeans on Kody's bed sharing pizza leftover from supper, while Zydeco music bumped from the boomer above the drumming rattle of rain.

"There somethin' wrong, cousin," said Raney. He unwrapped the bandage and studied the wound. "But, damn if I see what it is."

Matt leaned over Newton to look. "Wouldn't it be swellin' if it got infected?"

"What I can't figure out," said Raney.

"It only hurts once in a while," said Kody. "Maybe it's just a nerve or somethin'?"

There was a blinding lightning flash, glaring through even the heavy drapes, and the candle-shaped bulbs in their scones went out as a roar of thunder shook the house.

Raney looked at the clock in the parlor, dimly lit by the candles that burned at the Baron's and Ethu's feet. "It gettin' close to midnight, Kody. If Aunt Simone ain't back pretty soon we best take you to the clinic."

"We ain't supposed to leave the house."

"Wasn't no problem for you today."

"That was before we got all seven. This ghost is really dangerous, man. An' there's still Rick an' what's left of his crew."

Newton finished the last pizza slice, picked up the three little bottles and pressed them to his forehead. "I can't feel nothin' like dey was close."

Raney took matches off the dresser and lighted one of the gas lamps. "We could call Mr. Clay to come with his carriage. He can't be doin' much business tonight."

"No," said Kody. "They'll report a gunshot wound to the cops, an' I don't feel up for a drillin'."

Matt's slender body jerked suddenly tense. "Look in the mirror!"

A skull had appeared in the murkiness... and its own empty eyes were mirrors!

Raney cursed and grabbed a blanket, flinging it over the dresser.

Something battered one of the windows!

"DOWN!" roared Raney. Matt and Kody dropped to the floor, and Newton tumbled off the bed, but instead of bullets ripping the air a frantic fist hammered on glass.

"Kody!" yelled Raney. "Don't...!"

But, Kody had already scrambled up and thrown aside the drapes. For an instant he stared at a ghostly white face. Then he opened the window and Arlan leaped in, his long hair scattering rainwater jewels while blood trickled bright down his cheek.

"Some dudes got Michelle!" he panted. "They took her into the graveyard!"

"It was Rick!" cried Newton, staring into the little red bottle. "He in dat tomb wit' da skeleyton!"

Kody grabbed his sneaks. "C'mon!"

TWENTY-ONE

The lights were out all over the Quarter except for a few feeble flickers of gas or candle-glow showing in windows. Rain was still slashing down, sheeting from roofs and galleries, flooding swirling sewer grates and darkly frothing gutters. Lightning flashed and thunder roared as Kody and his panting posse reached the graveyard gate. The boys had run all the way, Newton clinging to Raney's back, splashing through the shadowy streets in murky water over their shoes. Despite the storm the air was still hot; the boys all shirtless except for Arlan who wore his sodden tank-top.

"How we get over the wall?" asked Raney as Newton slid off to the sidewalk.

"Use them muscles," said Matt.

"Yeah, give us a boost," said Arlan. "We'll help the others and then pull you up."

The boys were soon atop the wall and scanning the rain-lashed cemetery. Mist filled the grounds like a bayou at night, and only the taller tombs could be seen, their pale shapes rising out of the fog like a half-flooded city of death. Lightning ripped the sky again, and Kody searched around in its glare. "They gotta be in the Stafford crypt, back by the wall in the corner. But, it's gonna be hard to see down there."

"I can find it!" piped Newton, his young voice shrill above the storm. "First we go ta Marie Laveau's tomb."

"Ow! Dammit!" Kody cried, clutching his wounded arm.

Newton was staring into the mist. "Rick gots one of dem dolls from da store! He stickin' your arm wit' pins!"

"You see that?" asked Kody.

169

"Just for a second."

"But, *how* you see that?" asked Raney. "We don't got the bottles."

"I don't know, but I did."

Raney turned to Kody. "How he doin' that? ...An' what he done to Matt today?"

Kody shrugged. "Maybe he's usin' his natural magic." He smiled and ruffled Newton's wet hair. "Or maybe Ethu is with us tonight an' more than just in spirit."

Matt looked puzzled. "Thought you say them dolls don't work?"

"I said you don't need 'em," said Kody. "They're like a paint-by-number thing for people who don't know how to paint. All you need is... Shit! How did Rick get somethin' of mine?"

"It was your beanie," said Newton, closing his eyes for a moment. "He got some of your hair, an' it my fault for losin' it."

"No, it's my fault," said Kody. "I shoulda been payin' attention to details."

"How bad can he hurt you?" asked Arlan, shaking the streaming hair from his eyes.

"Depends on how much power he's got, an' where he's gettin' it from... probably Raleigh Stafford's bones. But if he could hurt me any more he'd probably done it already." Kody thought for a moment. "He might have been tryin' to bring me out, but he's got Michelle so he don't need me now."

"Think he'd really do it?" asked Raney. "Kill Michelle for a sacrifice?"

"That's what Raleigh Stafford wants. He needs a life to get up."

"Mean his skeleyton?" asked Newton.

"It's a figure of speech," said Kody.

"Yeah," said Raney. "It ain't his ol' bones, it what still in 'em."

Kody clutched his arm and winced. "Rick's bein' a fool stickin' pins in me instead of doin' what Raleigh wants. He's still playin' gang-baby games."

"We best hurry up," said Raney, "'fore he shoot Michelle!"

"Think the ghost know we here?" asked Matt.

"Don't matter now," said Kody. "It can only use Rick an' his crew to fight us. ...Until it gets a sacrifice."

"C'mon," said Arlan. "We're wasting time."

The boys scrambled down from the wall, Matt lowering Newton by the arms, the others splashing up graveyard mud as they hit the flooded ground below. Then Kody led through the slashing rain between the glistening rows of tombs. Lightning ripped the sky again, followed by a crash of thunder that rattled the doors of crumbling crypts and shook the skeletons inside. The narrow paths were muddy rivers, and steam rose up from glimmering puddles, shrouding the boys in ghostly gray as gravel crunched beneath their feet. At last they came to Marie Laveau's tomb with its plastic roses and drenched offerings.

"Hope she help us tonight," said Raney.

"So do I," puffed Kody.

Newton yanked up his sodden jeans, keeping them half on his butt with one hand and pointing with the other. "C'mon, dis way!" He slogged away into the mist.

The other boys followed amongst the tombs, the rain pelting down on their backs. Newton splashed through a steaming puddle, then stopped to point ahead. "Dere a light!"

Kody slitted his eyes against the rain and could just make out the glow of a window, a flickering candle behind crimson glass. Then he clutched his arm again. "You're only hurtin' yourself, fool!"

X   X   X

Rick lit another "Voodoo candle" and set it beside the skeleton, which lay grinning out on its dusty slab, while Terrel slumped against the tomb's iron door and sloppily guzzled malt. Rick had broken a dime-store mirror and shaped two pieces with a chunk of stone, fitting them into the skull's empty sockets to make a pair of ghastly eyes that now reflected the candle flames. He glanced at Michelle, who they'd dumped in a corner, her hands still bound behind her back. "Watch her, fool!"

But, Terrel was eying the moldy skull with its looking-glass orbits and stark yellow teeth. "Why you put them mirrors in there? It givin' me the creeps, man!"

"He gotta be able to see."

"The hell you sayin', Rick? That thing's way past dead!"

Lighting slashed the sky outside, glaring blood-red though the tomb's little window as thunder rattled the rusty bars. Terrel shrank back against the door and pointed to the skeleton.

"Swear to god I seen it move!"

Rick thought he'd seen it, too... an eerie quiver among the bones. "It just the thunder shakin' 'em."

Terrel drank again, spilling foam down his chest, bare beneath his half-open hoodie. "You really think this shit gonna work?"

Rick picked up a long wicked pin, one that had come with the Voodoo doll. The doll itself lay limp in its coffin on the skeleton's slab. It had no face or sign of sex, but Rick had used a Magic Marker to make it as black as Kody. Then he'd taken a scarlet ribbon and bandaged one of its upper arms, now stuck with several other pins. Last, he'd collected curls of hair from the ragged old beanie he'd found in the tomb and glued them onto the head.

"He told me it would if I called his name." Rick glanced at the jagged chunk of marble carved with the name

RALEIGH STAFFORD

"Who?" asked Terrel.

"*Him,*" said Rick, pointing to the skull.

"Man, you *are* crazy!"

"'Course he is!" said Michelle. "And you are, too, if you listen to him! What you're doin' is *evil!*"

"Shut up!" snarled Rick. "Both you niggers!" He savagely jabbed the doll's arm with the pin. Thunder roared above the tomb and the skeleton trembled again.

Terrel eyed the quivering bones. "How come I can't hear him?"

"'Cause you ain't worthy to serve him."

"So, what make you worthy?"

"He told me I was. Now shut the fuck up, I can't concentrate!"

Michelle had been trying to untie her hands... Terrel hadn't made a very good knot, and the wet bandanna was working loose. "Only crazy people hear voices!" She looked at the skeleton and shivered. "And we served that thing as slaves!"

"Shut up, girl!" yelled Rick. "You won't be hearin' nothin' no more, soon's as I done with Voodoo boy!" He viciously twisted the pin. "Everythin' was cool till he got in the mix!"

"You fucked with him first," said Terrel.

"Damn you, nigger! I said..."

Suddenly Michelle was free! She scrambled up, darted past Rick and shoved Terrel away from the door. Its hinges let out a ghastly scream as she slammed her shoulder against the iron and frantically battered it open.

"Get her!" yelled Rick, and whipped out the gun.

Terrel made a clumsy grab, but Michelle was too fast and escaped the tomb, vanishing in the mist and rain. Rick shoved past Terrel and charged after her, trailing the sound of her footsteps.

Left alone in the candle-lit crypt, Terrel regarded the rotted skull, which seemed to stare back with its bright mirror eyes. Thunder shook the bones again, and the skeleton's fingers trembled and twitched. Terrel grabbed his bottle and edged to the door. The thunder had died but... *those fingers still moved!* Keeping his eyes on the grinning skull, he backed out into the rainy night. Then he slammed the door and stumbled away, wishing to God he could lock it.

X X X

"The hell was that?" said Raney, as a scream ripped through the hissing of rain.

"The door to the Stafford tomb," said Kody, staring toward the red candle-glow.

"What we do now?" asked Matt.

A shadow burst from the darkness! Raney cursed and lunged to attack, but Kody caught Michelle in his arms. For a moment she struggled wildly and cocked a fist to punch, but then realized it was Kody.

"You all right?" asked Kody.

"Yeah," puffed Michelle, now clinging to him. "But there's somebody trying to kill you! Back there in a tomb."

"How many?" asked Kody.

"Two of them... Rick and Terrel."

"Devon prob'ly freaked," said Newton. "He just a little kid."

Michelle shivered against Kody's chest. "Rick thinks some old bones are giving him power."

Kody shook his head. "It's the other way around."

"Are they after you now, Michelle?" asked Arlan.

"Arlan! Thank god you're okay!"

Arlan showed his teeth. "Take more than a bump on the head to kill me."

Michelle turned back toward the dim bloody glow. "I heard somebody following me, but Terrel's so drunk he can barely stand up."

"Then it gotta be Rick," growled Raney. "I tear that dirty weasel apart!"

"Yo," said Matt. "Let me try an' talk to him. We used to be friends..."

There was gunshot! Matt staggered back and clutched his chest, but Arlan caught him before he could fall. Another bullet twanged off a tomb, scattering chunks of brick.

"Get in the doorway!" yelled Kody.

The tomb had a little alcove in front, and Kody pushed Michelle inside. Arlan followed, holding Matt, then Raney and Newton squeezed in. A third shot scattered whizzing chips from marble trim on the door post. Lightning gutted the tortured sky, and rain slashed down even harder.

"Let me see!" shouted Raney above the crackling thunder crash. He pulled Matt's hands away from his chest.

Kody regarded the glistening blood, black as oil on Matt's ebony skin. "Is it bad?"

"Missed his heart, but it bad enough!"

Another bullet ripped through the rain, scattering plaster over their heads.

"What kinda gun is it, Matt?" asked Kody. "How many caps?"

".32, an' eight in the clip."

"That leaves him four if the clip was full."

"It went off once," said Arlan. "When I was fighting him."

174

"Dat leave tree," said Newton.

"Dammit!" roared Raney. "Who care how many bullets he got! We gotta get Matt to a doctor!"

"Let me see," said Michelle. "I took a first-aid course at the center." She gently examined Matt's chest, not seeming freaked by the welling blood. "We need something for a bandage... have to keep pressure on the wound."

Arlan stripped off his shirt.

Kody peered into the misty darkness, slashed by silvery splinters of rain. "Listen up! I'ma run out an' he'll follow me. ...Raney, Arlan, help Matt. Head for the gate. Can you find it?"

"Gonna be hard in this fog," said Raney.

"I can find it," piped Newton. "First we go back ta Marie Laveau's tomb."

"Wait there a while," said Kody. "Give me some time to lead Rick away. ...GO!"

Kody dashed from the doorway. Another shot cracked from nearby, the bullet phutting past his ear so close he felt its heat. He darted between two crypts and paused a moment to listen.

Footsteps followed him, splashing through puddles. He raced around another vault. Lightning slashed the sky once more, and the tombs flickered pale in its lurid blue glare. He heard the footsteps come to a stop just before the thunder crashed. Then he dashed away again, cut across another path and circled around to the rear of a tomb. The footsteps followed, gaining on him. Kody grabbed a piece of stone and flung it into darkness. The gun fired again, and he saw the flash maybe thirty feet away.

Kody raced on through the rain, deliberately slapping his sneaks in the mud, hearing the other boy close behind. He splashed ankle-deep through steaming water, squeezed between a pair of crypts and crossed another flooded path. He was panting for breath when he stopped again at the rear of a castle-like tomb. He was too fat to keep running; he had to start using his mind!

The trailing footsteps also stopped. He could picture Rick trying to listen for him above the waterfall roar of rain. What now, he thought? Throw something else? Was Rick so stupid he'd waste all his caps shooting at shadows and sounds? There was one shot left if Matt had been right.

Then he recognized the tomb; the one he'd shown to the Trouts that morning. Quickly, he dropped to his knees in the mud and thrust his arm into the gaping crack. He found the leg bone and pulled it out. Then, puffing and panting, his jeans at his knees, he clumsily hoisted himself to the roof. Rain hammered down on his back, nipping his skin like splintery teeth. He heard Rick's footsteps creeping closer.

He held his breath and waited. Another three steps...

Kody leaped into rain-lashed space, crashing down on the other boy's back, smashing Rick flat in a splatter of mud. Rick fought like a zombie trapped in a net, kicking, clawing, trying to bite. He almost threw Kody off for a moment and jerked up the gun to fire. Kody swung the bone like a club, bashing Rick's arm away. The gun went off, spitting yellow-orange flame, the bullet drilling Kody's side. Kody slammed down on the other boy's chest, using his weight as a battering ram, driving Rick deep in a wallow of mud. Kody groped for the gun and got it, tearing it out of Rick's muddy fingers. He flung it away in the darkness, hearing it clatter on stone. Then he sat up astride Rick's body, dripping slime and panting for breath with blood running hot down his side as Rick struggled and cursed underneath him. For a second Kody raised a fist, about to smash Rick in the face, but jerked it down and panted, "Game over."

Rick tried to claw Kody's eyes, but Kody grabbed his wrists.

"No it ain't, nigger!" snarled Rick. "I gonna...!"

"You gonna what?" panted Kody. "Any more games an' you play 'em alone. 'He' ain't gonna help you no more."

"Liar!" Rick screamed.

"Wrong," said Kody. "*He's* the one been lyin', fool. All you been is his little house-boy."

Rick only spewed more curses.

Kody shook his head. "I know all the words. Any five-year-old does. An' screamin' 'em out don't make you a man. The *real* bad words got more than four letters... like ignorance an' stupidity."

Rick cursed again anyhow. "It ain't over, boy!"

"For you it is. We'll put down ol' Mr. Bones in the mornin'."

TWENTY-TWO

Lightning flickered distantly, and rumbles of thunder shivered the air, but the storm was slowly passing away. The rain had dwindled to less than a drizzle as Kody returned to Marie Laveau's tomb, pushing Rick ahead of him. He'd tied Rick's hands with the black bandanna, but carried the leg bone for backup. Their footsteps crunched through a patch of gravel, and Kody called, "We got him!"

Newton peeped around a crypt, and Rick jerked back as if slapped. "You damn little nigger! You started this shit!"

"No," said Newton. "You did."

Matt lay slumped with his back to the tomb amongst the scattered offerings, the sodden letters and plastic roses, while Raney, Michelle and Arlan knelt around him tending his wound. The rain had almost stopped by now, but the ghostly mist was growing thicker. There was only nighted silence, and dripping sounds from the glistening crypts.

"How is he?" asked Kody, dropping the bone.

Raney looked worried. "We gotta get him to a doctor!"

"And fast!" said Michelle. She pressed Arlan's shirt to Matt's chest. "Stay awake, Matt. Don't go to sleep."

Newton cried, "Kody shot, too!"

"Let me look," said Michelle. "Arlan, keep it tight to the wound." She got to her feet and came to Kody, checking the bloody gash in his side. "The bullet went through, just drilled your chub."

Rick scowled. "You won't be so lucky next time, nigger!"

"Shut the hell up!" bellowed Raney. "Or I kick *your* black ass till your chit'lins fall out!"

Newton stepped to Rick, still holding his jeans half on with a hand.

"Where Terrel?" he demanded.

Rick only shrugged. "Nigger ran away."

"You say that word again…!" Raney roared.

"There's a phone across the street," said Kody. "Arlan, think you can climb the gate an' call 911 for Matt?"

"No problem," said Arlan.

"What about for you?" asked Michelle.

Kody glanced down at his side. "Aunt Simone knows a doctor if she can't fix me herself."

Rick asked, "You gonna tell on me, Matt?"

Matt only looked tired. "You ain't worth the trouble of tellin' on."

A rusty scream shattered the silence!

Raney leaped to his feet. "The hell was that?"

Newton's eyes had flown wide. "Da door ta da skeleyton's tomb!"

Rick faced Kody and laughed. "Told you it wasn't over… boy!"

Kody grabbed Rick's shoulders and shook him. "Did you call his name?"

Rick laughed again. "Yeah."

Though hot and sweating, Kody shivered. "He played you, fool!" Then he turned to the others. "We gotta get out of here fast! Raney, Arlan, carry Matt! Take that path! Hurry!" He gave Rick a shove. "Get movin'!"

Rick planted his feet and stayed where he was. "No! He's helpin' me like he said he would!"

"You stupid shit!" yelled Kody. "He ain't comin' to help you, he's comin' to *kill* you!"

"You lyin' again! He said I was worthy!"

"To *serve* him, fool! Like the slaves he owned! But you failed him, Rick! You swore you'd give him a life but you didn't! An' now he's comin' for yours!"

"Liar!" Rick yelled.

"We oughta leave your stupid ass here an' let you meet your master… *boy!*"

Rick began to look uncertain, but Kody pushed him along at a trot between the mist-shrouded rows of tombs. The others followed, Raney and Arlan carrying Matt, while Michelle kept a hand on Matt's chest.

"This way!" called Kody. "Hurry!"

But then Rick stopped, his sneaks skidding gravel.

Kody shoved him. "Go on, dammit!"

But Rick stayed frozen, a little defiant yet looking unsure. "He comin'!"

Everyone stopped to listen. At first there was only the dripping of water. Then Kody heard footsteps slowly approaching beyond the swirling curtain of mist. They seemed to drag... and there was a *creaking.*

"Leave the fool here!" yelled Raney. "Let him find out how worthy he is!"

Rick hesitated another few seconds as the slow dragging footsteps and creaking came nearer, but then he spun around. "Back that way! I got a ladder!"

Kody untied his hands. "Let's go!"

The kids retreated along the path, Rick now in the lead.

"Can it run?" asked Raney.

"If it could it would," puffed Kody.

"Good, 'cause I can't!" panted Newton, holding onto his jeans.

Kody stopped and knelt. "Get on my back."

Newton mounted Kody, and everyone continued at a trotting pace.

Randy asked, "Can you put it down with a zombie spell?"

"It ain't a zombie, it's way too dead."

"What is it?" asked Michelle. "That skeleton in the tomb?"

"Mostly," puffed Kody. "How's Matt?"

"Still bleeding, and moving him's making it worse."

Again they came to Marie Laveau's tomb and everyone paused to listen. They had gained a little distance, but the footsteps were still coming slowly, crunching lightly through gravel patches, scraping over broken stones.

Newton, clinging to Kody, his jeans around his knees, shot a look over his shoulder. "Dis must be what it like when a zombie after you."

"Pretty much," panted Kody.

Rick stared around in the mist. "I don't know the way! I can't see in this shit!"

"Then how can it see us?" said Michelle. "Can't we hide some-where?"

"It don't need to see," puffed Kody. "It feels our life like trackin' a scent, an' we're the only livin' things here."

"But, you said it can't run."

"Neither can Newton. I can carry him, an' Raney an' Arlan are carryin' Matt, but we can't keep runnin' all night." Kody pointed. "Everybody! Get in front of Marie Laveau's tomb!"

"Yo?" said Raney. "What...?"

"Just do it!" snapped Kody. "Newton, Arlan, Rick, help me! Snag all those flowers an' offerings! We gotta make a circle! ...Hurry!"

Newton slid to the ground and pulled up his jeans, while Raney lay Matt in front of the tomb and Michelle knelt to slow his bleeding. Kody grabbed some plastic roses and lay them end-to-end on the ground. "Tear those letters an' notes into strips," he ordered to the other boys. "We only need half a circle 'cause we got Marie Laveau's tomb at our backs. But it's gotta be all the way closed. Don't leave any part open!"

Even by tearing the sodden paper there wasn't enough for a very big space, but, crowding against the tomb's marble front, everyone managed to fit inside.

Kody peered often into the mist as he double-checked the fragile circle, hearing the footsteps dragging closer. "Ethu!" he called. "Bless the circle!"

"How I do dat?" asked Newton.

"Use your magic! ...Fast!"

"Um..."

Kody dropped to his knees at Newton's feet. "Please, Ethu! Help us!"

Newton straightened his back a bit, and crossed his arms over his chest. "My children are safe in dis circle. Evil can't enter here!" He stared around as a faint blue glow appeared amongst the offerings. "Woah! Did I do dat?"

"It don't look very strong," said Raney, regarding the feeble light. "Brick dust woulda been stronger."

Kody shrugged. "I'll bring some next time a fool like Rick calls up somethin' he can't put down."

Raney glared at Rick. "You gonna be shittin' bricks in a minute!"

Kody studied the half ring of pale blue light, making sure there weren't any gaps, while listening to the creaking and footsteps coming ever closer. "These things belong to Marie Laveau so they're stronger than brick dust." He scanned the drifting mist again. "An' *he* ain't very strong. He shouldn't of used his own bones to get up, that's a pretty flawed spell."

"Don't give him no ideas," said Raney.

"It's too late now, he's stuck with 'em. He coulda waited for somebody else... another sucker like Rick. But, I guess he got tired of waitin'. ...How's Matt?"

"He's falling asleep!" cried Michelle.

Arlan knelt beside Matt and took his slender hand. "Stay awake, man!"

"I'm tired," murmured Matt.

"Think about life," said Newton. "Think about all da good stuff you done, an' all da good stuff you wanna do."

"I sorry, Matt," said Rick, kneeling and leaning close.

"I know," sighed Matt.

"Figure this gonna work?" asked Raney, coming to stand beside Kody. "We lettin' him choose the battle ground."

"It's all we can do," said Kody, tugging up his jeans as if preparing for a fight. He turned to the others. "Listen! This is gonna be scary, but don't leave this circle no matter what happens! An' don't put any part of you out of it! Even a finger or toe!"

Everyone pressed more tightly together, forming a wedge with Kody on point and Michelle and Arlan flanking Matt against the front of the tomb. For a moment an icy wind seemed to blow, hissing between the tombs and crypts, reeking of rot and ancient decay. Then, a pale shape came out of the mist, which swirled like smoke through its creaking bones. Kody had tried to prepare himself, but froze in shock for an instant.

"It's got eyes!" cried Michelle.

"Oh shit!" whimpered Rick, cringing back as the thing tottered closer.

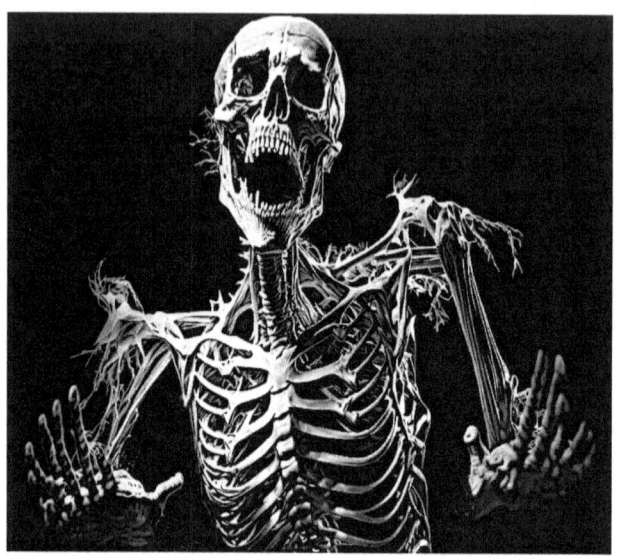

Kody stood his ground as the skeleton slowly approached. "They're only busted mirrors. Stay cool." He moved to the very edge of the circle and, despite his warning the others, thrust out an arm toward the oncoming bones, two fingers and thumb extended. "You have no power on us, Raleigh Stafford! We ain't your slaves no more!"

For a second the thing seemed to hesitate, but then it tottered forward again, its bony claws groping for Kody, who jerked his arm back in the circle. Three steps away... then two... then one...

There was a burst of blue fire! The thing stumbled backward, almost falling. Its jaw dropped open, and there was a scream that seemed to echo forever. One of the mirrors fell out of its socket and shattered to sparks at its grisly feet.

"Woah!" said Newton.

"All right!" yelled Arlan, thrusting a snowy fist toward the sky.

"G-guess your magic works," stammered Rick.

"Y'all best hope it does!" growled Raney. "It *your* dumb ass it want!"

Kody was dripping icy sweat... those fingers had been an inch from his face! He sucked a deep breath. "Don't leave the circle no matter what!"

Rick was cowering back against Raney, his wide eyes staring at what he'd called up. "H-how long we gotta stay in here?"

"Maybe till mornin'," said Kody. "Ain't much power left in his bones. An' he's afraid of the light."

"But he shoulda gone ta da light," said Newton. "A way long time ago."

"Yeah," said Kody. "But, hate kept him here in the dark so long he probably forgot there was any light."

Michelle shook her head. "Matt won't live until morning."

"If the sun comes up I'm toast," said Arlan. "Just so you know; but it's been fun."

"We'll think of somethin', just stay cool." Kody faced the creaking thing as it recovered and tottered toward him. Again he thrust out an arm, though keeping it inside the circle. "Go to the light, Raleigh Stafford! It's always there if you look for it!"

But the thing came on, its jaws still gaping, bone fingers clutching. Kody dropped his arm and braced himself, stepping again to the edge of the circle. Again the skeleton struck the barrier and staggered back in a burst of blue fire. Recovering, it again lurched at Kody. Its jaws snapped shut with their long yellow teeth an inch from Kody's nose. Kody stared into the single eye and saw his own reflection. "Go to the light!" he shouted as the skull jerked and gibbered while claws reached out.

There was another flash of blue flame, and again the thing was slammed away.

"Damn you!" bawled Raney. "You just some ol' bones! I bust you to pieces an' stomp on 'em!"

"Don't try," said Kody. "An' don't hate him; hate makes him stronger."

"He don't look very strong to me!"

For a moment the skeleton seemed to retreat, creaking backward unsteadily.

"What I say!" growled Raney.

But, the skeleton picked up a block of stone that must have weighed more than Kody! There was a grisly grinding sound as rotted bone strained and cracked.

"Don't move!" yelled Kody. "No matter what! It's tryin' to scare us out the circle!"

"But it gonna throw that!" squalled Rick as the skeleton slowly raised the block high above its grinning skull.

"Just. Don't. Move!" For a second Kody closed his eyes as the block came hurtling toward him. There was a crash like cannon fire as something exploded in front of his face, slamming him back into Raney. Sapphire sparks rained down though the mist, along with clattering chunks of stone. The skeleton screamed at Kody again, creaking, tottering, reaching out.

Kody gasped for breath as if he'd been punched in the stomach. "Still wanna wrestle it, cousin?"

"Matt's dying!" yelled Arlan. "We gotta do something!"

"Talk to him, Arlan," said Michelle. "Tell him what you told me tonight... how you feel about him. Give him a reason to live."

"I don't think I'm much of a reason."

Michelle reached over Matt's ebony chest to touch Arlan's snowy-white shoulder. "You're a lot more than you think."

Matt murmured, "I seen you around."

Arlan grasped Matt's hand. "I've seen you, too, man, dancing. You're, beautiful, Matt."

Now the skeleton seemed to grow cunning, stalking around the edge of the circle.

"It's tryin' to find a weak spot," said Kody. "Everybody stay cool."

The skeleton made a grab for Michelle. She cocked a fist to punch it, but more sparks flew and the thing staggered back.

Then Newton spoke, "Go ta da light, Raleigh Stafford." He stepped to the edge of the circle. "Can't be no peace in dem hatin' ol' bones. Go ta da light an' be free."

Slowly, the thing approached the small boy, creaking, shuddering, claws at its sides. The skull tilted slightly as if it could see through its one remaining mirror eye.

"Rick!" yelled Kody. "Your foot's out the circle!"

The skeleton caught Rick's sneak in its claws, toppling Rick to the ground and trying to drag him out of the circle! Rick screamed and kicked, thrashing wildly, clutching at handfuls of mud. Raney grabbed one of Rick's arms. Arlan grabbed the other. It was like a tug-of-war with Death. Then, Kody snatched up the leg bone he'd brought and swung it with all his strength at the skull.

Bone shattered bone and the jaw fell apart. Rick's shoe tore off in the skeleton's grasp. Arlan and Raney dragged Rick back inside, but the struggle had broken the circle!

"Fix it!" yelled Raney.

But, Kody only stood as the thing recovered and lurched for him, its jawless skull thrust forward, its single eye blazing triumphantly. "I can't! It's gotta be remade!"

He readied to swing the leg bone again, but Newton stepped in front of him, leaning way back in his awkward stance and looking up at the ghastly thing. "I feel sorry for you."

The skeleton slowly approached, but Newton stood seemingly unafraid. "I forgive you," he said. "Dey tole you lies when you was a kid. Dey taught you ta hate 'stead of lettin' you love."

Then, a light began to grow. It was pale at first, but brightened fast to a clear and silvery shimmer. It came from nowhere, and yet everywhere, and seemed to surround the small shabby tomb. The skeleton lurched to an uncertain stop a pace away from Newton. Rick looked up at the sky. "A cop helicopter?"

Then a woman's voice spoke, not in command but with kindness. "Come to the light, Raleigh Stafford. Come to the light and find love, poor child."

For another moment the skeleton stood, ancient, crumbling, rotten, dead, towering over the small black boy... then it simply fell to pieces, clattering down at Newton's feet.

"Woah!" said Newton.

Matt sighed. "I wanna go there, too."

Everyone gathered close to Matt as the shimmering light began to fade. Arlan gently touched Matt's cheek. "But, I never got to meet you, man."

Michelle whispered, "Think about dancing, Matt."

"C'mon, dawg," said Rick. "Hang on."

Then, a woman's voice spoke again. "You have much love and

beauty to give in a world of hate and ugliness. Please stay with us and dance."

Aunt Simone strode out of the mist.

"Woah!" said Newton, then looked at the bones. "You put him down, huh?"

"I did nothing, my child. It was you who made him remember the clear pure light of his own childhood before it was stolen from him with lies." Aunt Simone smiled. "Which is what Ethu would do." She regarded the tomb for a moment, and then the tumble of bones. "And Marie Laveau led him into that light." Then she gave Kody a frown. "You might have left me a note."

"Sorry," said Kody. "Did you have to climb over the wall?"

"I have, as you know, some skill with locks. And Mr. Clay drove me here in his carriage."

"Lord!" exclaimed Clay, also appearing out of the mist like an undertaker long overdue. He doubtfully regarded the bones. "What y'all been messin' with, Kody?"

"Just helpin' somebody lost in the dark."

Matt opened his eyes. "So, I ain't gonna die?"

Aunt Simone knelt at his side. "You must make that decision now. You have seen much of the worst of life, and to find the good may not be easy."

Arlan took Matt's hand. "Teach me how to dance with you."

"Yeah," said Kody. "The Undead Boys."

"Yeah!" said Newton. "You kill 'em!"

"But you gotta be un," said Raney.

Alan kissed Matt's cheek. "Please, man, I love you."

Matt smiled. "I just found somethin' good."

"Come, we must hurry," said Aunt Simone.

There was the sound of dragging footsteps! Everyone stared into the mist as a tottering figure materialized.

"Wuttup?" slurred Terrel, still toting his forty-dog bottle.

TWENTY-THREE

The skeleton clock in the parlor was showing a little past four. The Baron smiled from his candle-lit corner, and Ethu grinned at his own living image -- Newton, naked except for his horns -- who puffed a cigar in the plush velvet chair. Terrel, in just shorts, sprawled asleep on the sofa, while Rick, also in nothing but boxers, was scanning the slavery relics, and Raney in jeans was pacing the floor. Michelle came in from the kitchen with a big blue enamel coffee pot and delicate china cups on a tray, along with a plate of chocolate-chip cookies. She was clad in a huge purple bathrobe, one of Aunt Simone's, that draped her form like Mickey Mouse in *The Sorcerer's Apprentice*. "I hung our clothes by the stove," she said. "They should be dry in a while."

The door to Kody's room was closed, and the kids glanced to it from time to time while helping themselves to coffee and cookies. Then the door opened and Kody emerged clad only in jeans. A bandage was taped to his rolly side, another bound around his arm. "You can come in."

Matt and Arlan lay side-by-side on Kody's bed in the soft glow of gas. Alran was only in jeans, Matt in his wisp of leopard-skin, their bodies making a stark contrast of snowy-white and velvet midnight. They looked as different as two boys could be, yet something bound them together.

An elderly black man was tending that bond -- a primitive-looking red rubber tube -- while Aunt Simone stood near. Matt's eyes were closed and he lay very still. A bandage encircled his slender chest, but Arlan smiled as Michelle came in, followed by Newton, Raney and Rick.

187

"I'm a universal donor," said Arlan. "Like, I have everyone's blood."

Michelle smiled. "I'm not surprised."

Raney asked, "How Matt doin'?"

The doctor spoke with a Kreyol accent. "I believe he will be all right, young and strong as he is."

Matt's eyes fluttered open. He closed a hand over Arlan's and smiled. "Maybe we do the Zombie Dance."

Arlan smiled, too. "The Undead Boys."

"Dat make a lotta money," said Newton.

"Um?" asked Rick, coming to the bed. "Can we still be friends, Matt?"

"'Course," said Matt. "Just don't go playin' with dead things no more."

Raney added, "Or try to play 'em. They better at bein' dead than you."

Terrel appeared in the doorway. "The power's all in your mind."

"The real power always is," said Kody.

The doctor removed the needles and tube, taped bandages on the boys' arms, then turned to Aunt Simone. "The young man should rest. Give him plenty of liquids and hearty gumbo and he will dance again soon."

Arlan sat up. "What time is it?"

Raney parted the drapes. "Gettin' near dawn."

"I have to go home."

"You also should rest," said the doctor, laying a hand on Arlan's chest. "You have given much blood."

"That's okay, I can always get more."

"We'll keep the curtains shut," said Kody.

Arlan grinned with his fearsome teeth. "Thanks, but I rest better with the lid closed." He got easily to his feet, then bent over Matt and kissed his cheek. "See you tonight, my beautiful friend."

Matt smiled. "An' a lotta other nights, I hope."

"A goodnight to all," said Arlan, bowing then hurrying out.

"Guess I should go home, too," said Rick.

"Come back later," said Kody.

"...On the real?"

"Yeah, man, you're always welcome here." Kody turned to Terrel. "So are you." He took Michelle's hand. "An' you for sure."

Michelle pressed Kody's hand in return. "We still on for lunch today?"

Kody ruffled Newton's hair between his little horns. "With Ethu's blessin'."

"Oh sure," said Newton, munching a cookie. "If you bring me a doggie bag."

"Can I walk you home, Michelle?" asked Kody.

"That would be cool, but Mr. Clay is driving me." Michelle smiled at Aunt Simone. "Thanks for calling my mom and explaining why I was out all night."

"Let us say I explained enough... you were troubled by naughty boys and spent the night in my house. To tell everything... or perhaps not... that is up to you."

Michelle kissed Kody's cheek. "Bye, Voodoo boy."

"Um?" said Rick to Aunt Simone. "Could you do Voodoo to help my mom?"

"Perhaps not Voodoo, but I will try."

"C'mon, man," said Terrel, throwing an arm across Rick's shoulders. "We can get us some vampire teeth an' sell 'em in Jackson Square."

The doctor gathered his things and packed them into a black leather bag as Michelle, Rick and Terrel departed.

"Do stay for breakfast," said Aunt Simone. "Raney? Will you assist me?"

"Sure. An' I start some gumbo for Matt."

Newton plopped down on the bed next to Matt, leaned over and kissed him.

"What's that for?" asked Matt.

"For bein' cool you again."

"Yeah," said Kody and also kissed Matt.

Matt smiled. "Think I get one from Raney?"

"If he punches your shoulder it means the same thing."

Then Kody went out on the gallery. The Quarter was peacefully still at this hour, the sky just beginning to lighten. A tug hooted out on the river but there were few other sounds. Rainwater dripped from glistening roofs, and steam ghosted up from the sidewalks and streets, but the clouds had passed away and the morning star was shining.

Then, he noticed a figure below who seemed to be gazing up at the house. Kody peered down through the mist: it was the man he'd met in the courtyard after the ceremony last night -- well-dressed and wearing an old-fashioned hat -- though Kody couldn't see his face.

"'Mornin' Mr. Whitney," called Kody.

"Good morning, Master Carver." The man lifted the brim of his hat a little, but Kody felt more than saw a smile. "If I may presume, it's going to be a beautiful day. Always was after a rain."

"Yeah," agreed Kody. "You gonna be stayin' a while?"

A steam whistle sounded a long mellow note as the *Natchez* tested her engines, and the man turned his face toward its lingering echo. "I believe I've stayed long enough... 'guests and fish,' as Ben Franklin said. But, I wanted to have a last look at the house. I'm glad your aunt has it now."

Kody felt something, though not a chill. "You mean *this* house?"

But the man went on in a musing tone: "I didn't like that. Not at first. ...In truth, I was very angry. But I've learned a few things since then. About your aunt, and about you." He paused as the steam whistle sounded again; and now another seemed to join it, their notes overlapping each other. "My son is waiting. And now I know where."

"...Oh," said Kody. "We'll miss you, sir."

"You honor me, sir. Goodbye, Master Carver."

The *Natchez* sounded her whistle again, the bittersweet notes of a long-vanished time, and again another echoed it. Dawn was beginning to break in the east, and yet the man's figure grew harder to see as he turned away and walked toward the river.

Then Mr. and Mrs. Trout appeared, rounding the corner of Chartres Street strolling hand-in-hand. Mr. Whitney tipped his hat and wished the couple good-morning. The Trouts smiled back and wished him the same... but Kody watched him fade away before he reached Decatur Street.

"Woah!" he murmured.

"Hello, Kody," called Mr. Trout.

"You're up early," added his wife.

"Busy day ahead," said Kody.

Mr. Trout laughed. "Voodoo sounds like a lot of hard work."

"Gotta put all your heart into it."

Mrs. Trout said, "We've really enjoyed our stay."

"Seen everything you wanted?" asked Kody.

"I wish I could have seen a ghost and met a real vampire."

"Maybe next time," said Kody. "Folks always come back to New Orleans."

The Trouts said goodbye and strolled away.

Kody was about to go in when Raney parted the curtains. "Who y'all talkin' to, cousin? Nothin' dead, I hope."

"Everything's alive this mornin' in all the ways that matter."

Raney came out on the gallery and looked down over the rail. "I know Arlan strong, but it hard to believe he got up here last night. I couldn't climb over them nasty ol' spikes."

Kody laughed. "Maybe he turned into a bat."

"That just movie bull," said Raney. "Like zombies eatin' brains. ...But, y'all think he really might be..."

"A you-know?"

"We know he one of them you-knows, but you think he one of *them...* you know?"

"He's a friend, that's all we need to know, an' friends come in all colors, shapes and kinds." Kody laughed. "Even undead friends."

"'Long's he don't try an' bite me."

"I don't think you gotta worry 'bout that."

"...Why the hell not?"

Kody grinned, showing long gleaming fangs! "'Cause he already bit me."

Raney jumped back and made a sign, but Kody removed the plastic fangs, and Raney shook his head. "Had enough frights last night, dammit; don't need no more for 'least a week. ...Speakin' of which, y'all comin' out to the swamp? Go fishin' an' have us a barbecue."

Newton poked his head from the curtains, almost snagging one of his horns. "Barbecue yay! Can I come, too? Never been out da city before."

191

"Sure, little man," said Raney, taking Newton under the arms and setting the boy on his shoulders. "I teach you to wrestle a 'gator. An' we check out the ol' flooded graveyard."

"Yeah," agreed Kody. "We might meet a ghost who needs a good home."

THE END

ABOUT THE AUTHOR

Jess Mowry was born in 1960 near Starkville, Mississippi. When he was only a few months old his father took him to live in Oakland, California. Mowry's father was a voracious reader who introduced his son to books at a very early age. Jess attended a public school, but despite his love of reading, dropped out at age thirteen, part way through the eighth grade and worked with his father in the scrap-iron business. In his late teens, Jess moved to Arizona to work as a truck driver and heavy equipment operator. He also lived and worked in Alaska as an engineer aboard a tugboat and as an aircraft mechanic on Douglas C-47 cargo planes, as well as at a children's refuge in Haiti.

Mowry has written twenty-five books and many short stories about black children and teens in a variety of genres, ranging from inner-city settings to the forests of Haiti, the wilds of Alaska, the Arizona desert, the Caribbean Sea, and the African veldt. While some of his novels are set in Oakland and deal with social issues, such as poverty, violence, drugs, gangs, teenage sexuality, and school drop-outs, Mowry has also written ghost tales, as well as novels featuring Voodoo and African magic, in addition to sea stories, and compiled an anthology of Victorian ghost stories.

Jess Mowry lives in Oakland, California.

THIS BOOK IS ALSO AVAILABLE IN A KINDLE EDITION

OTHER ANUBIS BOOKS

AVAILABLE ON AMAZON

www.ingramcontent.com/pod-product-compliance
Lightning Source LLC
Chambersburg PA
CBHW070115030726
47506CB00002B/756